**She was an FBI agent. She wasn't supposed to be a mass murderer...**

From under the bed pillow, she drew out a black automatic and pointed at me. "Let's not be so damn hasty."

My hand went to my shoulder holster and I ducked low, trying to shove the table at her. It didn't work and I fell back with my gun up. I caught my balance and found we were in a Mexican standoff.

"Put it down," she commanded. "If they win, they'll destroy everything we've built up for almost two hundred years."

"You're nuts." True, but not the best thing to say under the circumstances. We held each other at gunpoint and I realized that I might actually have to shoot her. Worse still, she might shoot me. "Take it easy," I offered, wondering how I could get out of the room un-perforated.

In her free hand, she held up the two-way radio, a thumb on the power switch. "Thanks for this, Mr. Wade, but I've had Max rewire it." I'm sure my face looked like it didn't understand, for she went on. "It's now a detonator for George's camera bomb."

Bluff or insanity? I kept my gun trained on her and heard my voice say the fatal words: "Put them both down, or else."

She stood up and I almost fired. "They'll enslave us all. I'm going to kill them and you can't stop me."

A bead of sweat trailed down the center of my back. "Stop," I warned. "Right now."

She laughed like a child and placed the two-way on the table in front of her.

"Now drop your firearm," I ordered, extending my own weapon farther in her direction. I saw that I was going to win this standoff, so I repeated, "Right, now."

She laughed again and her tarnished eyes had something tortured in them. She echoed my phrase, first saying, "Right—" and then stabbing a hand at the radio's switch and firing her gun. "—now!"

Time slowed like an over-cranked movie camera. I'd gone one step beyond into the *Twilight Zone*. The radio was a transmitter? The camera was a bomb? This FBI agent was a crazed assassin, intending to shoot me and blow up her enemies?

In June 1959, America's TV superhero took a bullet to the head in an apparent suicide. But was it? And is he really dead? Stan Wade, a Hollywood PI, sets out to uncover the secret and encounters a host of Mob and Soviet intrigue that threatens not only his life, but the future of the world.

KUDOS for *Superfall*

"Faster than a speeding bullet, John Hegenberger's *SUPERFALL* sends you zipping through late 1950s Southern California on a supersonic ride. With the help of his kenpo-chopping girlfriend, a sub rosa Superman, the original TV frogman, and a hardboiled writer, private eye Stan Wade battles the Reds, the mob, and crazed federal agents in a mid-century modern yarn. It's clever, evocative and just plain fun." ~ Mark Coggins, award-winning author of the *August Riordan* series

"In *SUPERFALL* John Hegenberger takes us on an irresistible, hard-boiled walk down memory lane, with PI Stan Wade as the perfect tour guide. From George Reeves to Lloyd Bridges to Ross Macdonald, this is a historical tour-de-force." ~ Robert J. Randisi, President of the Private Eye Writers of America

"*SUPERFALL* gives us everything we need for a ripping adventure in 1950s Los Angeles: a wary private eye, a frustrated actor, gamblers, mobsters, Commies, and a labyrinth of twists and turns I never saw coming." ~ Martin Turnbull, author of the *Garden of Allah* novels

"*SUPERFALL* is a rollicking trip through 1950s Hollywood where Mickey Cohen still runs the Mob and the Ruskies are up to no good. If you like your hard-boiled fiction fast and sassy, you'll love *SUPERFALL*." ~ Matt Coyle, author of the Anthony Award-winning *Rick Cahill* crime novels

# SUPER FALL

John Hegenberger

*A Black Opal Books Publication*

GENRE: HISTORICAL SPY THRILLER/MYSTERY-DETECTIVE



SUPERFALL
Copyright © 2015 by John Hegenberger
Cover Design by John Hegenberger
All cover art copyright © 2015
All Rights Reserved
Print ISBN: 978-1-626945-01-2

First Publication: AUGUST 2016



Published by Black Opal Books **http://www.blackopalbooks.com**

# DEDICATION

*To George, wherever he may be.*

"Actor George Reeves, who solved mysteries as Superman on television with unearthly strength and skill, continues to leave them in death." ~ *The Tuscaloosa News*, June 25, 1959

Let's all remember that what follows is a work of "faction" based entirely on the author's dreams, recollections, and speculations. None of the names have been changed to protect anyone. All of the events almost occurred exactly as reported.

# PROLOGUE

*One day...June 18, 1959:*

L ook," George Reeves whispered. "I'm dead already. Can't we leave it at that?"

I hate my work. Well, not all the time. Just when I get a headache from dealing with bullheaded movie and TV stars.

Reeves sat in the booth in the Brown Derby restaurant on Wilshire, hidden under a heavy beard, dark glasses, and a darker wig that made him look like a dark Harpo Marx. A sketch of the real Harpo hung on the wall behind him among the rows of Hollywood caricatures.

The blonde seated next to him patted his hand gently. "You don't have to whisper, baby."

Her name, I'd been told, was Naomi Lugosi, but I figured that, like so many things in the Hollywood of the '50s, it was staged. Her hair was blonde, long, and flowing, making her look like Veronica Lake, except I could see both of her dark tarnished eyes.

My hair, on the other hand, needed a trim and had a white streak that ran from my forehead to my crown. I was a bit too thin to be considered ruggedly handsome, with brown eyes, five foot eleven, a habit of interrupting, and a persistent sinus condition from our wonderful LA air.

"I'm just tired of people mourning over me," George said, "like I was a god or something."

Seated across from him and the girl, I shrugged. "You were sort of a god to millions of kids, you know."

Reeves, of course, had been famous for his portrayal of the Man of Steel on the *Adventures of Superman* TV program.

"But I was a joke to adults. No one over the age of eleven took me seriously. Type cast into kiddieland. Do you know what Disney did to my role in that wagon train movie? He cut me down to a walk on." George scratched under his wig and above his left ear. "I think this rug is giving me head lice."

I knew full well what had happened to Reeves's part in Walt's *Westward Ho, the Wagons.* During the preview screenings, you could actually hear the audience gasp when George came on screen, and the hushed word, "Superman," rolled around the audience like muted thunder.

"Not to mention what happened in *From Here to Eternity*," the big actor in the trench coat complained while he fiddled irritably with the saltshaker in our booth.

The same unwanted recognition had occurred at the pre-screening of the Columbia Studios' Burt Lancaster feature. George's meaty part was cut down to nothing, because audiences recognized him the second he appeared and the director knew that it broke the film's narrative flow.

It was all too much for Reeves. He became totally fed up with acting and, in the end, took the easy way out when the circumstances presented themselves. He had come to me weeks earlier, looking to hire me to help with some of those same circumstances. On top of everything else, George had gambling issues and local mobsters, like LA's finest hood, Mickey Cohen, and his known associates were starting to send not-so-veiled threats about paying up.

The blonde Lugosi lit a Camel with tiny, butane lighter. I didn't know much about the lady, but George vouched for her when we'd set up our meeting today here at the hat-shaped restaurant. The plan was to see if he and I could identify a small-time hood who had been muscling Bob Cobb, the restaurant's owner, into offering patrons off-track betting "under the tables" at the Brown Derby. Horse racing. Derby. Get it? In the city of angles, everybody has one.

George looked at Naomi, his face a scowl. "This was not part of our original deal, you know. I'm supposed to be on a train east to Pittsburgh."

The long-haired blonde patted his hand again. "The Bureau has it covered, baby. We spot this creep and we'll have the connection we need. Then you can go on to your new life."

There was a firm assured tone in her voice that made me understand that the Lady Lugosi wasn't just any dumb blonde. I studied her for a moment. "I get it now. You're his handler. You've got his back covered."

She smiled broadly at me. "Baby, I've got his whole body."

George grinned and pulled down his shades, winking at me the way he used to at the end of a TV episode.

"Bullshit." I laughed, sitting back in the padded booth. To our right, another TV actor named…Something …Coburn was enjoying lunch with director Bud Boetticher.

The undercover girl with the phony name cooed, "Georgie, or should I call him Ralph now, is faster than a speeding bullet. And I'm no Lois Lane."

She was no Gracie Allen, either, as they sat there looking deeply into each other's eyes and ignoring me.

I was here this bright summer's day to perform one act that would help two clients: George and Mr. Cobb. George had asked me to help once again with his mob and gambling problems—problems so severe that they caused him to go into an FBI program that promised to protect him with a new identity, if he'd bear witness against local racketeers. Mr. Cobb needed and expected my help, because lately I'd been working out of a temporary office in the crowded, noisy rear of his restaurant. Cobb kept me on retainer to "police" the premises in general and lean specifically on any free-loading Hollywood talent who wouldn't pay their bar bills. We'd had this arrangement for several months now and I'd almost forgotten how much I owed him, until he told me about the racing tout.

The Derby was a classy place to meet clients and prospects and I got plenty of eats while running my professional investigation business out of a cubbyhole office back where all the other employees clocked in and washed their hands. It wasn't what I'd imagined when I'd started out as a PI years ago but, like George, I'd taken the easy way out when circumstance presented themselves. Also my old office in the Farraday building had been torched.

As it turned out, the same race tout whom Mr. Cobb had wanted muscled off the premises was also the "creep" that the blonde FBI agent had wanted identified for Mob connections.

When the creepy tout entered the front door of the restaurant, I noticed right away the small and quick movements, the thin face, and pointed nose. He made a show of scanning the tables and booths from the front of the room and then strolled over to speak with Tennessee Ernie Ford who was dining with, as it happened, Dinah Shore.

The BD was known for the celebs who graced its tables and the framed sketches of same that adorned its walls. I didn't think Ford or Shore were the gambling type, and it appeared that I was right, because the little man soon shoved off with a wave and headed for the sandwich shop that adjoined the restaurant proper. Something in the gesture seemed familiar. I'd seen it before, recently.

"That him?" asked the Bela babe.

George and I spoke in unintended unison, "Yep." Then he went on, "They call him Nicky the Nose, because he knows the inside information from the Santa Anita track and how to get a bet down."

"The nose knows?" I asked.

Reeves ignored me. "He has a direct line into Cohen's gambling organization. I think he's related somehow. You track him, you get the Mick."

"Okay," Lady Lugosi said, nudging George and sliding from the booth. "Let's go."

"Wait a minute." I hissed them to a halt. "Something's wrong here."

"What?" George and the woman said in unison.

"You say that guy's with the Mob? I've seen him before and know that he's also a high-level closet commie."

The disguised, dead actor and his blonde handler disappeared before my eyes and I was sitting across the booth from two concerned and confused individuals, who spoke in unison: "Bullshit!"

I started getting that old headache again.

# CHAPTER 1

*Earlier*:

This particular headache began for me on Saturday, April eleventh, my twenty-ninth birthday.

The longer you live, the more stuff accumulates around you. I was sorting through stacks of old mail, old files, old newspaper clippings, and the remains of an old sandwich—all crammed into my cramped office at the back of the very same Brown Derby restaurant. I was drowning slowly in an ocean of yellowing paper. Twenty-nine felt positively ancient.

Cindy Pyle wrapped her knuckles on and then poked her pretty, blonde-haloed head in the open doorway. "George Reeves is up front at the maître d' station, Stan, asking for you."

I knew she wasn't kidding for two reasons. One: as the office bookkeeper, she never does. Two: Reeves had called me earlier for an appointment. I checked my brother's aviator watch on my left wrist and saw that Reeves was almost a full half hour early. Must be important. "Can Carlos seat him in a booth for lunch? I'm not nearly ready for him yet. This place is still a mess."

She glanced around the room, so small that her cute head didn't need to move. "Why don't you just use Mr. Cobb's office? It's bigger and a lot neater. He's on vacation, you know?"

"Clever girl. Wish I'd thought of that." I smiled. "Give me a minute to settle in there and shoo him in, *shweetheart.*" I gathered up a pen and notebook and stepped into the short hallway, past the time clock.

Norman Weirick caught me as I was navigating around a couple of waitresses on break. "Happy birthday, Mr. Wade," he called out, adjusting his glasses self-consciously on his lean nose. Norman often looked like he'd been stunned by an oncoming truck, but today his expression held nothing by anticipation.

The waitresses stared at us and snickered something to each other. I couldn't tell if they were smirking at me or Norman. Probably both. Norm followed me past Cindy's desk, as she tickled the keys of her adding machine. It too snickered.

Cobb's office was larger, but had at least as much stuff as mine. The BD was celebrating its thirtieth year in business and there were stacks of red and black anniversary menus piled on the floor, blocking access to a row of filing cabinets. I'd recently stopped smoking, so I couldn't help noticing with distaste the large amber ashtray on the desk overflowing with bent butts. Still, it was, by and large, better than my cubbyhole office.

Norman brought out a shopping bag from behind his back, holding it out to me. "Here, this if for you," he grinned, glasses sliding down. And, as if I couldn't figure it out, he added: "From me." He took a proud breath and stepped back.

I automatically accepted his gift. "Why, thanks, Norm. You didn't need to…" I peered inside the paper bag from A-1 Electronics and saw what looked like a couple of small Japanese transistor radios and a jumble of wires for their earplugs.

"I built them myself by combining the miniature radio units with civil defense equipment we had at the store." I must have looked baffled, so he added, "They're a set of two-way radios."

I shook the bag. "You mean these Dick Tracy things actually work? That's pretty cool."

"They're more like the communicators that Captain Midnight used on his TV show to signal the Secret Squadron." He pushed his glasses up. "I was a charter member, SQ7."

I didn't know what all that meant, so I went with, "I'll bet."

"I got the idea from the new issue of *Electronics Illustrated*." He pulled a folded copy of the red-covered magazine from the back pocket of his wrinkled slacks. "You can use them when you're out on stakeouts or tailing some crooks." Tinkering with radio and TV equipment was Norman's true calling, despite his yearn to learn detective work and/or write the great American science-fiction novel. "They transmit and receive up to a mile and three-quarters, even farther after sunset."

"Sun spots and interference," I nodded. "You told me about that the other day. Thanks again, Norm." I made sure he saw me place the little two-ways in my jacket pockets. If they worked, great. If not, my office would acquire new stuff. "I'll give them a real work out and let you know the results."

He snickered. "You find any bugs in them, I'll squash 'em."

Seemed like everybody was making that sound today.

Cindy popped in, took a pencil from between her teeth "The kitchen's preparing his lunch order, so he's on his way back here to see you. Ready?"

"Ready." I settled into the padded swivel chair behind Cobb's desk and told Norman, "I've got a client meeting now. You'd better scoot."

Norman put his hand up to his mouth as if he were speaking into a microphone. "Roger, wilco. Over and out." Swiveling to the door just as Reeves walked in, he froze.

My perspective client winced from under a fedora too large for him. "Excuse me," to Norman before turning my way.

Norm's mouth opened, but his tongue was a Gordian knot.

I gestured to Reeves, offering him the plush, customer chair. "Have a seat, please."

Norm went, "Uh…" without moving from his spot.

Reeves sat, but didn't remove his wide-brimmed hat.

"Thank you, Mr. Weirick," I called to Norman. "Glad I could help you with that diamond theft. And I'll send you a full report on that homicide. You're in the clear and can go—now."

Reeves looked around from his chair and scowled.

Norman hung there, swallowing, as he eased toward the door. Finally, he spoke one word, "Jeepers."

It was my turn to snicker. "Sorry about that. He doesn't get out much," I said, making a show of rearranging some papers on the desk, as if I owned it. "What can I do for you?"

"He's a little weird, but it's all right," Reeves said. "I get that all the time." He took off his hat and ran his fingers through his surprisingly gray hair. I saw for the first time the gash and stitches along his forehead and was reminded of the bad guys in a Katzman B-movie about creatures with atomic brains. The wound on Reeves's head didn't look like makeup.

"I understand from a mutual acquaintance that you

might be able to help me with a small matter." The actor gestured at his injured head. "I got this Thursday morning when the brakes failed on my Jag and I hit a stone wall near my home. Twenty-seven stitches."

"So much for the man of steel," I said.

He shook his head like he'd heard that one before—repeatedly. "There's a guy who claims that I owe him money. Now he's starting to get nasty about it."

"Who's the mutual acquaintance?"

"Another type-cast TV personality, Clay Moore."

"Ah, yes," I said, leaning back in the swivel chair and almost losing my balance. "The lonely kemo sabe. One of my favorite clients." I'd done a piece of work for Moore a few months back, when a woman and her "husband" had tried to pull the badger game on him. The case had resulted in my old digs getting torched, which was why I was currently operating out of the phone-booth-sized room in the back of Derby. "But I'm sorry, Mr. Reeves. I don't do strong arm work."

"Call me George," he offered. "I understand and I'm the last person you'd think who'd need to hire muscle, but the guy I'm talking about claims I welched on a gambling debt. The truth is, I paid him, got back what I thought was my IOU, and tore it up in his office."

"Oops." From out in the hall came the harsh clatter of dishes. I got up and closed the door.

"Yes," Reeves said. "It was a dumb move." He put his hat back on, possibly to hide both his physical and mental pain. "A couple of weeks later, he claimed that I still owed him. When I refused to pay the second time, he threatened to have someone rearrange my face."

"And naturally you didn't want to go to the police," I said, carefully settling back down behind the desk. "Like I said, I don't do strong arm work."

"The police concluded that my car crash was all an accident, but I know better."

I looked down at the mysterious ink-stain designs that covered the blotter on the desk.

The actor elevated his voice with just the right professional touch of urgency. "I don't want him leaned on, if that's what you think. I just want you to talk with him, so he'll know that I have professional help on my side. Sort of an advocate."

"Who are we talking about?"

"His name is Eddie Wexler. He has an office on the eighth floor of the Capitol Records Tower over on Vine."

I made a note of making a note on my notepad. "And who's the muscle behind Wexler?"

"I don't know his name. I think he's an ex-wrestler. Speaks with a lisp. I've heard he's part of Mickey Cohen's local mob."

I leaned forward slightly, watching him. He seemed drawn and lethargic, but it was probably the effects of his pain medication. "You sure you're all right?"

He shrugged. "I know a lot more about Mickey and his gang than you might think. It's a family thing. I took my real last name, Bessolo, from my step-father. Sam Goldwyn changed it to Reeves when I appeared in *Gone With The Wind*."

As it happened, I knew quite a bit about Mickey myself, from several previous encounters with the little giant gangster. But I didn't think he employed a lisping thug. "I guess it wouldn't hurt to have a little talk with Wexler on your behalf. Understand, I can't guarantee any results."

There was a faint knock at the door and Cindy called, "Your lunch order is ready, sir."

"Come on in," I replied as Reeves got to his feet. He reached into his back pocket and brought out a wallet. "A hundred ought to cover a day's work," I advised.

Cindy opened the door. "We're ready for you, too, now, Stan."

Reeves placed two fifties on the desk, next the filthy ashtray. "I'll pay another hundred, if you get results. Hand me your pen and I'll write down a number where you can reach me."

I complied, while Cindy said, "Stan. They're waiting…"

I pocketed the bills and shook the actor's hand. It was surprisingly gentle. He tipped the brim of his hat to Cindy as he went back out into the main dining room.

"He's even bigger than I imagined," Cindy said, her neck beginning to redden.

I laughed and she guided me through the restaurant to a table where a cluster of people waited. I could see that she had giving her son, Jimmy, a trim to save a few bucks. The eight-year-old didn't seem to mind his bird's-nest head. He grinned proudly as he lighted a candle on a small cake. I got sung at by everyone for what seemed like five hours. Now I was the one reddening. A quick peck on my cheek from the blonde bookkeeper and a flurry of back pats later, I saw Norman rush back in, holding copies of a comic book. "Is he still here?"

The cover of the comic showed Superman hog-tied by golden bands shot from a small spaceship hovering over the city. Norman gave one of the comics to Jimmy and they immediately headed over to the booth where Reeves sat eating with a guy who looked like Dabbs Greer.

One of the waitresses started cutting the cake and another wheeled in a cart with dishes of vanilla ice cream.

"Thanks, folks," I said, trying to appear casual. "You didn't need to—"

"Of course, we did, squirrel," said a rumbling female voice from behind me.

I turned to find Alexis Iglesias holding up a package

of three large cigars. "Hi, Lady Lex," I said, greeting.

"Don't tell anyone," she hissed in mock confidence, her grin lopsided and her short coiffeur more salt than pepper, "but they're Cuban!"

Everyone in at the party went, "Woo…"

Lex nodded, playing to the crowd. "Well may ya woo, people. Cost me a buck apiece."

"Thanks," I said, "But I'm pretty sure that I told you I quit smoking a couple of weeks ago."

Without hesitation, she grinned and moved the cigars to behind the backside of her slacks. "Then I owe you a case of Coors."

"Take a look at what Norman gave me," I said pulling one of the miniature two-way radios from my coat pocket. "He says they'll transmit over a mile on a clear day."

Lex laughed. "Hope they work through smog."

Cindy tapped me on the shoulder, presenting me with a copy of Raymond Chandler's last novel, *Playback*. I had purchased and read the book last year and she knew it. "It's signed by the author," she said with a bright smile.

Outstanding. I returned her peck on the cheek. "Like wow. You're the ginchiest?"

And the crowd roared.

Jimmy and Norman were back, the boy almost in tears. "I don't see why he got so mad."

"Okay," said Norman, ruffling the kid's hair. "It's okay."

"What's wrong?" I asked.

"Here, look." Norman held up one of the comic books and pointed to a page where Superman was being shot by a policeman. Instead of the bullet bouncing off his indestructible body as usual, Superman grabbed at the back of his left shoulder, saying, "Uh—I'm hit!"

"He said they were destroying the character," Norm

explained, "and he wouldn't autograph it."

"I don't understand," Jimmy said. "You can't shoot Superman, can you?"

I knelt down. "You're right, cowboy. I guess we'll just have to read the story and see how things come out."

"Hey, Jimmy," Norman piped up. "Since it's Saturday, how about we take in a double feature at the Pantages? If it's okay with your mom, we can go see the Killer Shrews and the Giant Gila Monster."

The boy brightened, still clutching his comic. "Okay."

"Not okay," Cindy said. "He'll have nightmares for a week."

"Ah, Mom…"

Norman appealed to her with logic. "It's only a movie, Mrs. Pyle."

Jimmy applied further logic. "I just stick my fingers in my ears and close my eyes."

I nudged things forward a little. "Let the boys go have their fun. I'm sure they'll be all right."

"Well," she conceded. "I do need to get caught up on some work here in the office—

"Yea!" Jimmy bounced like freshly popped corn. "You coming too, Stan?"

"Uh, not this time."

A faint "I want" line still sat between Cindy's eyebrows. "Can you have him back here by five o'clock?"

Norman nodded, glasses loosening. "Oh, indubitably."

Jimmy did a full 360-degree turn and tugged at the sleeve of his new best friend. "Let's go see some giant killer screws!"

Reeves sat alone now in his booth, totally forgotten. I nodded to him, but he ignored me like a strange visitor from another planet.

# CHAPTER 2

*Within minutes*:

As the celebration wound down, I went back to my office and called Mickey Cohen. One of his goons came on the line and I told him who I was.

He told me to "Hang on a minute, the boss is getting a manicure."

I heard muffled background sounds for about twenty seconds and then Mickey's voice echoed, "Just hold the phone closer to my head, you putz."

Cohen was known throughout most of the free world as the main made man in greater LA. Over the years, he'd risen gradually to the top of the mob-heap, despite several attempts to put him down and under, as well as a four-year stretch in prison for income tax evasion. Since then, he had fronted floral shops, paint stores, nightclubs, and even a gas station in the Los Angeles area. But behind these various facades, he was always the man to see to get a bet down on practically anything.

Last month, he'd flown to Washington DC to be grilled by Chief Counsel Robert Kennedy regarding illegal gambling and union pension fund investments. Nothing much came of the hearings, except to boost the image of both men in the national press. Cohen now over-lorded the local syndicate and managed an ever-expanding gang of goons and bookie joints. Some people believed that Mickey Cohen was involved with the hit on Bugsy Segal, but that made about as much sense as Mickey Mouse being involved in a hit on Bugs Bunny. Hmm…

Anyway, I'd had a recent run-in with one of his underlings, who had tried to take advantage of Cohen's absence from the west coast. In the end, the maverick "lieutenant" had drowned ugly, and Mickey had apologized, claiming he was in my debt. He sent me a dozen, full-stemmed carnations which I gave to Cindy without revealing their source.

"That you, Wade?" his juicy voice spat at my ear. "How's it hanging, kid?"

I tried to sound gruff. "Hanging like a hammer, Mickey."

He chortled or gargled. I couldn't tell which. "A ball-peen, I bet. What's cooking, kid?"

We talked for about five minute and I had the uneasy feeling I could smell his cologne. Cohen acknowledged that the lisping thug that Reeves described was indeed one of his low-level mugs. He also knew who Wexler was and could arrange for me to meet the guy at the Capitol Tower tomorrow at ten a.m. While the Mick and I continued to jaw, Lex came to the door of my office with a good-sized helping of ice cream and cake.

Cohen blabbed, "I may have a piece of work for you soon. Off the books. I need a cute babe followed for a couple of days, you know?"

"Sure, Mickey. Getting behind babes is my favorite pastime."

He liked that one and gargled again before telling someone, "Just hang it up, dummy."

The line went dead and the phone receiver in my hand seemed like an old sweat sock, so I hung it on its cradle to dry. I looked at my hands and felt an urge to go wash them.

Lex forked cake and ice cream. "Did I hear you're going to Capitol Records?" she asked as I two-stepped around her considerable form in the doorway. "Lots of big-name stars do recording sessions there," she informed me.

"You can't go," I said. "If you want to see stars, got to Forest Lawn. It's safer."

The autograph hound in her gave me a disappointed, "Ahwww…"

I went back out to the dining room to give Reeves the news, but found that he had already flown. The BD was packed with afternoon tourists now, so I walked back to my messy office to find Lex gone, but the mail delivered. There was a birthday card from Tobias and Carman Pevsner and a small, hand-sketched illustration from Walt Disney. The sketch showed Mickey and Minnie arm in arm with a cartoon figure wearing a sagging trench coat. Beneath the figure were the words, *World's Best Sleuth*. It was nice to know that I was appreciated by good people, even as I eased into middle-age. *What the hell?* I thought. *It's my day, so why not leap a tall building and take the rest of it off?*

I hefted my gift from Cindy, locked the office, and mooched a steak sandwich and Pepsi from the kitchen on my way out to the parking lot, feeling young and fair and debonair. Strolling past the garbage cans, I discovered that the windows of my 1953 Kaiser Manhattan had been soaped with the inscription, *Birthday Boy*. Lex. I drove a couple of blocks west on Wilshire to a new drive-thru carwash and ate my lunch while riding through a foamy thunderstorm. It was better than Disneyland, but one of the patched bullet holes on the car's right rear door still leaked.

I caught Route 66, while rivulets crawled up the windshield, and drove to Santa Monica to take the PCH south. Traffic was lighter than usual for a Saturday, but it still made me edgy. I turned on the radio for comfort and got three stations in a row playing Pat Boone's "April Love." Nineteen more days until the end of the month and then they'd stop playing that sappy song. I switched to LA's only hilly-billy station, while cruising down Culver Boulevard, and listened to "The Battle of New Orleans." The car phone that Norman had installed under the dashboard hadn't been working the last few days—sunspots again, I guessed.

Nearing home, the clouds in the pale blue sky were arranged in a washboard pattern that matched the waves rolling in to shore. The sea breeze came through the cranked down window as I drove along short residential streets to the tiny harbor where my boat was moored.

The *Cervantes II*, a thirty-six-foot Taylor Cabin Cruiser, lay docked near the entrance to the Del Rey Lagoon. The muddy marsh put me in a similar mood. A group of ambitious businessmen had started dredging a canal into the muck. Next year, these high-class developers figured to make a fortune by converting the low, mosquito-infested swamp into a massive marina for pleasure crafts and small yachts. They'd soon be moving in, like a new breed of gold-rush prospectors. Right now, though, my newest neighbors were brown swill and piles of mud on the banks of Ballona Creek. I thought about my own prospects as I gazed down at my rippling dun reflection.

I'd survived a couple mean cases in the last year. There had also been several offers to join one of the larger investigation firms in town, like Nick Harris's agency, but I always preferred to play a lone hand on small—and low paying—cases, rather than work what felt like a pointless portion of a bigger case for a larger corporation. I knew that meant I'd never be famous or a big success, like some of my clients, but so what? My dark reflection started to say, "George Reeves. He's got it all. What have you got?" when a late-model Ford pick-up truck cleared its throat as it eased into the parking space next to my Kaiser. The horn blurted the evening air.

I walked over. "What are you doing here, Lex?"

She was smoking one of the Cuban cigars. The cloud of prime tobacco still smelled wonderful to my nicotine-starved system. "I've got a surprise for you, squirrel." She had tagged that name on me years ago, because she'd thought a lot of my hunches were nuts. "Come on." She reached over and opened the passenger door. "We're go-in' drinkin'."

I shook my head. "We've already celebrated my birth-day, remember?"

"Yeah, but that's the surprise." She was having a hard time talking around the stogie. "My birthday is next week. Get in."

I said, "What—" as she blew a cloud of smoke big enough to fill the cab and float my somber mood away, "—the hell. Why not?"

೧೫೧

The sun melted into the Pacific as Lex and I melted in-to our third double Bushmills.

The Blue Phrog seemed to lean more than usual. We were in a beached tugboat that had been converted into a bar and grill. Its owner, the inscrutable Sunny Goh, had constructed rough-plank tables, benches, a short bar, and a shorter stage at an angle that compensated for the grounded boat's tilt. Saturday night and the place was packed—not because of my birthday, but because Sunny had scored big and booked a folk-singing act better than Woody Guthrie.

Like just about everybody else on the west coast, I'd heard the Kingston Trio strum and sing their songs on the airwaves, especially their number-one hit about Tom Dooley. Sunny had connections with the people who run the Hungry Eye in Frisco and had booked the trio for one night only while they were in LA recording at, of all places, Capitol Records. Banjo-strumming, foot-stomping, hand-clapping music literally rocked the boat. The trio regaled the small SRO crowd with a rollicking blend of tunes about a man named Charlie in a Tijuana jail with a zombie jamboree.

When they got to the lyric, "What nature doesn't do to us, will be done by our fellow man," I was feeling pretty much invulnerable to pain. We forgot about Lex's truck and stumbled back the four blocks to the *Cervantes II*, talking like fools about putting out to sea for some night fishing. Since neither of us could recall exactly how to get the engines started, we concentrated on listening to the distant surf and drinking a few more beers. The last thing I remember was an open can of Coors rolling out of my palm and across the deck, leaving a slurry of foam all the way to the fantail.

~∂~∂~

The next morning, I awoke inside a super-villain's evil plan. A slight storm had come in from the west, causing the cruiser to rock back and forth and my head to thump repeatedly against the bullhead.

Lex was already up, but moving with infinite care. "I used the last of your Crest toothpaste," she growled.

I wanted to tell her, "Look, no cavities," but my

tongue felt like a dead slug. Tasted like one, too. Or what I figured a dead slug might taste—ah, hell, I needed coffee, bad. And that's what I got, because she already had a pot of brewing on the hot plate by simply dumping the grounds into boiling water.

My left eye wanted to stay blurred, probably due to a recent injury. When I found a hand-mirror and studied it, it finally cleared and I saw that I needed a shave—or a whole new head.

"Okay, no more Bushmills for at least a week," Lex said. "Until then, I'm switchin' to Jameson."

I started to chuckle and almost chocked. I caught my breath. "Yeah, well, I'm switching to Pepsi."

"That stuff will kill you."

I discovered where the boat's head had gotten to and hit it hard. A few minutes, or days later, when I opened the hatch and came topside, I caught Lex pitching the last of the Cubans over the side into the drink. I burped and nudged her elbow on the rail. "That's the stuff that'll kill you."

She didn't say anything, just shifted her gaze out to sea.

Since I didn't get much of a response, I added, "Did I ever tell you the time that a cute redhead knocked me out with a Dr Pepper?"

"Whadshedo?" Lex asked in her gruff voice. "Hit ya with the bottle?"

"No. She put knockout drops in the soda before serving it to me."

Lex tightened her dark eyebrows, looked straight at me, and said flatly, "A doctored Dr Pepper. That's a bad joke."

The wind picked up a little and the boat slowly rocked. I checked my stomach and watch. "Damn! I'm late for a meeting."

She spat overboard with the wind. "A meeting? On a Sunday?"

I rushed below deck to wash and brush, misquoting the Pinkerton slogan: "We never oversleep. I've got to see a man about an IOU."

I heard Lex grunt, "I'll go with ya. We can hold each other up. And maybe get an autograph."

# CHAPTER 3

*That night*:

Wait." I almost hit high C. "It's not your birthday. You were born in October."

"So what?" Lex pulled her truck to the drive-up window of a Fatburger on Sepulveda. "It's my un-birthday. And I wanted a way to tag along. Might meet some celebrities."

"You're star-stuck."

"And you need someone to watch over, squirrel. I'm always watchin'."

We gulped decent coffee from paper cups as we drove through the city under a clearing sky as pale blue as Crest toothpaste.

"Ya look terrible," Lex complemented me. "Ya sure yar up for this?"

I yawned and quoted a Kingston Trio line from the previous night. "I'm worried now, but I won't be worried long."

"Oh, yeah," she replied. "You're a mean motor scooter and a bad go getter." She found a parking space about a block north of the Capitol Tower on Vine. "Place always reminds me of a pile of pancakes," she said, making my stomach growl.

The building was LA's non-leaning tower shaped like a stack of 45-rpm records with wide curved awnings fanning out from the windows of each floor.

Johnny Mercer was coming down the steps to stop at a street vendor's hot dog stand as we neared the entrance. He wore a light brown jacket, an open collared yellow shirt, and a startled expression when he saw Lex. "Say, little lady, I know you." He snapped his fingers to jog his memory. "You were with that old private eye back when this place first opened in '56."

Lex did a little curtsy. "Right ya are, sir. Some East Coast boys were offering you a batch of paid DJs to play your recordings, for a price. We escorted 'em out and almost got hit by their limo."

The songster of "Stardust" and "Accentuate the Positive" and co-founder of the company smiled, spread the mustard on his dog, and chewed like a young boy. "You cats had some nice moves, little lady."

My stomach made itself known publicly, so I purchased a hot dog of my own. They were referring to one of Mr. P's cases that I had not worked, since back then I was still sort of an operative-in-training.

"Still do, Johnny," Lex said.

I handed a dog to her and started stuffing my face.

Mercer gave a wide smile, exposing the gap between his top front teeth, and turned to look up at the round building. "I remember that day. We were the first label based on the coast and the Tower was the first circular office complex in America. The Sound Capitol of the World."

I wiped my fingers on a paper napkin and counted. "Thirteen floors, right? Unlucky?"

"Nah," Mercer said. "We'd have gone higher if the

zoning commission would've let us."

"And the first album recorded here was by Sinatra, right?"

Mercer's eyebrows rose and his high forehead wrinkled. He studied me as if I'd just walked up, so Lex finally introduced us.

I shook the man's hand and explained, "I read the trades."

He nodded. "Why you cats here?"

"Stopping by to see a cat named Wexler," I said.

I saw Mercer grimace. "Not our best tenant. He's up on the eighth floor."

Two men came out of the building's front entrance and down the steps to join us at street level. They wore extremely dark glasses and English-cut trench coats with loosely-tied belts. Foreign agents or incognito entertainers on a warm day? A cream-colored stretch Cadillac pulled to the curb and kept its motor purring.

"Here now," Mercer said, "on the other hand, comes our number-one man. Along with another august gent."

"Come on, Jack," Sinatra said, "We've got to get to the airport."

Lex had her mouth open.

"Hold on there." The other "gent" pulled his glasses down and looked at me from under a cloth cap. "You're the kid who got cut up when we were shooting *High Society*. Frank, you were there, remember? This fine lad tackled the miscreant who came at me with a knife."

"Hi ya, Mr. Crosby," I said. "Sort of old home week, eh?"

"Shit fire," Lex said in awe and started searching for something that could be signed.

Crosby pointed to my hair. "That white streak is the remains of the tussle, I'll bet."

"You mean it's real?" Mercer asked. "I thought it was

just another hip and crazy hair style."

"Will you two baldies knock it off?" Sinatra complained. "I've got to catch a jet to Vegas."

The rear door of the Caddy opened and we felt a gush of air-conditioning. The two singers ducked inside to join a third man seated next to the car's tiny bar. I was pretty sure I caught a glimpse of Dean Martin's smooth smile as the door closed and the car sped south on Vine to Hollywood Boulevard.

Lex held a limp napkin and looked like she was going to cry.

Mercer turned back to us, explaining. "They're trying to put together a deal to get Capra to direct the life story of Jimmy Durante. It'll be huge, if they can get the financial backing. But I'm glad they got the hell out of here, before Bobby arrived." He pointed to a hat with a man about my age under it, coming down the sidewalk from the parking lot on Yucca Street. It was Bobby Darin of "Splish-Splash" fame. I figured his new "Mack the Knife" tune would go all the way.

Lex's eyes distended enough to make Tex Avery proud.

"Keep it quiet, but Frank is leaving to start his own label," Mercer told us, "so I'm courting Bobby to replace him. You're looking at the new King of Cool."

Darin seemed intent on his own thoughts as he walked toward us, digging a pinky finger in his right ear.

Mercer called to him and he ambled over, sliding his excavating hand into a coat pocket. "Hi, fellas. I'm ready to cut that test disk." He must have mistaken Lex and I for studio execs, because he brought his hand back out for me to shake. Mercer saw that I was staring at it and steered Darin up the front steps without introductions.

Lex watched. "He's gorgeous. My knees are weak."

"Looks like the new King of Cool cuts his own wax,"

I said. "And you're gushing again. Leave them be."

We followed the two entertainers into the building at a discrete distance. The hangover smog inside my head was finally lifting.

Once in the mezzanine lounge, Lex and I rode one of the three elevators up to the eighth floor and found Wexler Investments. Inside, we encountered a cute girl behind an empty typewriter, with triangular glasses and cherry-red nails and a large man on a peach-colored sofa, with a burr haircut and flat nose. I made the guy with the short hair as either Rocky Marciano or the goon Reeves had described. I would have liked to have made the girl, period.

"I'm Stan Wade, here for Wexler. My partner and I have an appointment."

The girl rose and stretched, showing off the curves of her long hair and longer figure. "I'll see if Mr. W is in."

The three of us exchanged glances during the short time she was gone. Then the girl came back from an inner office and the same three of us all went in.

The room was done up in modern show-room furnishings, elegant and impressive in the peach motif. Two TV monitors where mounted into the side wall, next to a second closed door. The sound was turned down or off on both sets. One showed a horse race at Santa Anita and the other played a boxing match from an unknown place and time, but I thought I recognized Archie Moore getting punched.

Eddie Wexler sat behind a desk and in front of a series of curved window from which he could keep an eye on the roof of the Bank of America building across the street. He looked like a man who had tried hard and made it big, like a hungry immigrant who had come a long way, like nothing to worry about. Just a pleasant guy with a long jaw, close-set eyes, and red-white-and-blue striped tie, who would gladly take your last buck. "I understand," he told his telephone. "You can rely on me to turn up the heat. Yes." He hung up, glanced up, and got up. "And you are…" He looked down a scribbled piece of paper on his desk. "…Mr. Wade Samuels?"

I didn't bother to correct him.

"And I understand that you and your associate—" He indicated Lex. "—are connected with Mickey Cohen?"

I didn't bother to correct that either. After all, we were in the heart of Hollyweird.

A commercial for Gillette Blue Blades came on the TV with the boxing program. Nobody shook hands or sat down. Short meeting?

"We're here about the Reeves marker," I threw out. "The one he's already paid."

Wexler glanced at his goon.

Lex stifled a cough.

I went on. "He doesn't want any trouble from you and neither do we."

"You want trouble, pal?" the thug behind me asked.

I stepped back so I could keep both men in sight. "What did I just say?"

The tough guy ping-ponged his eyes to Wexler and back to me. "I—I wasn't listening." Then he added, "Wise ass," and rolled his shoulders like Jimmy Cagney.

"Hold your tongue, sonny boy," Lex said.

Wexler made a raised-hand gesture for peace, as his man took a step toward Lex.

"Why you sick old bat—"

I started to insert myself between them, when Wexler said, "Easy, Ray. I'll handle this. Let's all start over. Since you're friends of Mickey, I think I can let this slide, a little."

I relaxed and thought everyone else did too. "Cancel Reeves's debt and we all walk away happy."

"Is that a threat?" Ray demanded. He didn't seem to be the smartest round in the cylinder. "One thing I can't stand is a threat."

"Well," I answered, "I'm glad there's one thing."

Eddie Wexler stepped around the desk, adjusting his tie. "I wasn't thinking of canceling it, just giving him more time to pay up, at regular rates. It's true that he's already paid once. I think he'll do it again."

Wexler was turning out to be a world-class ass.

"Someone ought to slap your face," Lex growled, stepping toward Wexler. It was the wrong thing to do. Ray the Goon reached under his arm and brought out a short revolver. It was a lot like my .38, which I had neglected to bring to the meeting.

I lunged and caught his arm, twisting his wrist, until he dropped the weapon. He was big, but not fully committed—yet. A new horse race started on one of the muted TVs.

Lex took two steps and contributed her right knee to Wexler's groin. He winced, bent, and went over on his side. I had seen her do this before and knew what came next. She stepped back. "Timber!"

Ray pulled away from me and we squared off, trading fists.

I briefly saw all the stars in Hollywood, and a couple of Tweetie birds flew around my head. I wondered why Walt didn't do Mickey and Donald cartoons anymore. I'd have to ask him the next time we talked, but right now I swung a hard right and heard a crunching noise when I connected with Ray's previously pounded nose.

Blood flowed down his chin onto the carpet and next to his gun. Everybody took a deep breath except for the boxers on the TV. Ray groaned deep in his throat like something from the zoo and yanked open the side door. I glanced back to be sure Lex was okay, telling her to get the cops, and then followed Ray out of the office.

He dashed down the hallway past a water cooler and out of sight. As I came around the curve, it was the Goon by two lengths, followed by Wade on the outside. I caught sight of the door to the service stairs slowly closing.

A heavy clanging of footfalls went up the stairs, just as Lex caught up to me, breathing hard.

"I told you to git, lady." I started up the blood-spattered stairs.

"Okay," she puffed. "I agree—one-hundred proof—but we're going to get—the SOBs—on an assault charge."

"You get the cops. I'll get him." I took the stairs two at a time to the ninth floor, but the red trail continued higher. *Why is he going up, instead of down?*

I moved along as quickly and quietly as possible, panting like Rin-Tin-Tin and listening for the sound of his footsteps, or any door he might open.

He kept going higher.

I caught the bittersweet smell of Mary Jane on the landing as I passed the executive offices on the thirteenth floor. Then the glare of sunlight struck the sidewall of the stairwell and I charged through an access door out onto the bright, round rooftop.

I ducked and rolled to avoid being jumped, but he didn't pounce.

Over the edge of the roof and down below to the north, traffic whizzed by on the 101. The spectacle pulled hypnotically at my eyes. Even though I knew it was blocks away, I felt I could reach out and pick up the cars and trucks as they sped toward or out of Cahuenga Pass.

I shook myself and turned back to the center of the tower. Through a forest of TV antennas and aerials, I saw the thug hunched down by the elevator building.

"No use trying to hide up here," I told him.

He came up, pulling something out of a large metal tool shed and I finally knew why he'd kept going up, instead of down. He turned and came my way, cradling a Thompson machine gun with a twenty-round stick.

When the hell had he brought that monster up here. And why?

Naturally, I raised my hands in surrender and began speaking to him as if he were a skittish colt. "Easy, fella. Whoa there."

He came forward, red still dribbling from his chin. Maybe I'd get lucky and he'd pass out from lack of blood.

Distraction seemed like a good plan at that point. "I walked into an antique shop and asked what's new," I said in a low voice. "They threw me out."

He came closer. "Huh?"

I shrugged my shoulders and stepped nearer. "Just thought I'd lighten the mood a bit." I batted the gun's barrel with my left palm and moved in with another solid right to the center of his face.

The chopper ripped a half-dozen .45 rounds into the afternoon sky.

I clawed at his eyes and yanked the weapon from his hands.

He moved his shoulders and butted into me head down, as the Thompson spiraled in a brief arc to clatter into the four-foot white cement wall that encircled the edge of the roof.

I felt a sharp pain as something under my right arm went "crack." I staggered and he was on me, hefting my body over the edge of the building. I twisted frantically through blinding pain and slammed my left elbow into his jaw, forcing it upward and causing him to tilt sideways.

He let loose of me and we rolled over the side of the retaining wall, falling down through the warm wind from Mount Hollywood.

# CHAPTER 4

*Seconds later*:

The right side of my body felt like it was on fire from the waist up. I dangled over 100 feet above the city, hanging at half mast from a louvered awning on the twelfth floor. Ray had fallen below me, but I didn't know or care how far.

Someone, who looked a lot like Stan Freberg, slid aside a window panel and began hauling me in. I hooked a foot inside and collapsed onto the carpet, wheezing. The guy, whose looks reminded me of Norman, helped me up and we shuffled and wobbled together to the elevators.

He said something and so did I, but they were just words amidst the stabbing pain in my side.

Another nice mess.

I stumbled into the elevator car and shoved Darin back into the hall. "Call an ambulance for that other guy."

The doors to my elevator started to close as I heard the other two cars go bing and Darin say, "Other guy?"

I rode down and started shuffling through the lobby, past the neon oval with its four stars and picture of the capitol dome. There was a lot of excitement going on in the lobby and I tried to look amazed by it all.

I almost made it to the front exit, before two security guards hung up their phones and came in my direction with a determined stride. Mercer called out to them and it was enough of a delay for me to get outside.

On the street, Lex stood next to the hot dog stand. I signaled her off and went south on Vine, trying to catch my breath. The Hollywood branch of the Brown Derby was a very long block farther down the street, but it felt too far away for my pain to allow. I crossed to the west side of Vine, hoping it would break the line of sight, if the security guards decided to follow.

A squad car swooped up the street, its driver ignoring my J-walking, as I shambled along holding my side like the Mummy, headed in the direction of Hollywood Boulevard. An ambulance screamed by. I needed a place to go to ground, before the Lead Investigative Officers tracked me down.

I leaned a palm against an ornate façade and realized I was in front of the Hollywood Playhouse. Breathing was becoming a serious challenge and black spots began floating before my eyes. I turned around the side of the building and looked back. Lex strolled casually out of the gathering crowd and in my direction. Cops were just beginning to confer and look around.

I found a low casement window that was open an inch and managed to widen the crack enough to allow me to climb into the building. The two-way radios in my coat pocket clattered against the window frame. I set one of them on the ground, hoping Lex would find it, and pulled the window shut after me.

It was dark and silent inside the theater. For nearly forty years, the Playhouse had been a place of grandiose and ornate style. Now it was the site of the *This is Your Life* show, but not on a Sunday like this. I was alone surrounded by the Spanish Baroque red-and-gold leaf lobby and black-iron flowing staircases. I hobbled through a world of chandeliers, bronze statues, adobe walls with dark mahogany woodwork and shell-shaped light fixtures. William R. Hearst would have loved it. For all I knew, he probably had the place built back in the '20s as a place to store his collar buttons.

Just around to the left of the main entrance, I found a smaller, carpeted stairway leading down to the dressing rooms. I followed an ordinary hallway stretching beneath the theater seats on the floor above. Eventually, this darker passageway took me to a vast room under the stage, where the walls were stacked with wooden and painted flats and forgotten props. The ceiling was chalk-marked with trapdoors in the stage overhead and a gap yawned where once a freight-lift had elevated an organ up to the audience level.

Had Wexler given my description to the cops? There was no way that they could know I was here. I kept telling myself that if I stayed here long enough, eventually they would give up trying to find me. So I was safe, for now, maybe.

I sat down for a time in an old rocking chair and pressed a cushion against my right side to minimize movement and pain. Switching on the two-way and screwing the plug into my ear, I waited as the pain lessened. Hissing static. No reception down here—maybe problems caused by those supposed sun spots.

I would have to go back up, if I wanted to have any chance of getting through to Lex, assuming she'd found the other two-way. Carefully making my way back up the darkened hallway to the stairs, I listened for any signs of trouble in one ear and a radio signal in the other. Halfway up the steps, I whispered, "Hello?" into the handheld unit, but got no response. I loathed going all the way up to the lobby.

Slowly, I climbed two more steps and the earphone squawked in what sounded like English. I felt my heart thump in my injured chest and called in hushed tones, "Lex? You there?"

"You can come out now, Squirrel," she grumbled. "They're gone and I didn't get a single damn autograph."

☙❧

"Ya need some serious help," Lex said, as she bundled me into the cab of her truck.

"I need to lie down and rest. I just leapt a tall building. Take me to Suzi's place up by the Bowl," I told her.

"Ya need to see a doctor first," she answered and steered the pick-up two blocks south of Sunset to a doctor she knew at the Hollywood Hospital.

An elderly physician prodded my ribs, rested his bifocals on the top of his balding head, and pronounced the universal medical term: "My, my." He lectured me like I was nine-and-a-half years old and wrapped me in girdle of white tape, while Lex made a call to my girlfriend.

When we left, I was full of Darvon and feeling better, but had trouble following the episode of Johnny Dollar that came from the truck's radio—something about a fair-weather friend. I wondered again how much Wexler and his goon had told the police about our visit. Maybe he'd kept mum for fear of Mickey's involvement. Maybe not.

"Get me to Suzi's," I repeated. "She'll take care of me."

"I already called and told her what happened. She ain't happy, but she knows we're comin'."

I raised an eyebrow without feeling any additional pain. The tape on my ribs was already starting to itch, as we neared Suzi's rambling complex. Through the open window and the darkening pine trees, I could hear the Philharmonic rehearsing in the Hollywood Bowl. I caught a glimpse of the dancing-water fountains shooting up from the reflecting pool in front of the stage, and then we rounded a drive to stop where the ex-Mrs. Sunset stood, waiting to take me in.

Suzi was a vision in bare feet, casual white blouse, and lime-colored pedal pushers. I had known her for more than a dozen years, and it seemed that she'd grown more beautiful every time I saw her. Her face looked tight under her platinum bobbed hair, her mouth drawn down in an expression of concern and derision.

I gave her a "Hi, babe."

"Lex said you fell off a building, Standy."

I loved the pet name she'd hung on me when we were teens.

The two women helped me into the front door of the apartment.

"You should have seen the other guy," I answered, feeling stiff as a surfboard in all the wrong places.

They got me over to a couch next to a kidney-shaped coffee table and Lex dusted off her hands like she'd just set down an antique. I knew the feeling.

"I'll make tea," Suzi said.

Lex backed toward the door. "Boiled leaves? That stuff gives me enough gas to drive to Pittsburgh. Guess I'll be shovin' off. Take good care of him."

Suzi's deep blue eyes looked down at me. She shook her head, displaying her impish smile. "I'll give him a great—big—hug."

"Don't you dare!" I said, trying with little success to find a more comfortable spot on the sofa.

After Lex left, Suzi kissed my forehead and settled down next to me. "Are you glad to see me?"

"Great horny toads."

She nuzzled close. "So, how was your day at work, hon?"

I blew and sipped piping-hot Lipton's from a china service, while answering all of her questions.

The premiere episode of a western called, *Bonanza*, played on her color TV.

She ignored it and listened to my tale as I tried to make it all sound like nothing to worry about, just another day at the office.

She didn't appear to be buying my off-handed approach. "You should call Cohen right away. Get out front of this and let him know what happened. He's not someone to leave…hanging."

"Hanging? Very funny." But I knew she was right. She was almost always right about how to best handle an investigation. The small agency she'd inherited when her husband had died kept her instincts sharper than mine would likely ever be. It occurred to me again that we'd do well to form a merger. For now, I just settled for: "Hand me the phone, will you?"

Once I'd got him on the line, I learned that Mickey had already heard all about my little meeting with Wexler. There was no love lost between the two men, but Cohen had arranged to cancel the disputed debts, telling me, "I warned him off, kid, so now my debt to you is paid, too. Get me?"

"Uh, right, Mickey," I said, with a trace of dread. "I understand. Now, we're even."

"Got that right," he shot back and hung up.

I pinched the bridge of my nose between forefinger and thumb and then dialed the number Reeves had given me. I told the actor that "all bets are off" and I'd be sending him a special bill for my time and pain.

Suzi sat quietly, taking it all in. After I hung up, she

seemed oddly focused on the base of a black metal floor lamp.

"Hey, what's wrong?"

She got up slowly and turned down the sound on the television. I noted how the room's dim lighting made her hair shine like precious metal. The colorful cowboys were now engaged in a silent shootout. "I've been thinking about the way we live," she said.

I looked around at her modern furnishings, as my head began to ache. "You live pretty well. I live on a dumpy boat."

She gathered up the teacups and took them to her kitchenette, while I admired her lithe figure. "I don't mean that, Standy. It's just that lately it seems that our work pulls us apart and makes us almost strangers. Do you feel it?"

I didn't have an immediate response, but was captivated by the delicate turn at the corner of her mouth and the sweet scent of her perfume.

"This business," she went on, "draws us into more trouble than we deserve. It almost forces us to be loners." She rubbed her shoulder where she'd been wounded a month ago on another case.

I found my voice. "Easy does it there, kiddo. Don't get all worked up. What's really bothering you?"

"I don't know. I don't really know if I can keep doing this messy, dangerous work—and I'm not sure you should either."

My eyes watered slightly as I stared at the salmon-colored throw rug under the coffee table. "I think I know what you mean, but it's part of the job. We have to work in confidence and play a lone hand. It's in the name of our profession. We're not public investigators, we're private."

A yellow cat strolled in from the bedroom.

"I know," Suzi said, "but neither of us is getting any younger."

This seemed like the perfect opening to get down and propose, but something about her mood and my physical condition felt like it was the wrong time. Yes, we wouldn't want to look back and think we'd come together out of pity, or weakness, or frustration.

Suddenly, I was taken by a powerful urge. The explosive force of my sneeze caused the cat to jump and my ribs to burn as if we'd both been stabbed by a red-hot corkscrew.

I moaned through tearing eyes, "Allergies." My chest clinched in pain as I sneezed again. "Cat." And again.

Suzi and I rushed to leave her apartment and get me to the fresh sea air at my boat. She drove her new Studebaker Lark through the spring night, apologizing for having taken in a stray to protect it from coyotes. I blew my nose into a wad of Kleenex she'd pulled from her glove compartment and tried to make light of the matter by saying, "Cats are my Kryptonite."

The quip helped and, by the time we arrived at the *Cervantes II*, I could breathe easily and my head was back to what, for me, passed as normal. I fell asleep in her arms while the boat gently rocked us.

In my dreams that night, I found myself in Cincinnati where a black-and-white clown played records and danced the Madison with Bing and Frank. Then he floated up and blended with Superman, waving from behind his cape and sailing off above the birds and planes and tea leaves. I tried to fly up and join him, but found that my left wing was broken.

# CHAPTER 5

*Several weeks later*:

And that was the last I had any thought of George Reeves for some time. During the days between April and June, my ribs gradually got better, while my life in general and the world at large didn't.

At large, guy named Castro started showing signs of turning Cuba communist, ninety miles off the coast of Florida. The Dalai Lama stayed in exile and the Russians continued to kick our butts in the Space Race. Peace talks with Premier Khrushchev seemed to go nowhere. Mao Tse-tung stepped down as China's chief of state, but remained chairman of his country's Communist Party. The secretary of defense said that the Soviets could soon have a three-to-one advantage in ICBMs.

In general, I'd conducted a few brief standard investigations for clients like the Brown Derby and Uncle Walt. Suzi began martial arts training to help get her strength back. I decided to put off proposing to her until she fully healed. Norman and Lex came up with a crazy project to build remote controls into an old Packard, but their plan soon bombed out, since neither of them had decent skills as an auto mechanic. And a good German friend of mine passed slowly away from the effects of a lingering disease.

Then on Thursday, June eighteenth, I drove Lex out to the old RKO studios in Culver City, when she asked me to act as moral support in dealing with her son, Alex Church.

"He seems more distant from me than ever," she said. "He's got a new job, working on a cops-and-robbers show for Desilu and I think he's ashamed to have me around."

"It'll pass," I advised as I turned on Ince Avenue and drove my Kaiser past the guard station and studio gates. "Most things change in Hollywood every few months."

"Well, I ain't waitin'," she grumbled. "I need him now."

I wondered why the rush. Lex was usually more easy going, but lately she'd become generally impatient. "Is there something you want to tell me?"

A tall man consulted a clipboard and ushered us onto a set that looked like a 1920s speakeasy.

"Not now," she said, pointing. "There he is over by that camera."

I recognized Alex's lean back bent over a gimbal used for elevated shots. We waited while he argued with a technician about planes and angles. Robert Stack sat nearby in a camp chair, turning the pages of a script.

"Hi, honey," Lex said in coaxing, yet basso voice.

Her son turned his sandy, crew-cut head toward us, said, "Oh, Mom. Give me a minute," and went back to his discussion, moving his hands like toy airplanes.

We waited some more, surrounded by carpentry sounds and the voices of grips and gaffers overhead, calling to each other like strange birds interested in the position of bright, heavy lights.

I was beginning to get bored. Lex actually began tapping her left foot.

Finally, Alex turned back to us. "What's he doing here?"

Church always thought my investigative work was a bad influence. There was more to it than that, but that's how he usually started a conversation when I was around. He had a point, I guess. I'd certainly caused her some jeopardy back in April at the Capitol Tower, but Lex always preferred to steer her ship wherever the winds would take her and nobody could tell her how to chart her course.

"You were too busy to come get me," she told him. "So I asked Stan to bring me,"

Nothing moved in his face, except his flint-gray eyes. "I told you I was tied up with this *Untouchables* shooting." Then he slumped a little, as if he'd just grown younger. "I'll go to the doctors with you, if that's what you need."

Lex hadn't mentioned anything to me about a doctor's appointment, but I had a strong feeling that it would be good way to bring family members together, so I said nothing. Their conversation went back and forth for a while and they settled their differences without me, eventually leaving together in Alex's maroon station wagon.

I wandered back to my Kaiser Manhattan and that's when I bumped into a fuzzy-headed, bearded man on the arm of a slender blonde. He turned away when he saw me, as if I were the one who needed a doctor. The expression on what I could see of his face struck me as embarrassed or guilty. I figured he was some well-known actor in heavy make-up, ready to shoot a comedy scene. I followed the couple for a minute and then had an eerie inspiration.

He gave me another furtive look from under the thatch of dark, curly hair and I recognized the lines of his face and the carriage of his build.

I searched my memory and called, "Mister Bessolo?"

The couple stopped dead, conferred quietly, and turned back in my direction.

"Actually," the man said to his companion, "I think this guy might be able to help."

The woman stood alert beside him, her body taunt, ready to move away. "Who is he?"

I glanced around the parking lot, wondering if they really meant me, but we appeared to be alone.

The man approached, looking over the top of a pair of dark sunglasses. "A local PI who worked for me a couple of months ago. Name's Wade, right? Stan Wade?"

The woman followed him. "He's a private eye named Spade? Are you kidding?"

I winced at my oldest challenge. "Wade, lady. Stan Wade. Spade is a fictional character—in books."

Reeves, for unbelievably that's who it was, chuckled. "Just like in the funny papers."

"You should talk," I told him. "What the hell?" I almost sputtered. "How can you—"

He cut me off with a genuine "shush."

I looking appealingly for grace from on high and started again, quieter, calmer. "How the hell can you—"

Now, the woman shushed me. Were we in a library?

Reeves leaned forward and cleared his throat. "Something new. Witness protection program. I told you I knew a lot about the local Mob." The woman pulled at his sleeve, but he ignored her. "I get a new identity and out from under all my problems in exchange for identifying a few hoods, like that guy I saw at the Brown Derby the day I hired you."

The woman finally conceded to join the conversation, confessing, "We've got a new life now, so keep it under your hat."

"This is impossible," I protested. "It was in all the papers. It's still in all the papers!"

Reeves gave every indication that he was enjoying my confusion. "That's exactly why we came here to the studio. Testing my disguise to see if it's effective, even around people in the industry."

The woman glanced around the area, as I had done moments before. "You're the only person here who's spotted him. What tipped you off?"

Her hair began to look fake to me, too. Hollywood: City of Shapeshifters and Shoplifters. In all honesty, I wasn't sure what specifically had tipped me off, so I fell back on a tried and trite expression: "I suppose, because I'm a trained detective."

"Yes. Yes, you are," George declared. "Saved my ass and it only cost me a couple hundred bucks."

"I'm thinking of raising my rates," I hastened, beginning to overcome my astonishment. "Who's this guy you say you saw that day at the Derby?"

"A little guy with a funny nose," Reeves said, scratching the back of his head and causing his wig to move down farther on his forehead. "A racetrack tout who goes around clubs and restaurants, making book with customers."

The woman carefully eyed another couple who were weaving their way in our general direction between the parked cars.

I said, "Yeah, I've heard of the guy. He's a nuisance for the Derby"

The blonde snapped her attention back to me. "You have?"

"The management at the restaurant wants me to catch

him in the act and boot him out. He's been showing up a lot and is probably there now."

"You see?" Reeves said to the woman. As an afterthought to me, he added, "Oh, Naomi. She knows everything."

I rubbed the back of my neck. "I'm glad somebody does."

He smiled. "Her last name is Lugosi."

I looked at him and slumped.

The Lugosi lady glanced at her wristwatch. "We've got time. I guess we could drive over and meet him there."

My amazement and curiosity took hold again. "I can't believe you're alive. There was a body—and witnesses in the house where—"

They shushed me in unison and we went to our cars to meet undercover at the place where you eat under the hat.

❧❧❧

A half hour later, after I'd recognized the tout as a high-level closet commie and my companions had both said, "Bullshit," the Bela Babe took control of things and commanded, "Come with me."

George and I followed her out the front entrance of the BD and down the street to the Beverly Hills branch of the Pacific Federal S&L.

It was late afternoon, so the financial institution was already closed, but Lady Lugosi flashed an ID at a guard inside, who had the looks and nature of Buster Keaton. We were granted access, as if we owned the place.

Moving together across the echoing foyer, we went down a short flight of stairs to the basement vault. The stone-faced guard spun the dial and gestured us in. Lugosi didn't hesitate, but George and I just stood, looking at each other.

"You first," I said.

"Both of you heroes get in here," the woman instructed.

I began paying a lot closer attention to her as we stepped across the curved threshold. Undercover. Underground. Under control?

"Okay, Fred," she called after the actor and I entered. "Soft close."

"Yes, ma'am." And the guard pushed the vault door shut with a quiet clang, sealing us inside.

"Sound proof?" I asked.

The woman nodded. "Keeps out the radio waves, too. We started using it last year when J. Edgar Bergen and his dummy Clyde got nervous about a couple of our freelance operations."

"So, you're saying that we're perfectly safe," George said. "For how long?"

"There's enough air for a couple hours, but we won't need that long, if your friend, here, tells us all he knows."

I studied the numbered, metal faces of the safety-deposit boxes. "What I know is that your Mob contact tout was highly placed and active at a communist meeting that I infiltrated a few months ago."

"What meeting?"

"The American Workers Alliance, which is a front for a commie cell here in LA."

She nodded. "I can probably confirm that. What were you doing there?"

"Part of a case for a client."

"What client?"

"Can't tell you that. Privileged information—unless you want to explain a few things first."

"Bullshit. I represent the federal government."

"Dealing with communists wasn't part of our, uh…deal," Reeves said,

"It is now," she answered him and turned to square off again with me. "Does this client of yours have big ears?"

I thought about it. "What do you mean?"

"Does he talk in a high, squeaky voice?"

I started getting the picture, but I strung her along further. "You mean like Walter Cronkite?"

She blinked at me. "Another Walter."

"Winchell?" Reeves guessed,

I'd had just about enough. "We're talking FBI, right?"

"Of course," Naomi answered. "And you know what? I realize now that I've heard of you, Stan Wade. Your client is the Grey Seal. He runs you, doesn't he?"

That last part baffled me. "I'm sorry?"

She let out a long breath. "His codename is the Grey Seal. The Bureau let him pick it years ago, God knows why. His real name is too well known to the public."

"Lemme guess," Reeves said. "James Garner."

She wrinkled her brow. "Who's that?"

I said, "How about Richard Carlson? You know, the actor in *I Lead Three Lives*?"

"Oh, good pick," Reeves said.

"I was wrong," Naomi said, leaning back against the wall. "We are going to run out of air."

I gave her my most serious face. "I'd like a look at those credentials now, please."

She came back off the wall, literally and figuratively. "You know as well as I that those things can be faked. What's important now is that apparently the communists are starting to work the Mob, from the inside."

Despite all I'd seen, I still wasn't convinced. This whole meeting was like something from a Bob Hope movie.

"That's absurd."

"Is it? They've already tried to infiltrate just about every other industry, union, local government, even the colleges. Why not organized crime? Just ask your contact."

"My what?"

"Your client. The Grey Seal. You know who I'm talking about. Let's call him."

"I give up," Reeves said. "Who are we talking about?"

She went over to an intercom unit on the safe's interior wall. She pressed the button there like she wanted to bend the steel in her bare hands. "Okay, Fred. We're coming out."

The round door eased open and minutes later I placed a call from office of the S&L's vice-president to a private number that I'd memorized.

George removed his wig and wiped his head with a handkerchief. His stitches had healed nicely. The woman stood by. "Tell him its Amelia Earhart's sister."

I put my hand over the mouthpiece. "You're serious?"

She nodded slightly. "He'll recognize it and talk freely. You can decide what to do after you two talk." She motioned to Reeves. "We'll wait outside."

George followed her into the hall and closed the door. Great Caesar's Ghost.

I spoke briefly with Uncle Walt. The Old Man readily acknowledged the Earhart codename, especially since it came from me. I said, "She's all excited about communists working undercover within the Mob. It's nutty, but she genuinely seems to want my help."

"Yes," Walt said. "I've heard rumors and seen recent reports about the possibility. If those two groups got together, it would mean grave danger for the country."

I knew from past experience that Walt worked undercover as a special agent in charge for the FBI. He'd started operating as a SAC during World War II and had continued behind the Hollywood scenes during the cold war. I owed him big time for covering my back during an earlier case involving the AWA. He was fighting the good fight, but the public would probably never know. I'd kept all this private, but recent first-hand experiences with a couple of crazed party members had turned me to the Old Man's way of thinking and sparked my interest in stopping commies any time I thought I could.

"How would you feel about sitting in on this one for me, Stan?"

I wasn't quite yet a determined commie-hater like my friend Norman was, but I still wanted butter on my bread. "Double rates?" I pressed Walt.

"All right," he responded. "I think it might well be that important. Follow her lead and keep me advised."

When I hung up the VP's phone and came out of the office, I told Naomi that I was now on the payroll. "Where do we begin?"

She'd anticipated my question and didn't miss a beat. "You boys are going undercover with me tomorrow in Vegas."

Reeves beamed. "Isn't she wonderful?'

I almost responded by saying, "Bullshit," but I was afraid that if I did, it would become my codename.

# CHAPTER 6

*The next morning*:

I had a feeling that the day would be grueling, long, and ugly. Spooning coffee into the percolator and plugging it in, I turned on the portable TV and watched *LA Morning with Maude* on channel eight. She was interviewing Roy Rogers and Dale Evans about a chain of restaurants they were opening in the valley. While I dressed, the Tommy Lynn Trio played a Latin-beat version of "Dancing in the Dark" as the camera panned across the waving audience. I made toast, poured hot coffee into yesterday's dirty cup, and selected a twenty-year-old tie and a fishing-rod clasp that Mr. P used to wear. I turned off the TV in the middle of a cartoon dog-food commercial, got into my Kaiser, and made a left on Sepulveda, wondering if I'd unplugged the percolator.

In quick order, I arrived at FBI headquarters and met up with George and the small squad of agents run by Naomi Lugosi. "Good morning," I said and extended my hand.

She looked at it without moving and I realized I was

still holding my car keys. "Nice tie," she said, turning away. "They're wearing them thinner this decade."

Being the new guy, I was asked a lot of questions, some I preferred not to answer directly. It was not easy joining this group. They were exclusive and mistrusting. I became suspicious that they suspected something suspicious of me. The main thing that won them over to my side was Norman's little two-way radios which I'd begun using over the last few weeks. Transmissions from the devices were not secure, but the mere idea that brief code signals could be exchanged among team members was near intoxicating to this cautious group of federal agents. Naomi and her second-in-command, a wiry, dark-skinned guy named Max, wanted one immediately. I phoned Norman at A-1 Electronics to see if more units could be made available and he said all I needed to do was stop by the shop later and he'd have them ready. He also asked me to pick up the latest issue of *Popular Science Magazine*. His subscription had run out.

As it happened, there was a meeting that evening of the AWA, so Reeves and I were assigned to attend it and report back any additional Mob members we might find there, before rejoining the team that night in Vegas.

I left the FBI office before noon and went back to the boat to pack a valise. It was too early to meet up with Norman, so I listened to "Sorry," "Along Came Jones," and other top ten tunes on KFWB, while driving over to Suzi's place to let her know I'd be out of town.

My girl was just returning from a class she'd started taking in Pasadena to strengthen her upper body and gain more confidence. "It's inspirational, as well as physically demanding," she said, while we lunched on her patio overlooking a part of Laurel Canyon, and thus avoiding the cat. Mild smog was better than the allergic reaction I had to that creature.

                                    

I looked skeptically at the small container of pale gunk she was spooning into her pert mouth. "What's it called?"

"Kenpo."

"Looks disgusting."

She glanced down at what she was eating. "Not this, Standy." She raised the container to eyelevel. "This is yogurt. My training is called Kenpo. It's a serious martial art, combining mind and body discipline."

"Like judo?"

"Ummm…more like karate."

"Ah, karate I've heard of." I finished my baloney sandwich and leaned over to inspect her trim figure. "It seems to be having a good effect on you, too."

She nodded appreciation. "Thank you, sir. I believe it is indeed. You should try it."

"It still looks disgusting."

"Not the yogurt, the kenpo. It's empty-hand combat, mostly about those karate-style chops used to break bricks. Only you use them instead to strike and stab at sensitive parts of your opponent's body." She raised an open palm vertically in front of her face and jabbed it in my direction.

"Okay, chop, chop, when do you want me to start training?"

"Not for another week, at least. I'm busy on a case."

This was both surprising and encouraging. Suzi hadn't taken a case for months, due to her injury and generally sulky mood. Apparently, things were beginning to look up for her. I showed my interest. "What's the case?"

"Don't get me wrong," she said, easing back in her chair and gazing out over the late afternoon light that filled the canyon. "I'm still planning to quit the business. It's just too…too demanding…on my spirit."

Kenpo talk? "Oh, I don't know—"

"It pulls me off center and leaves me feeling used and empty."

Yep. Kenpo talk.

She shook herself and sipped ice tea. "But the case is for my cousin, Bethany. She works in the wardrobe department at Paramount and is accused of stealing Danny Kaye's Diner's Club card. There are two other people working with her there, so I'm going to find out which one took it."

"Danny Kaye, huh? Sounds interesting. I think I read he's working on a bio-pic with Bob Crosby and Louis Armstrong. How do you plan to find out which suspect stole Kaye's charge card?"

She warmed to the question, as we cleared up the remains of our lunch and moved inside. "I'm going to grill them hard, Sherlock, and ask where they were on April thirty-first. The one with a good alibi will be the culprit."

Holy frijoles, that was brilliant. She had a completely different investigative technique from mine. I'd have demanded answers, hoping to gain truth by intimidation, while she was content to trick people into trapping themselves.

I told her a little about my case and that I expected to be back in town in a few days. We spent some intimate time together and I finally started sneezing from the Krypto cat around six o'clock, so I left her to head off to the TV repair shop.

ℰℐℰℐ

"Okay," I said. "You'll never guess this one: 'Dinner in the diner. Nothing could be finer.'"

Lately, whenever we spoke, Norman and I had started challenging each other to a game of "guess the next song lyric." One of us would supply a line from a song and the other had to respond with the next line. Extra points if you could also supply the name to the tune, itself.

"Got it," Norm smiled. "'Then to have your ham and eggs in Carolina.' 'Chattanooga Choo-Choo.'"

"Damn. And I thought I'd stump you with old band numbers."

"I get to listen to a lot of songs on the radio while fixing electronic equipment." He had three more radio units and twenty-eight pages of his new novel waiting for me.

"It's a murder mystery set on Mars. I'm calling it "Reds on the Red Planet" and my private eye, Clem Picasso of Triple Eye Investigations, fights telepathic commies who are trying to take control of the planet."

I knew better than to question him about his book, or I'd quickly get a headache. I tactfully eased the subject back to something a little closer to reality. "Commies, again, huh? Why, Norman, do you have this hate for communists?"

He shrugged and placed the radios and manuscript pages into a paper sack for me. "It's not something I like to talk about," he said.

I waited, mostly out of courtesy, rather than curiosity.

He toyed with the dial of a pre-war Philco table-model radio. "They'll do anything to get what they want. They tried to blackmail my uncle who taught physics at Harvard back in 1950." Now he picked up a battered Tom Swift novel and then carefully placed it back down in the same spot on the work bench. "My aunt and cousins were still over in Poland." The pain in his eyes made me feel like a voyeur. "Now they're gone."

This was much more than I'd expected. My throat felt tight. My eyes caught sight of a black and white drawing leaning against a rack of TV tubes next to a slide rule. It looked like the original art from a Sunday comic page, something called "Lance." I reached out to touch it.

"I got that straight from the artist, Warren Tufts," Norman warmed to the new topic. "And Alex Toth was there too. He gave me a cool sketch from the Bret Maverick book he's illustrating."

The pen and ink art was fine-lined and polished from a skilled hand like that of Hal Foster's Prince Valiant, only this drawing was of characters in the Old West.

"A girl I know works at Western Publishing and I got to meet Alex and Warren there. Alex is working on concept art for a spider-bat monster in a new sci-fi movie, *Angry Red Planet*, and Warren is doing a Zorro comic."

I admitted that both drawings were impressive. Almost like real art.

"Oh, you think so, huh?" he grinned, coming back to full normal Norman. "Mark my words, Mr. Wade. Someday there'll be entire conferences about the artists and writers of comic books and newspaper strips. It's an American art form."

"That's pretty amazing, Norm."

"The part about the comic conventions?"

"No. The part about you're knowing a girl."

I had to dodge a Brownie camera that came sailing at my head.

ↁↁↁ

"Which one is the Old Duck?" Reeves whispered.

"Can't you tell?" I hissed back. "The guy with the white hair and bristle-brush mustache in the center of the stage."

I'd known that the American Workers Alliance met in an empty warehouse on Olympic near Santa Fe, since I'd attended, or rather snuck into, an earlier meeting there while on a previous case for Walt.

"Nope," Reeves mumbled. "I don't recognize him as part of the Mob."

Having first grabbed a bite to eat on the way over, I'd met George here in his phony hair and fedora around ten o'clock on a cloud-covered night.

"You look different without your beard," I said to him.

He ran a palm over his chin. "Damn thing itched worse than this wig."

I wouldn't know, since whenever I tried to grow any heavy hair on my face, it came in weak and spotty.

We'd followed the crowd filing into the hanger-sized meeting hall and selected chairs far back in one of the last rows. Out of the corner of my eye, I saw Nicky, the race tout from the BD, shaking hands and moving up to the stage area at the front of the high-ceilinged room. The Duck greeted him warmly, like a close relative. The older man was slightly overweight and sat in a cream-colored suit, with his hands on his knees, like a Kentucky Colonel.

Various Party members rose to the occasion and spoke before the audience, detailing their various successful endeavors. One short guy that Reeves quickly identified as part of a gambling syndicate had something going on with jukeboxes in pizza parlors. A plump woman wearing a pillbox hat smugly told the crowd that she chaired book club meetings where pro-commie works of fiction were introduced to middle-aged housewives. If I'd had a portable tape recorder, I could have secured enough evidence to launch a dozen Bureau investigations. I made a note to see if I could get Norman to build me something lightweight.

"I think we're done here," Reeves spoke into my ear. "I don't recognize anyone else from the Mob,"

I leaned in his direction and mumbled, "Keep looking. There are a lot of people moving around in this place."

He agreed just as the meeting took up a new activity. From the stage, the Old Duck rose and stepped forward before the crowd, looking like Mark Twain. He dusted off his 'stache and began talking about the importance of being a loyal party member. I hoped he wasn't going to pass the hat.

He pointed to someone in the audience and directed that they stand up and tell the group, "why you're a loyal party member."

"Uh, oh." I nudged the actor next to me. "We'd better get going." Reeves adjusted his hat and fuzzy wig and we got up to leave, just as the Duck pointed our way.

"You two comrades," he called out and all heads turned to face us. "Thank you for volunteering.

I bent down slightly and whispered, "Shit," but George stood tall as if in the middle of a spotlight. The audience's eyes were on him like Texas and he held their attention as if her were Douglas Edwards with the Evening News.

"It's not enough to be only a loyal Party member," he told them in a modest, commanding voice. I stayed in a half crouch, as he went on: "We must be ever vigilant, comrades. Many of us have friends or family behind the iron curtain and constant vigilance is the price we all must pay for their continued safety."

"Here, here," the Duck called out.

I looked up at George, but the actor was buried in the role.

"We must always remember," he said with a sweep of his hand, "that there is no business like Party business."

Someone to our left shouted "Here, here," and the Duck nodded agreement, holding up open hands of encouragement.

"Everything about it is important," Reeves went on. "Nowhere else do you get that special feeling, than when you're vigilant to your party vow."

The Duck applauded loudly and the crowd joined in

before another "volunteer" was chosen and attention shifted away from us.

"Come on, Hamlet," I said, pulling Reeves's elbow.

Two men, each the size of frost-free Frigidaires, moved in on us. "Come with us, comrades, if you please." His breath was as strong as a mountain-climber's socks.

This was not the time to start a fight in public, so we followed the refrigerator twins to a small room off to one side of the main hall and waited twenty tense minutes, until the meeting broke up.

The Duck and two additional men entered the windowless room, which now felt awkwardly crowded with all seven of us standing in a group. I began assembling some sort of bluff in my mind when the Duck came over and handed Reeves and I his business card.

"I want you men to have those," he said, pruning and lighting a Havana. It wasn't a business card, rather an official AWA membership card with, of all things, a red seal on the back. "Your extemporaneous speech tonight was inspirational to us all."

The rest of the crowd, including Reeves, nodded like the Supreme Court. I felt very alone, especially when I noticed that one of the guys in the room was Nicky, the tout. A toothpick dangled from his mouth. He caught my eye for a second and then told the group, "Just a minute. I know this guy. He runs security at the Brown Derby."

I immediately felt the single focus of everyone's attention. "So? What of it, comrade? It's simply my cover." I looked around. "We all have cover stories and secret identities."

"I say they're cops," the tout charged. "Or they've been planted here by the cops to get evidence against us. Lousy spies."

The Duck's eyebrows went down. He gave out a cloud

of cigar smoke, gestured toward me, and told to one of the Frigidaire Boys, "Search him, Claude. Just to be sure."

If they found the two-way radio on me, I might not be walking home tonight in one piece. I took a step back and looked at George. His eyes moved left and right. And then he took his Clark Kent horn-rimmed glasses out of his breast pocket and said, "Here's my cover story, comrades. I'm really Steve Allen, see?"

He switched his sunglasses for the pair he'd taken from his pocket and mashed his hat and wig farther down. "Hello, folks. This is your old Indian sportscaster with all the sports news for all you sports out there in sportsland."

A guy the size of a boxcar gave out a booming laugh. "Hey, he's right. I seen that act before on TV. This guy's hilarious."

George shamelessly hammed it up. His laughter was infectious and even the Duck chuckled around his cigar.

I saw Nicky approaching me, but his attention too was drawn to Reeves who pounded his fist into his own palm. "The 1959, ouch, baseball season is getting underway..." He giggled, adjusting his fedora. Almost everyone in the room watched and laughed with him. "And the score is still tied, three to five."

A howl went up from the group and the Duck moved over to shake George's hand. "Very nice to meet you, Mr. Allen. I did not recognize you at first."

"My friend and I work hard to keep our party loyalty a secret," George said, continuing to milk his part until the right moment. "That's why I'm in disguise here tonight."

"I understand," the Duck puffed. "I've had cause to do the same before myself, but I'm proud to make you a card-carrying member of our cell." He patted George's broad shoulder. "However, like you so aptly said earlier tonight, we must be ever vigilant, correct?" He turned to me. "Claude, search that man. And then, our friend, Mr. Allen, here."

Nicky the Nose smiled cruelly, waiting for confirmation of his claim that we were government plants.

Rough hands roamed over my chest and back. I watched another guy pat down George's arms and legs. Nothing suspicious resulted from the actions and the tout immediately protested that we should be searched again. This time to the skin.

I threw out, "How 'bout we search you, too, pal?"

The Duck paused and puffed. Then he nodded.

Seconds later, they found the two-way that I'd slipped into Nicky's coat pocket. He actually seemed to turn a little green. "What's that? That's not mine. They planted it on me."

George raised his chin. "Everything's a plant with you, isn't it, comrade?"

The Duck screwed the radio's earpiece into the side of his head, flipped the switch, listening.

Everyone was respectfully still, as if we were in church, so I silently composed a prayer.

The Duck spoke into the radio, "Hello? Can someone there hear me?"

"It's not mine, I tell you," the tout shouted. "It's his!" He came at me and I moved away, bumping into George. One of the Fridge Boys belted Nicky in the back of his head with a fist that looked as solid as a sewing machine. The tout lost his toothpick, going limp as a sack of grain.

At the same moment, the Duck dropped the two-way onto the concrete floor and stomped down, sending a crunching noise and small pieces of plastic and metal across the room.

"Take out the trash," the Duck told the two blocky guys and they carried the sack of Nicky out of the room.

"You boys have done us a good service," he said to George and me.

Reeves took in a deep breath. "Ever vigilant," he declared.

I was relieved, but still concerned about our future.

The Duck continued to blow smoke and nod. "I want you both to keep those special Party membership cards. They'll identify you as loyal, trusted, and vigilant members."

Not far away, perhaps at the other end of the vast warehouse, I heard a voice cry out, followed by a single sharp report of a firearm. I felt my face flinch. It wasn't the result I'd intended when I'd slipped the two-way into Nicky's pocket. I'd hoped for an easy way to avoid being caught red-handed, not a homicide.

"Gentlemen and comrades in the great cause, let these events inspire you all to greater loyalty," the Duck calmly advised us all.

I felt sick and my hands shook a little when we finally left the building for the cool night air. The stars were still hidden by cloud cover. I had always stopped short of killing anyone straight on, unblinking, and thought I always would. A good investigator could find another way out of a grueling and ugly situation. Solving a case was not worth taking a life, even indirectly.

Or was I dead wrong?

# CHAPTER 7

*Later that night*:

Whomp-a-whomp-a-whomp-a-whomp-a…
Over the rhythmic thudding of the helicopter's blades, Reeves asked, "So you've been to Vegas before?" His alter ego smiled at me, still wearing the goofy full-head toupee and hat.

I simply shouted, "Yes."

"Me, too. I love it there."

I yawned and felt my ears pop. Yep, he was a gambler, all right. And it was true I'd visited Las Vegas a year or so ago, but I'd never traveled there by copter before. It was an unbalancing experience. Lex and I had foiled a casino heist and almost gotten arrested, before we could make it back across the California border.

I strained to see out the window past my reflection at the hundred-mile-per-hour, moonlit landscape passing below. Buffeted by desert winds, I felt myself soar and dip among the air currents. George and I had caught the night flight about two hours ago, loading on the suitcases we'd previously packed and strapping in for a low fast swoop across the desert to America's Newest Showplace.

As soon as we'd left the AWA meeting earlier that evening, I'd used my car phone to call Captain Seidman at the LAPD and report a shooting or possible homicide. Neither George nor I knew Nicky's full name, so there wasn't much else we could say or do. Still, it bothered me that I'd indirectly contributed to the death of another human being.

Strangely, it didn't seem to bother Reeves at all. He was a lot more cool-headed than I'd expected—or at least that's how he acted. We were operating under cover together with people who didn't hesitate to kill for their political principles and George sat calmly inserting a Philip Morris into his cigarette-holder and lighting it as if he were FDR. The pilot hollered to him to put it out, but Reeves just clamped it in his teeth at a jaunty angle and blew smoke toward a crack in the Plexiglas window of the whirlybird's side door.

Whomp-a-whomp-a-whomp-a-whomp-a...

"This silly disguise of yours is starting to wear thin," I shouted.

George nodded emphatically. "Starting to wear on me, too."

"I know the FBI somehow faked your death and you're beholden to them, but how much longer do you have to wear that get up?"

"Few more days," he shouted back. "They had another body stashed in my bedroom closet that night and I went out the window."

That fit with the accounts I'd read in the newspapers. His friends had heard the shot and ran upstairs to find a naked body that looked like Reeves with a bullet hole in its head. The world was all upset over his "death," but I could see that George was enjoying his new identity, even if it required him to wear sunglasses at night.

"What made you think you could pull off that Steve

Allen routine with just a pair of ordinary glasses?"

He shrugged and crushed out his cigarette on the helo's floor. "Hey, the writers made it work in every episode, so I figured why not try it in reverse?"

Whomp-a-whomp-a-whomp-a-whomp-a…

We tilted and the engine noise dropped a few decibels. My ears popped again.

It was windy in Vegas as we disembarked the helicopter of the ironically named Icarus Air at the darkened McCarran airport. The night air was blast-furnace hot. When I looked around, I saw that the airport was small and somewhat jerrybuilt. In the distance, I could see a blaze of wattage that pinpointed the city and its casinos. To the south, a few miles away, sat the low structure and a few DC-3s of the Hacienda Airlines. Nearer at hand, there didn't appear to be any signs of life, except for a single, waiting lime-green taxi. I grabbed my grip and walked toward the vehicle almost parked on the tarmac. Grit blew into my eyes as the chopper lifted, tilted, dipped, and flew off into the inky night.

The cabbie was tan as a copper penny. George and I rode in quiet awe past a giant flying saucer that our driver said was the recently opened Vegas Convention Center. We drove along the Strip and saw the huge, new casinos sprawled across a sandy stretch of badlands leading to nowhere framed in the distance by the timelessness of the desert and the hulking mass of the Black Mountain.

Cruising briefly up Fremont Street, I caught sight of the Golden Nugget across from the Mint. How could I miss it? It was lit up like a Hollywood premiere. Farther down the perpetual day of "Glitter Gulch" were the Lucky Strike and the neon cowboy smoking and waving welcome to the city's hungry pleasure palaces. The double highway was chocked in both directions.

People here simply did not go to sleep. Chumps of

every persuasion were streaming toward the casino's glass doors with the excitement of kids heading for the big top. Cowpokes, servicemen, overweight middle-Americans in Bermuda shorts, even a bum in sunglasses. Fancy-dressed women with what looked like off-the-rack suited accountants and druggists. The swarm of hopeful patrons glided through the walls of arctic air at the entrances of the most perfect machine, since the government, ever designed for the continuous extraction of money.

Back on the Strip, our taxi finally dropped us off at the Riviera Hotel and Casino, a big block of a building that reminded me of Uncle Scrooge's money bin number one. The sign out front said that the Ritz Brothers were playing here and I thought I caught sight of Liberace beside the illuminated pool as we made our way inside.

"I'm for the roulette tables," Reeves said, checking his bag at the registration desk. His back was already moving away from me, when he added, "Let me know when Naomi's train gets in from LA."

I was tempted to join him, but I was also one tired bloodhound. I couldn't find a bellboy, so I hefted my bag up to my room on the fifth floor and planned to call it a night. The room had a nice-sized double bed with a shower and tub that smelled of lavender. There was a five-dollar chip on my pillow and a color TV where I watched the tail end of Jack Parr before drifting off to dreamless sleep.

The sound of twittering birds woke me and I found that it was the phone ringing beside my bed. During the night, I must have gotten up and undressed, because my clothes lay in a heap on a chair beside the curtained window. My wallet and gun appeared undisturbed. The phone call advised that I had a message from another guest room. My mouth felt as if I'd eaten a mud pie. I actually had eaten one years ago when Suzi had served it to me, so I knew what one tasted like. "What time is it?"

A crisp female voice said it was sorry, but there were no clocks in Las Vegas and transferred the call. I thought maybe I was still asleep, until I heard Naomi say, "Get your lazy ass to the crap tables. George is winning."

I slipped the Twist-o-flex band of my watch onto my wrist and saw that it was 9:15. The sliver of sunlight at the bottom of the window curtains told me it was Anti Meridian.

Dressed casually, without the broad tie and fishing-rod clasp, I found my way down to the modern, busy casino with its tidal wave of noise and color. The dizzying carpet around the crowded roulette tables and tutti-frutti hues of slot machines with their relentless chinking conspired to dazzle and attract me.

A swarming hive of hope and frustration filled the dimly lit cavern of chance. Guys with manicures and top-dollar ladies. A gray-haired man sat placidly smoking on a corncob pipe in a wheelchair steered by the buxomest blonde I'd ever seen.

The place had the ambience of an ocean liner. A long bar and its group of cocktail tables were separated by a running half partition from the main gambling area.

I found Naomi and her man, Max, standing close to our disguised actor making passes before a medium-size crowd at a dice table. The rack along the table's edge in front of the actor was full of five-dollar chips. "There are plenty of Syndicate men all over this place," she said to me in a low voice, "but it looks like the AWA leader is here, too." She indicated a small group of men off to one side also watching George shot the works. Among them, stood the Duck.

"Who is that guy, anyway?" I whispered.

"His name is Reed and he's in oil from Texas."

"How do you know?"

She moved as sleek as a princess phone. "Max has one of your little radios and was able to listen in when they spoke briefly with George a few minutes ago. They called him Mr. Allen and invited him to a meeting later this afternoon."

"Is he in danger?"

"George? Hell, no. He's in hog heaven here and I'm keeping a weather eye on him. There was mention a few minutes ago of plans for launching a casino in LA, but I don't know if it's to be run by the Mob or the party, or both. What have you heard about it?"

The pitman at George's table had his hand up, signaling. Reeves wanted a smoke. A cigarette girl came over and George selected a pack of Kents and dropped a five-dollar chip between her full breasts.

"Me? It's all news to me, lady. Communist gambling? It doesn't make sense."

"Exactly, man," Max said. "I think I can jimmy this radio to get better reception, but the casino might notice and won't like it."

"Too big of a risk, Max," Naomi cautioned quietly. "We'll use your wiring skills another way, another time. This assignment is taking on new proportions." She turned to me. "Can you contact the Grey Seal and see if he knows anything about plans for a casino in Southern California?"

I had a few other things I wanted to talk to Walt about, so I said, "Sure, where will you be?"

She looked at George in his wig, hat, and sunglasses. He was still the shooter, rattling the bones. He even blew on them before his next pass. She sighed. "I'll have my hands full with him. Come to room 612 in an hour."

I thought about calling Walt's number from the quiet of my own room, but opted for a pay phone instead. That way, it seemed there would be less chance for someone else to be in on the call. I strolled outside and found an empty phone booth out near the highway. I listened to the hollow sound of coins dropping and bells clanging within the long-distance phone system. After I got my "client" on the line, I explained the situation as best I could without using any specific terms.

As it turned out, Walt had heard reports of a possible re-opening of a casino on Catalina Island, but there was no mention of an affiliation with the Party. He encouraged me to find out as much as I could, even if only the usual "organization men" were the ones planning the operation.

"And keep an eye on Amelia's sister for me, too," he said. It sounded like he was asking me to lend a helping hand to a fellow agent. I agreed automatically and rung off.

On the way back to the hotel entrance, a family was exiting a taxi in front of me. They were obvious tourists—father, mother and mop-haired son. While the parents were gathering their bags, the young boy ran out almost in front of an on-coming bus. I caught him in time and his folks gave him hell for "acting up again, Stevie!"

I grinned at that and they thanked me, following me back inside to the registration desk where I heard them sign in as the King family. The kid kept giving me weird looks through his thick glasses. Maybe he'd seen the gun under my left arm.

The crowd had broken up when I got back to the crap table, so I sat and played blackjack for about twenty minutes and ended up a couple of bucks up. I moved to a neighboring roulette wheel, went back and forth on red and black for the rest of the hour and took my modest stack of chips to the cashier's window.

I left the clank of the slot machines and the drone of

dealers and caught the elevator to the sixth floor, feeling like a lucky, modern day Robin Hood.

ﻌﻌﻌ

By the time I got to room 612, it was half past eleven. George and Naomi were seated there, enjoying a coffee service. I would have preferred some Irish in my coffee, but I guess J. Edgar's agents didn't drink on the job.

"So your final task is simple," said the woman to the actor. "Since they now accept you, you can easily make the drop and go on."

"Thank God," George said. "I can't wait to be done with all this spy stuff. You people strike a hard bargain."

"That was our deal for your new identity. You get a fresh start and we get inside information. The fact that we're now dealing with Reds as well as the gambling syndicate changes nothing. One more little performance and you're on your way." She handed him a Polaroid camera on a plastic strap. "Just leave this at the meeting and it'll record everything."

Reeves started to open the back of the camera, but Naomi stopped him, saying it would damage the tape machine inside.

"Won't they be suspicious?" he asked.

"Act like every other tourist in town. Tell them that you even forgot you had it with you. Set it aside anywhere within ten or fifteen feet of them and it should pick up their conversations. Then you can leave. Max will pick it up later."

I listened to this and reached for a piece of toast. "What did I miss? Where are we going?"

"You're staying here," Naomi said. "I had you two come to Vegas because we'd learned there's a meeting today between select casino representatives and your friends in the AWA. George has been invited to join them at the Convention Center."

Serious spy stuff. "Sounds risky," I said, pouring coffee into a clear glass cup and saucer. "I think I should at least go and follow him to be safe."

"I already have Max stationed outside the convention building. He's there now."

"Is that the place that looks like a landed UFO?"

"Yes." She nodded. "Welcome to the space age, Mr. Wade. George will be all right, and I need you here."

"It's the last thing I have to do to fulfill my part of our pact," Reeves said. "Then I can catch my flight out of here and put all this behind me."

Naomi came to him and they slipped into an embrace. "You know that I'll miss you, you big lug," she said. "Just drop off the device and get on with your new life."

George tousled her long blonde hair. "Madame, I'm yours to command."

I cleared my throat, but they ignored me. Maybe I was invisible.

She rose up on tiptoes and planted a light kiss on his cheek. "You're performing a great role for the good of country, baby, and I'll miss you."

"Miss you, too," he said, strapping the camera around his neck. He looked at me. "It's been fun, pal. I guess you can take it from here."

"Sure," I said, not sure exactly what "it" was, or where I could take it.

He pulled at the rim of his fedora in a gesture of respect and opened the hotel room door.

"Wait a sec," I said. Even in his goofy make up, he looked strong. Happy, too. I went over and shook his firm hand. "Enjoy your life as a disguised actor. You've earned it."

"And you keep up the good fight for truth and justice."

He smiled. "See you in the funny papers." That was his exit line.

I swallowed more coffee and vowed to myself to someday find out exactly what that meant.

Naomi huffed audibly through her nose. "Thank God, he's finally gone for good."

I chuckled and eased into the comfortable chair where Reeves had sat. "You don't like him?"

"No wonder he couldn't get a job acting as anything but a big hunk of ham."

I knew that FBI agents often had to stretch the truth and twang it like a rubber band to extract the information they wanted, but this seemed unduly harsh.

I studied the carpet for a moment and then asked, "What's your real name, anyway?"

"That's need to know and classified." She looked as comfortable as a kitten on a cushion.

I leaned back. "Okay, Miss Classified, what do you want me to do? Why am I even here?"

"I like you, Mr. Investigator. We have a lot in common. We both like to get at the truth and we both hate commies."

"There's that." I shrugged, although I felt she was pushing the last point. "Now what's the real reason?"

She rested her long legs on one of the other chairs at the table. "First, let's talk about Disney."

"Okay."

"You know, of course, that he's a double agent."

I placed my glass cup in the center of its saucer and became more aware of the weight in my shoulder holster. "What do you mean by that?"

She stood up and moved to the window, becoming framed in the noon sunlight. "Please don't play dumb with me, Wade. I know you've been running special assignments for him over the last few years. You think you're in his confidence, but there's more to it than you could possibly know."

I uncrossed my legs and began inventorying the room. Nothing seemed out of place. No secret equipment or hidden weapons that I could see. "You're right, of course," I answered. "I've worked with Walt and he does have things he keeps to himself. But he's no communist."

"How do you know he's not a closet Red?" She went to the unmade bed and sat there picking up the two-way radio I'd given her. Was someone listening? Was I being tested? "They're all Reds," she said in an even voice.

I watched her carefully, but said nothing.

"I had a family once. They knew the risks involved with my profession, but they accepted it. Until they were taken from me. My husband and son. I haven't seen them since."

She was no Betty Davis, but her anxiety at that moment seemed very real.

"I know the Russians have them and I'll kill every damn Red if I have to, in order to get them back."

Why tell me all this? Was she playing me for some reason? Or was she a little unstable? I decided to try and appeal to reason. "Look, I still don't know why I'm here. Why do you—"

"You're here as insurance, Wade. I needed George to follow through and you helped. I need a hold on Disney and you're it."

I made my voice calm, but firm. "Just a minute there, lady—"

The phone on the bedside table next to her began to ring. She took it up and listened, watching me come to my feet. I honestly did not know what to do next. I could leave, but there were too many unanswered questions still hanging in the air. Her actions and comments in the last few minutes had thrown me off and made little or no sense at all. I was hooked like a fish, dangling on her next line.

She spoke into the phone. "Very well. If you think they've spotted you, get out. I'll take care of it from here." She hung up. "They're on to Max. If they capture him, they could find out where we are. We can't let them take over."

"Then George is in danger, too."

"No, you heard me tell him to find a reason to get away after he's dropped off the fake camera. That part has been done. The camera's there and he's gone."

I came back with, "You don't know that for sure. Listen, I can contact Walt for you and you can—"

From under the bed pillow, she drew out a black automatic and pointed at me. "Let's not be so damn hasty."

My hand went to my shoulder holster and I ducked low, trying to shove the table at her. It didn't work and I fell back with my gun up. I caught my balance and found we were in a Mexican standoff.

"Put it down," she commanded. "If they win, they'll destroy everything we've built up for almost two hundred years."

"You're nuts." True, but not the best thing to say under the circumstances. We held each other at gunpoint and I realized that I might actually have to shoot her. Worse still, she might shoot me. "Take it easy," I offered, wondering how I could get out of the room un-perforated.

In her free hand, she held up the two-way radio, a thumb on the power switch. "Thanks for this, Mr. Wade, but I've had Max rewire it." I'm sure my face looked like it didn't understand, for she went on. "It's now a detonator for George's camera bomb."

Bluff or insanity? I kept my gun trained on her and heard my voice say the fatal words: "Put them both down, or else."

She stood up and I almost fired. "They'll enslave us all. I'm going to kill them and you can't stop me."

A bead of sweat trailed down the center of my back. "Stop," I warned. "Right now."

She laughed like a child and placed the two-way on the table in front of her.

"Now drop your firearm," I ordered, extending my own weapon farther in her direction. I saw that I was going to win this standoff, so I repeated, "Right, now."

She laughed again and her tarnished eyes had something tortured in them. She echoed my phrase, first saying, "Right—" and then stabbing a hand at the radio's switch and firing her gun. "—now!"

Time slowed like an over-cranked movie camera. I'd gone one step beyond into the twilight zone. The radio was a transmitter? The camera was a bomb? This FBI agent was a crazed assassin, intending to shoot me and blow up her enemies?

We both fired our weapons and I felt a tug at my coat sleeve.

Her outstretched hand missed contact with the radio and even the table. She fell over, her torso thrown to the side, hiding her head, her face, and the bullet hole I knew I'd put there.

My gun was an anvil in my damp, shaking hand. I'd crossed the line and killed, coldly and intentionally, and now a loud pounding came from the hotel room door.

# CHAPTER 8

*As time seemed to stand still*:

Now I was a killer.

Attorneys, doctors, policemen, and soldiers—all professionals remained calm under stressful situations. I was just plain numb for several seconds.

I'd killed a federal agent, but I'd saved lives. Hadn't I?

The pounding at the door made me want to run, but I was still frozen in place by the thought of what I'd just done. Consequently, as the door to the room came open, I turned, gun still in hand and faced down a guy with thin arms and legs, a sturdy body, and high forehead.

"Whoa, buddy," the heavy-set Fred Astaire said, raising his hands, one of which held a ring of keys. "Hotel security. I don't want any trouble."

I lowered the gun. "Me too neither." It came to me that I was "in a world of shit," as Lex would say.

The cautious house dick stepped eloquently into the room, saw the body on the bed, and looked at me for an explanation. "How 'bout you give me the gun, buddy?"

It seemed like the right thing to do, but my hands had their own ideas and slide the .38 back into its shoulder-holster. "She was going to set off a bomb. I—I had to stop her."

He stretched out a thin arm and felt the side of Naomi's neck. "You stopped her, all right."

I clinched my eyes, which is why I didn't see the other people gathering at the room door. But I heard a gasp and a "Holy Ike."

From out of the huddled, yearning mass, shouldered a middle-aged man wearing a freshly pressed suit, carnation, and pencil-thin mustache. Behind him came two other guys. One of them was the commie leader, Reed. "Okay, Andy," the official with the flower said to the hotel cop. "I'll take it from here. You keep mum, until I tell you, check?"

"Yes, sir," Andy said. He was ushered out of the room, the door closing behind his ample, gangling form.

I watched all this without comment, partly from fear and partly from shock. I stared at my palms, but saw no signs of blood there. The bitter scent of cordite bit my nostrils and I failed to suppress a sharp sneeze.

The Duck, Reed, came over and wished me, "Gesundheit," as I pulled out a handkerchief and blew my nose.

The hotel official leaned over to inspect the body. He looked up at us. "You'd better get out of here, Mr. Reed. I'll see that this is taken care of. It's not the first clean up I've had to handle."

The snow-haired Duck and the other man, who had come in with him, hustled me out, past Andy, who was clearing the last few stragglers from the hall. "You're the fellow who was with Steve Allen last night," he said steering me to the elevators. "You two will have to join our little get together tonight."

I still couldn't fully shake the feeling of numbness. "Uh…Steve can't make it. He's been called back to Hollywood for a show, or something."

"That's all right," Reed said. "Come along with us, then. We'll see that the management here takes care of this mess. What was your name again, son?"

"Wade. Stan Wade." The killing kept replaying in my mind as we walked together across the casino floor. People swarmed around the gambling tables as if afraid the games would close before they could lose their money. Someone chattered, "Seven a loser. I'm afraid he's fallen big time."

"Sounds like I've heard of you," Reed mused, ignoring all of this. "A detective, right?"

"What?"

"I said, some sort of detective, eh?"

"Yes. Some sort." I was having trouble concentrating. "How'd you get here?" I asked dumbly, as we approached a limo parked in front of the Riviera's entrance.

"We caught a man at the convention center and learned about the bomb and how to find the FBI agent who was going to detonate it. We sure owe you our thanks, comrade Wade." He stroked his mustache. "We'll see that most of this doesn't hit the newspapers, but with so many people involved now, some part of the story is bound to get out. You understand." He gestured toward the open door in the side of the limo. "Come. Let us show you our gratitude."

I felt as dull as the hum of the highway. Their gratitude consisted of dragging me to almost every live floor-show and lounge act in Vegas. I saw Joey Bishop at the Sands, Tony Martin at the Desert Inn, and some guy impersonating Elvis at a club I couldn't remember. This town had more stars than MGM, but it was all a lot of sound a fury to me.

At each stop, new members were added to our group, until there were nearly twenty of us. The idea seemed to be to move me around enough that I'd have a decent shot at an alibi, if necessary. I kept quiet throughout most of it, making mental note of the people who joined us and picking up bits of information. This was a busy crowd.

Reed and his cell appeared to have completely accepted me as one of their members. They spoke freely before me about their plans to infiltrate the Mob. They even planned to use the connection with organized crime to tap Union pension funds, hoping to gain further control of the "idea factory," which is what they called the movie industry. As a Texas oilman, Reed bankrolled the operations, directing Party members to work on projects both here in Vegas and back in LA. The plans were so grandiose and widespread that I knew there was no way in hell they could pull them off.

We all had dinner at the Sahara and watched Bobby Darin perform as the opening act for George Burns. Seeing the boy wonder again finally brought me back to my old self. Seeing Burns made me want to smoke a cigar.

At their meeting that night, back at the Convention Center, Reed puffed on his own Havana and introduced me to Dandy Phil Castle, who was trying to buy ownership of the swank Tropicana.

"I want Wade here to work with you and Sam," Reed said.

Castle looked me over and grunted. He was a moneyman from back East. Short, middle-aged, with a wide, thickset body and a shock of unruly black hair, he walked with a swagger that showed self-pride.

I raised my chin in greeting. Reed gave me an assignment as part of a group attempting to set up a "floating casino" between greater Los Angles and Catalina. I was mildly surprised to find that one of the men in charge of the program, Sam, was the Elvis impersonator. Without his wig and makeup, I saw a touch of hardness around his mouth and eyes. He outlined his plans to the group for redesigning and moving an oil platform from down in Long Beach to set twelve miles outside the city in the Catalina Channel, but Reed seemed cool on the idea. He listened, nodded, brushed a finger along his thick mustache and announced even grander plans and a new public slogan for the overall operations of the American Workers Alliance: "My Independent America." I had the impression I was inside a political party's smoke-filled back room. My sinuses began to swear alliance and my head began to throb.

Later that night, we all went back to the Sands and caught the rambling, impromptu act of the Rat Pack. In the middle of Dean hoisting Sammy up and presenting him to Frank as an Academy Award, I looked to my left and recognized the grinning face of Eddie Wexler, staring at the stage. He knew me from our tumble at the Capitol Tower and might blow my cover. He looked as dangerous as an overloaded electric socket. The tip of his cigarette glowed in the darken room as he inhaled deeply.

Sliding farther down in my seat, I thanked Reed and gave him the excuse that I'd had enough excitement for one day. He seemed to understand and handed me the key to a room at the Hacienda, one of the older casino/hotels out by the airport. "You did fine work today, comrade. You've earned a decent rest," he whispered through his cigar smoke.

I couldn't believe that he was letting me leave on my own. "Super, man."

"Pinky will go with you back to our rooms," he continued and nudged a short, fragile kind of guy who looked cool and fresh in spite of the late hour.

Pinky, with hair too thin and red for the crew cut he wore, led me outside in the ninety-degree night air. I wanted to catch a cab down Highway 91 to the train station and get the hell out of Vegas, but I was in too deep now. I was an accepted member of the communist party who knew too much about their plans and I was a killer. They'd use that against me, if I tried to rabbit.

Sand swirled from the vacant lot next door and bit my face with abrasive force. I felt as dull as a dial tone.

Pinky drove me to a long, low sweeping building with a red tile roof and wings that ran back on each end to enfold a pool-centered patio. We used a side entrance to avoid notice. Reed had a suite up on the top, second floor with a full bar of premium stock. I poured and drank down four fingers of Johnny Walker and flopped exhausted in one of the empty bedrooms.

જીજી

I slept fitfully, watching the clown visit my dreams, doing back flips. For a second, it looked like Naomi was going to join the act, so I did that thing where you force yourself to wake up. I felt as old and yellow as a World War I-era newspaper and went to the sink for a glass of cold water. My watch said it was 8:47 and I smelled fried eggs and bacon. My suitcase had been gathered and brought to the room. I showered, shaved, and climbed into fresh cloths. I even chuckled when I thought about a Red named Pinky.

"Ah, here's our sleeping beauty." The oilman from Texas was in full Duck mode. "Good morning, sir." Seated in the sunlight pouring in from the room's huge windows, he casually folded his newspaper and raised a coffee cup to me in grand salute. "Come and join us for a bite, comrade. We were just reading about the bombing attempt."

I eased past the windows and looked down at bathers splashing and sunning below. There was a small balcony, maybe three feet across, and a trellis that ran down to the ground. "Just coffee," I said, holding my stomach. "And perhaps a bit of toast."

I figured they were wondering about my early exit from the festivities last night. Obviously, it looked a little suspicious, so it might be a good idea if I feigned illness. The truth was, I still didn't feel fully in focus. I kept flashing back to the moment when I'd so easily squeezed the trigger.

Pinky grinned from a nearby couch. "Try the boissonberry marmalade. It's superb."

Reed quickly corrected, "Boysenberry," and unwrapped the cellophane from a cigar.

I wondered what best to say or do to ensure that they remained convinced that I was still a loyal party member. And what was that business last night about a floating casino and Catalina Island? Maybe the gambling operations of the Mob were coming back to California but, if so, what was the Communist connection?

I needed to find a way to make contact with Walt and validate my whole purpose of being undercover with these creeps. For now, all I could do was shrug, fake a burp, and ask, "What's in the paper?"

Reed held up the front page so I could see the headline. *BOMB SCARE AT AWA MEET.* Beside it was a story about how another Vanguard rocket launch at Cape Canaveral had gone off course and a sidebar saying that the Soviet Union planned to sell an atomic bomb to China.

"Pretty explosive night," I commented.

"Don't worry," Reed said, folding the paper. "We made sure that your part of the local story stayed out of the press. Why do you think we kept moving you around last night? Wouldn't want any nosey reporters to learn the details of your shootout, would you comrade cowboy?" He chuckled deep in his throat.

I reached out with the courtesy lighter that I still carried and offered him a light for his stogie. I hadn't noticed before, but his mustache was the same style as Walt's, except Reed's was almost completely white.

"The party thinks that, to achieve our goals, it is vital to control the press. The account in the paper here describes the foiled explosion, but nothing about your…uh, activities. To us, you are a hero. You saved dozens of lives…and only took one," he puffed on as I buttered and munched on a slice of toast. "To the rest of the world, you're an unknown and we plan to keep it that way."

Until it suits your purposes, I thought. They now had a threat they could hold over my head. I wondered what they'd done with Naomi's body.

"Tell me something," I said, pouring a cup of black coffee. "Why are we here? I mean, how is it that our people are so well allied with casino and hotel owners here in Vegas? I would have thought that the party would never associate with money-grubbing capitalists."

He set his pungent smoke in an ashtray. "Not what you'd expect, is it? Which is exactly the point, son. The members of the various organized crime families are not, strictly speaking, capitalists. Nor are they all that well 'organized.' We have an opportunity to undermine the true capitalists of this decadent country by joining forces with established enemies of democracy."

"I get it now." I sipped from my cup, even though I wasn't thirsty. "The rule of the masses and mob rule are almost the same thing."

He answered with one word: "Almost" and then changing the subject. "Now let me ask you nearly the same question: why are you here? Why did you join the Party? We've checked into your background and it seems you've been associated with several shady business dealings over the last half-dozen years, but…"

I knew I was walking a tightrope here and he could knock me off, literally, by questioning my reason for being a Communist. I had to convince him that I was a true Party member. "The truth is," I lied, "I attended some meeting back when I was in college. Nothing where I signed anything, of course, but I learned the basics of the Cause and read the manifesto."

He nodded. "But what drove you to join? What inspired you to take action against your country?"

I sat there, a PI working for the FBI, undercover with the Reds who were infiltrating the Mob—and it was time to tell a whooper. I inhaled and let it out slowly. "I'm convinced," I said, keeping my face perfectly still, "that the Feds were behind my parent's death in a car crash late in the '40s. They went over the side of a mountain at night, for no apparent reason."

His white eyebrows went up and he leaned back a little. "That's something we'll certainly check up on."

"Are you questioning my veracity?" Where had I come up with that word? "Or are you threatening me?"

"I am," he said, placing his cup on the table, "concerned about what you'll do next, son."

I set my cup down as well, smiling. "I'll do as I'm told—comrade."

"At least," Pinky said from his seat on the sofa, "you knew who your parents were."

Reed and I both looked significantly at him. The little man shrugged and adjusted the knot in his tie.

"Things have a way of working out for the best," I advised Pinky. "Scout's honor."

The silver-haired Red turned his attention back to me. "I've read a fair amount of detective fiction and I must say that I expected a man like you to be a bit more brash and bolder. You know, comrade, 'my gun is thirsty' and shooting people in the stomach. That sort of thing."

"I hate to spoil all the camaraderie, but this is reality, sir, not fiction. Besides, I did kill a woman for you."

"Point taken," he said, tossing down his napkin. "And we have definite need of your investigative services. There's another vital operation—this one at Marineland—and we need to know that our underworld contacts there do not suspect the party's involvement."

"This has something to do with the floating casino project off the coast of LA?"

"Something."

So, we were back to one word answers again.

"For a party leader, you're a hell of a businessman, Mr. Reed."

There was a hard rapping at the door. Pinky got up and let in Dandy Phil and his buddy Sam, who I had to admit, did have a passing resemblance to Elvis.

"The guy we picked up outside the convention hall got away."

"When?" Reed demanded with unveiled concern.

That would be Max, I thought. Just how much did he know about the bomb, Naomi, and me?

Phil swallowed. "About an hour ago."

"What happened?" Pinky asked.

"He overpowered Comrade Krofft at the neon sign shop," Phil explained. "But he couldn't have gotten far on foot out there on the edge of the desert."

"Find him at once," Reed ordered.

I was in the belly of the beast and knew it was time to find a way out. "Lemme get my gun and go along," I told them, going back into the bedroom and closing the door. I immediately opened the window, hung a curtain out, and ducked into the closet. It was a move I'd seen once in a late night movie. A minute later, as I hid in the dark confined space and listened to the sounds of them rushing around outside the thin door, I quickly questioned my strategy, safety, and sanity. I held my .38 at the ready and heard Phil shout about the window in my room and the trellis. Then it grew quiet, so I stopped holding my breath.

# CHAPTER 9

*Scant moments later*:

I eased open the closet door, went to the window, and peered carefully over the edge of the balcony. Pinky was halfway down the wooden trellis, but none of the other comrades were in sight.

I gingerly left the bedroom, coming back into the suite.

Nobody.

The door to the hallway hung invitingly open.

I dashed for freedom like a fugitive from behind the Iron Curtain. Maybe I was panicking, but buddy, it felt good to be in action again. This maneuver just might actually work.

I surfed silently down the carpeted hall, past a maid's cart, where I snatched a hand towel to cover my revolver, reached the far end of the passage and a single flight staircase, thanking the gods that the iron steps were thickly carpeted, leading to a glass exit door. Within careful seconds, I was out in the dry heat of the late morning in a half-filled parking lot, tossing the towel and tucking my gun into its shoulder holster, near giddy with excitement.

This maneuver was going to work—except every car door that I tried to open was locked.

A fat guy in a loud Hawaiian shirt, solid as a chest of drawers, noticed me and grew interested. He flicked away his cigarette in a short arc, while I tried to appear casual. Maybe I should whistle. The big guy looked back over his colorful shoulder, when Pinky and Phil came skidding on the gravel walkway around the corner of the building.

I impulsively ducked down and the Hawaiian guy started yelling and pointing in my direction. So much for giddy.

Up to that point, I hadn't actually seen any of my comrades packing heat, so I decided to use my own to get what I desperately needed. I approached the guy in the bright-colored shirt and let him see my holstered .38.

He eyes grew wide. "Look now—let's not be too hasty."

It stopped me for a full second and then I saw Pinky dash back out of sight around the building, probably going for more help. Phil went low behind a two-tone Dodge.

"Toss me your car keys, Big Kahuna," I said in a tough-guy voice. "Now!"

The Hawaiian guy fished out a jingling bundle from his pants pocket.

From the edge of my eye, I saw Phil moving in. I couldn't be sure he didn't have a gun.

The guy in the shirt underhanded his key ring to me, asking, "Can I go now, please?"

I caught the ring on this crazy merry-go-round. "Which car is yours?"

He didn't answer.

"Come on." I reached for the gun. "Where is it?"

People were starting to notice.

I acted like Bogart. "Where's—your—car—pal?"

Phil popped up, aiming his arm in my direction. Sunlight glinted there. Pinky and Reed hustled over to join him.

The Hawaiian wet himself, whining, "It's in the shop getting a brake job. Don't kill me!"

I heard some fool say "Shit," as a bullet whizzed and smacked into the frame of a station wagon behind me. The comrades started to spread out among the parked cars. Somewhere a woman screamed. I kept low and searched furiously for safety.

A late model Buick sedan kicked up gravel in the lot and almost ran down Phil, skidding and slowing as it roared toward me.

"Get in," Max shouted from the open passenger window and fired once over my shoulder into the air. I raised my hands and opened the door to the back seat.

Max gunned the engine, spraying grit, and steered for the highway.

I shouted, "Home, pardner. And don't spare the horses."

He floored the gas pedal, heading back into town, instead of the open spaces.

"Are you nuts?" I said, leaning over the seat. "They'll be right behind us in a sec."

"Exactly." Max tried to see around me in the rearview mirror. "And let's get one thing straight. We ain't partners and we're not friends."

Through the rear window, I saw a rust-red convertible rocket out onto the road and speed in our direction.

"I heard about what you did to Naomi," he growled, hunched over the steering wheel.

"Hey now, she was talking crazy and going to blow up the whole—"

"Exactly," he yelled, screeching onto Fremont, headed west to the Nugget. "She was very nuts, all right. I saw it coming during the last few weeks. She set you and your actor-buddy up like bowling pins."

The red convertible followed at an unreasonable speed, almost hitting a woman wearing a sundress and floppy hat.

"You knew about the bomb?"

"No, but I suspected it. That's why she staked me out at the convention center, away from you guys. Any closer, and I'd've been blown to shit."

Our car made a sharp right turn and bounced down a ramp into an open parking garage. Max skidded the Buick around a panel truck and parked in a slot beside a dark-green Chevrolet. "Come on," he commanded and jumped into the Chevy's driver seat.

I caught on to his plan and felt about as bright as the radium dial of my watch, underwater. The FBI had a car planted here for emergencies like ours. As I dashed to the passenger side and joined Max in the second car, I glimpsed the red convertible zoom past the garage entrance, headed north up the alley.

I hadn't paid much attention to Max before. As we went south out of the garage, his wide, cruel mouth and hard eyes made him seem like the world's most determined agent.

I gave him an edited version of my last dozen hours in Vegas before the commies witnessed my "rescue." It occurred to me that I could now convince them that I was a valuable asset, because of my supposed affiliation with the FBI. Despite my elaboration, Max remained glum and didn't talk much during our "leisurely" drive out of the city. Eventually, I leaned back as we cautiously followed the sun and the two-lane blacktop ribbon across the dry lonely desert.

My nerves were shot and, despite my allergies, I yearned for one of the cigarettes Max smoked. Almost four hours later, we passed a new housing development, where each lot included its own fallout shelter. Max pulled in for gas at an Esso station off Highway 91 in San Bernardino, still fifty miles east of LA. I was starving and bought four packs of Twinkies and two stale Babe Ruths from a rack in the gas station. I washed them down with a warm bottle of Pepsi, while I called Suzi's agency and left word that I was back in town. Then, from the ancient phone booth next to a pyramid of oil cans, I dropped another dime and dialed the man who was paying me. A yellowing sign over the pay phone told me: *Buy Bonds.*

"Yes. I just heard about it," Walt's firm voice said in my ear. "The word is that she had some sort of illness that affected her thinking. We're not sure how she contracted it. She was fine last month at her last psych evaluation."

"I don't care," I told him. "It doesn't make any difference to the fact that I'm still the one who gave her brain a bullet."

"You saved lives," the Old Man counseled. "You made the hard choice for the good of many."

"She was a human being. She had a husband and a son who were killed by the commies. She wanted revenge."

"That was a delusion, part of her mental disease. She had no immediate family."

"What?" I felt like I'd just touched a high-voltage fence.

"She used to be a fine agent, but recent accounts have her starting to act queer."

"Queer?"

"Not that kind of queer. The reports said, odd. Off balance. At least, Stan, you're safe now. And Max is an excellent operative. Tell me what you've learned of the AWA plans."

I loosely described what little I'd heard of a floating casino off the coast of Los Angeles.

"Yes. I've heard about that, too," he said. "What do you want me to do?"

"What do you want me to do is more important."

"Most of the Mob's attention lately is focused on Havana and Florida." I could tell he was thinking out loud. "Events in lower California have taken a backseat at the Bureau. It would be a perfect time for the communists to try something here."

I went back to swallowing my cream-filled Twinkies. "Kind of thought you'd say something like that."

"What else can I say?"

The shoulder holding the phone slumped and I caught the receiver in my free hand. "You could say forget the whole thing."

Max hit a short blast on the car horn to urge me to hurry.

"Is that what you want me to say?" the voice in my ear asked.

I said that it didn't matter.

"I know what you're thinking, Stan. But at the risk of repeating myself, I'll say again that you did the right thing back in Vegas. It was your duty to save lives, so take a trip down to Marineland for me, all right? Let them think you have an in with the FBI that they can use."

"A double-double agent?"

"Yes. I'll see about getting a couple of agents to keep an eye on you."

That got my dander up. "No thanks. If I do this, I don't want any more of your Bureau friends anywhere near me. I'll handle it my own way, or not at all. That's final."

The horn blasted again and I took satisfaction in hanging upon him.

*⁓⁕⁓*

Roughly an hour later, as the golden ball of the sun melted into the ocean, Max dropped me off at the short pier next to my boat and we compared notes a final time.

"Let's get our stories straight," Max said.

"I'll say that you thought you were rescuing me—"

"I was!"

"I know, and I'll tell them that eventually I escaped from you. They think that the FBI and the CIA are dopes."

"We're not dopes."

I let that pass. "Look, I've gained their confidence, even though you appear to have yanked me away from them They know my name and profession. Everything will check out."

He thought about it. "So when they eventually catch up with you, they'll think that you're still the same comrade who saved them from being blown to shit."

"And they'll still think they can use me to gain inside information from the FBI. Get it?"

"Got it."

I wanted so much to say, "Good," but instead, I got out and went around the front of the car to offer my hand. "Thanks for saving my ass, back there."

His eyes were still and brown. Stubble covered his shining chin. "This double-double business is highly risky, pard. Are you sure you can do it? You don't want to end up floating face down out there in the Pacific."

I sniffed the fresh ocean breeze and gave him back his favorite phrase: "Exactly."

He grimaced, put the car in gear, and drove off.

I climbed aboard the *Cervantes II*, past the teak foredeck, wicker chairs, and brass fittings that needed a polishing.

I was weary and beginning to understand why PIs were loners.

Up on deck, someone clanged the boarding bell twice. "Ahoy, the boat," I heard Suzi sing out.

My heart soared and soured. I wanted to see her, but this didn't feel like the right time.

"Down here," I shouted and she came aboard down the ladder, hauling a picnic basket. She wore pink pedal pushers, a sleeveless white blouse, and a checkered bandana that matched the red-and-white cloth covering the top of the basket.

I greeted her with a kiss and a "What's this?"

"A celebration. I solved my case."

"Suffering succotash. How long have you been out there waiting for me?"

"When you called, I decided to meet you here." She opened the basket, extracted the checkered cloth, and spread it on the chart table. "Besides, my spies are everywhere." Next she took out some wax-paper containers and a bottle of cranberry juice.

I grimaced. "I'll make us some Kool-Aid."

While I pumped water from the reserve at the sink and mixed in a packet of red power, Suzi pulled out a baguette, cut off a few slices, opened the wax containers, placing them just so on the table cloth. "Pasta salad with spinach, thin sliced roast beef, fresh fruit, and for dessert, your favorite: Hostess Twinkies."

Ugh. More cream filling. I switched on the radio and found a classical station.

"And the best part is," Suzi smiled, "we don't have to wash any dishes."

"So," I asked, forking pasta and avoiding spinach, "Did your April thirty-first gambit work?"

"Did it ever! The culprit was the guy in charge of hats and shoes in the warehouse. A young kid from NYC, who had a history of fashion back in New York."

I chewed beef and bread. It was totally delicious. "Okay…"

"He made a dash for it when I accused him, tripped over the leg of a klieg light, and almost electrocuted himself. Got burnt and cutup pretty badly."

"You sure you didn't just Kenpo him?"

She threw a grape at me. I caught it and popped it into my mouth, grinning. "What about your cousin?"

"She's completely exonerated. Taking a week off to visit our family up in Santa Barbara. Funny thing was, Danny Kaye got a new Diner's Club card and now the company is planning to back him in a movie deal."

She seemed in a hundred percent better mood than the last time I'd seen her. "See there—" I swirled my cherry Kool-Aid and raised my jelly jar in a toast. "—you're a better detective than you thought."

The radio played Mozart's Eighth Symphony, I think. I used to hear it in the basement lounge of the girl's dorm at college, while a cute brunette and I—well, never mind that.

Suzi didn't raise her glass back. Instead, she looked down at her pasta. "I still don't know…" Then she looked up. "How's your latest assignment?"

I gave her the same edited version I'd used with Max, ending by telling her I was planning to look into rumors of off-shore gambling around Marineland.

"I arranged for a friend to get a job there last year," Suzi said. "She's an ex-B-girl."

"She sounds interesting."

"Don't get your hopes up, sailor. She's completely reformed and now studying hard to become a marine archeologist."

"She sounds interesting and hot."

Another grape sailed my way. I caught this one in my

mouth, like a trained seal gobbling a sardine.

Suzi scowled at me, sipped her Kool-Aid, and scowled some more. "Do you have any ice I can put in this?"

I got up, bowed from the waist, and stepped across the cabin. There was a note from Lex taped to the front of the icebox, which must have been there for at least a day. Her loose, pencil scrawl read: *Doc says I got throat cancer.*

# CHAPTER 10

*Minutes later*:

"**M**y god," Suzi breathed when I showed her the note. "We have to go to her."

"Right now?"

Her eyes were as wide as searchlights. "Of course, right now. Absolutely."

"Absolutely."

We took separate cars for maximum mobility in case of an emergency. She knew the address of Lex's place at 625 Palisades Beach Road. Lex house-sat the main, beachfront property for some studio muck-a-muck in exchange for free rent.

As I drove north on the Pacific Coast Highway, I tried to reach Norman on the jerry-rigged car phone that he'd recently installed under my dash, but there was no response. As a result of my fooling with the phone, Suzi beat me there. I pulled in and parked next to her sky-blue Renault Dauphine.

Since the stucco and marble home sloped down toward the beach, it was what we Angelinos call a "one-and-a-half story." I took the thirteen wooden outside steps two at a time to reach Lex's door above the wide garage. I huffed for a sec and then knocked.

She answered the door, lines in her face, bags under her eyes that I didn't remember being so deep before. "Come on in. Coffee's brewing."

Lex was a loyal and faithful friend from way back. She'd saved my life once or twice. Come to think of it, I'd saved hers twice, too. Once when she'd almost drowned during a sudden storm off the Santa Monica coast not far from where we now stood and once when she'd been trapped in a cave-in of an old gold mine up near Placerville. During that one, everybody else had given up on her, but I'd kept digging until my hands were like raw meat.

She glanced over at Suzi sitting on a horsehair couch from the last century and back to me. "You look like shit, squirrel. Suzi been keeping ya up at night?"

I went over and gave Suzi a "Wadimiss?" look. She shrugged ignorance back at me, so I sat down next to her, while Lex brought in steaming mugs of coffee.

"I'm all out of bourbon, so you'll have ta take it straight."

"It's fine," Suzi said and blew ripples across hers.

I set mine aside on a fancy TV tray from Pan Pacific Auditorium. "Naturally, we got your note," I explained lamely.

Lex gave a rumbling cough, set her chipped mug down next to a folded-back copy of TV Guide on the shelf of a wooden floor lamp. "What note?"

"Ha. Ha."

"Just kidding. I appreciate you kids comin' over to see me. I—I ain't got no immediate family."

"Except for your son, Alex," I offered.

Her eyes shot daggers at me. "And he's an ungrateful jerk."

Suzi handed me her coffee and I set it next to mine. "What did the doctor say about your…" She made a gesture toward her own lovely neck.

"My prognosis?"

I couldn't help blinking.

"Didn't think I knew that word, did ya? Ya learn new stuff every day." She took a ragged breath. "He's got me seein' a specialist on Monday. Pretty sure I'll need an operation on my throat." She swallowed some hot coffee and grimaced slightly.

"Look, Lex," I said, "If there's anything you need that I can—"

There was a knock at the door. Lex nodded to me that she understood and got up to see who was calling.

Suzi reached for my hand and held on like a hammerlock.

"Oh, hi, boss," Lex said, clearing her throat. "Come on in." And Peter Lawford joined us from out of the night, wearing a genuine lounging jacket.

"Sorry, to disturb you this late," he said in a soft, cultured pearl of a voice, "but I have to ask—"

"Hey, no trouble at all," Lex said, perking up. "Just chattin' here with a couple of old friends." She turned to off-handedly indicate us.

I got to my feet and came over to shake Lawford's tennis-grip hand. So, this was the muck-a-muck for which Lex house sat. She was right about learning new stuff every day. "I really enjoy that *Thin Man* show of yours, Mr. Lawford," I told him. "You're a pretty swanky private eye."

He self-consciously touched the gray at his left temple. "Well, thank you, but the last episode airs on Friday next. We're on at 9:30 opposite that *77 Sunset Shit* and got crushed in the ratings."

"Geez, boss," Lex moaned. "I'm sorry ta hear that."

"Not to worry. There's always something else on the horizon." He bounced once on his toes. "Alexis, I came up to ask one of your friends to move their car, so Pat and I can get out of the garage. We're off to a late dinner at the Zanuck's."

"I'll get it," I volunteered and went out with Lawford to maneuver autos. By the time I got back, both women were seated on the couch and slightly weepy. I asked, "Wadimiss?" again, but got no useful insight. There are many mysteries in this life that a male professional investigator will never solve.

The three of us talked for a while and it was finally decided that I should go and Suzi should stay. I wanted to stay and offer some sort of support, but who am I to fight city hall? I told them that I'd call in for any news and Suzi lead me gently to the door. She gave me a gentle kiss, too. "If I think of it, I'll bring some cranberry juice tomorrow. It has healing powers."

"And it tastes like crap," Lex said from back at the couch.

I nodded glumly. "Good night, Suzi and Alexis," and drove to the Blue Phrog to hoist a few beers.

❧❧

I hoisted more than a few beers that night. I stayed and yakked with Sunny Goh and learned that it was his big idea for Suzi to take up that Kenpo training. Seems it's a big deal in Hawaii. It felt good to gulp down foam from a frosted mug, for a change, and I stared at the flickering image of the late show movie on the TV over the bar, until the end when Bogart said, "The stuff dreams are made of," and Ward Bond said, "Huh?"

It was soon so late and drunk out that the first half of the Sunday paper was delivered. The front page would come in a couple of hours, but I got a chance to glom the want ads and the comics. I looked at Dennis the Menace. "What do you know? Today's Father's Day."

"It's also the first day of summer," Sonny shouted back. "So what? Want me to check your horoscope?"

Thoughts of my own father came over and sat next to me. He was a cheerful, yet stern man, who liked baseball and fishing when I was growing up and seemed ultra-busy as we both grew older and further apart. He and my mother had both worked at the Lockheed plant, north of Burbank.

Sunny came down the tilted bar and said over my shoulder, "What'll you have?"

"Black Label," a guy behind me said. After he'd been served, the guy stood there, kind of close.

I waited, while the TV started giving out ball scores. The gray-haired guy with grizzled beard and mustache didn't look my way. He drank his beer down and went out. I never saw him again.

It suddenly overwhelmed me that I knew almost nothing about my grandfather. I knew that his father had come from Germany in the 1800s, because of a famine or something, but that was all I had. I felt a little alone again and the cold night seemed to touch my shoulder. What was I doing here? I had to get moving.

Sunny brought me coffee that he said was as strong as the smell of a mountain climber's socks. I thought that was a bit too much hyperbole, if you'll excuse the ex-pression, but didn't argue with him about it. Instead, I relaxed, rocking on my stool at the bar, and spent the next ten minutes drinking steaming cupfuls of the stuff and checking on the latest events in the lives of Moon Mul-lins, Bugs Bunny, Kerry Drake, Lance—that western of Norman's—and, yes—Superman. He was up in Alaska, dealing with Lois Lane's kryptonite vision, which was enough to sober up any man, steel or not.

When I finally got moving and carefully drove my Kaiser back to my boat, the sun was burning over the mountains to the east and I figured I'd try to call my buddy, Norman Weirick, again on the car phone. He picked up after two rings. I told him about Lex and her illness. I also told him that I was going undercover with the commies and not to over-react. He immediately over-reacted anyway, saying he was certain I'd be drugged, or hypnotized and converted into a communist puppet.

"Look, Norman," I said, parking next to the shabby pier where the cruiser was docked, "what do I have to do to convince you that I'm not going to turn communist?"

"That's exactly the problem," his voice chirped. "They can get to you like smoke through a keyhole. They can turn you and you wouldn't even know it—just like the body snatchers."

I told him that I thought I'd know it.

"Did you ever read any Lovecraft?" he said. "The narrator always thinks he's sane until the end of the tale when it too late and he starts raving about Ancient R'Lyeh and Nayarlathotep."

"Oh stop it, Norman." I started to get out of the car and realized I was still on the phone. "We don't have time for raving, especially yours. I'm not now and never will be a member of the communist party."

"That's exactly what they all say."

I felt an unfair rage building behind my eyes, beside a pulsing headache, and almost called him what a lot of other people call him: "Weirdo" Weirick. Logic, right now, was not my strong suit. "You win." I laughed like Elmer Fudd. "I'll be vewy, vewy caweful."

That stalled him long enough for me to say, "Happy Father's Day," and hang up. What a maroon. I weaved up the gangway and fumbled to get the hatch open. I could usually handle Norm's nonsense without resorting to sarcasm, but I'd put in a full day—and night—and my body needed solid sleep.

I yawned deeply and switched on the light to see Sam and Phil standing there with guns drawn. I automatically raised my hands. "Eh, what's up, dopes? Is this a purge?"

❧❧❧

They hustled me into the back seat of a gray Pontiac. Sam the Elvis drove. Dandy Phil sat in back with me, holding an automatic like it was a filter-tip Viceroy cigarette. When I asked where we were going, he told me that I had a nice boat. They weren't going to talk, even when I mentioned that we might want to stop for Late Mass on such a fine Sunday morning.

We rode easily through the light traffic around Pasadena. They were either going to take me somewhere to grill me or kill me. Probably both. I began to think that they weren't smart enough to consider me an asset who had access behind the Berlin wall of the FBI. I decided to nudge their minds in that direction. "We need to see Reed right away," I coaxed them. "I found out a lot of key information while I was with the FBI. They don't suspect I'm a true party member."

"Take it easy," Phil advised in a voice that held a touch of sneer. "We're almost there."

I leaned back, trying to appear relaxed, but I kept plotting ways to get at Phil's automatic.

Sam wheeled the Pontiac off Route 66 to Huntington Drive and I suddenly knew where we were going. I saw the three-story grandstand and blue and white attached buildings of the wide-sweeping stadium at Santa Anita. We pulled up between the main building and the fountain where the names of past-winners were inscribed. Sea

Biscuit, Azucar, Top Row, and others. Phil gestured for me to get out, while Sam drove off to find a place to park. Phil kept his gun in the pocket of his jacket, but I felt pretty comfortable about the way things were going. They wouldn't risk shooting me here among the crowds streaming in the entranceway.

I boldly stopped to buy a hot dog with mustard and dropped a quarter in the tip jar for luck. Sweat built up on Phil's forehead and upper lip. "I've been meaning to ask you," I smiled. "What'd you do with the body of the woman I shot?"

His eyes flinched and he looked around, hoping no one had heard me. He took the hot dog from my hand and placed it back on the counter, showing me he was in control. "And I've been meaning to ask you—ever heard of Lake Mead?"

So, Lady Lugosi was sleeping in the deep waters near Hoover Dam. Did they first get my bullet out? Would they keep it to use as blackmail against me?

Sam strolled over to join us and we went up the stairs to the top of the grandstand. In addition to the offices of several track officials and radio announcers, there are small, exclusive rooms where exclusive people can view the races from on high and enjoy a day's pleasure without odor of horse and people sweat. August Reed, Pinky, and Eddie Wexler were waiting for us in one of these knotty-pine paneled rooms, along with a dark-haired and eyed lady introduced as Miss Francesca Fortuna Degarre. She looked me up and down like a cat finding a sparrow and offered her hand to be touched or kissed.

Reed looked like an elderly George Armstrong Custer in his pale cowboy hat that befitted a Texas oilman. His belt buckle was so big that he could have used it as a frying pan.

He sat me down in one of the chairs beside the large

plate-glass window that overlooked the track and offered me one of his cigars.

"No thanks, Comrade," I declined. "I'm more of a Marlboro Man."

He shrugged his wide shoulders. "Someone give Mr. Wade a cigarette."

Pinky started patting down the pockets of his plaid jacket, but the rest of the team stood still.

"Never mind. I'm fine without," I told them and turned back to Reed. "I figured you'd find me after the FBI finished rescuing me. I assume you have an assignment for me to learn all I can from my 'friends' at the Bureau."

"That would be interesting," Sam said.

"If we can trust him," Wexler added.

I tried to act cooler than I felt. "By now, you should know I can be trusted, comrades." The Degarre woman watched me closely from the side, as if I might spontaneously combust.

"Indeed," the silver-haired leader told the group. Curls of smoke from his cigar floated around his head as he turned back to me. "During your time behind the lines with the Federal Bureau, we've checked up on what you told us about your parents' death."

I felt my pulse quicken. The story of their death at the hands of the FBI was a pipe dream that I'd made up and told them back in Vegas. Now I was going to have to pay the piper. "Yes, but—" I started.

Reed cut me off, flicking ashes to the floor. "It seems that your story is true and both your mother and father were indeed members in good standing with the local party community of their day. Furthermore, we know that they were on a special mission when the FBI had them killed."

Wexler looked as stunned as I felt. Were my parents

truly Reds after all? Or was Reed bluffing? Or what?

"As a result," Reed went on, "we brought you here, son, because not only do we need you to stay interned with the FBI, but we need your investigative skills to solve a problem that is interfering with a major operation."

I bit down on the inside of my left cheek to see if I was dreaming. It hurt—and I didn't see any black-and-white clown anywhere, so this all must be really happening. I honestly was as confused as a first-time audience of Hawks's *The Big Sleep*. I wanted to play for time, but Reed gave me a broad smile like a proud papa. "Come. Let's all watch the first race from down at the rail."

# CHAPTER 11

*Not long after*:

As a group, we descended the stairs and worked our way toward the rail. It was a warm summer day. Half the men in the crowd wore hats and half did not. In the distance beyond the oval, dirt track, I could see the San Gabriel Mountains and a gleam of sunlight from Mount Wilson Observatory, where Mr. P had almost died a few years ago, until I'd tackled the guy who was trying to push him over the side.

Reed handed me a twenty-dollar ticket for Blue Lark to win at thirty-five-to-one odds. The old trumpet sounded off, and the starter's pinto pony came out of the paddock. A little mare came next, and then a beautiful chestnut, High Heels.

"The horses are going into their starting-stalls," Miss Degarre commented. No one in our party questioned her. "High Heels is the favorite at even odds."

I watched the horses sliding in and out of their stalls, dancing.

"They're off." Royal Bed, the favorite's stable-mate, led to the quarter pole. "He always does that," the dark-haired woman explained. She seemed to be the authority on the subject. "A promising career as a sprinter had been sacrificed when his owner found out that High Heels was one thoroughbred who wouldn't wear himself nervous trying to catch a fast pacemaker. The pair has been unbeatable all season."

No horse could keep up the start that Royal Bed had made. He dropped back going into the back stretch, and a couple long shots went with him, run down. Whadaheck was left up there with High Heels and Blue Lark. The horse with the funny name was leading now, but there was foam at his bit.

Slowly the other two horses came up, neck and neck. Blue Lark was a fine horse, honest and fast. It was just his tough luck that he had to compete with the High Heels-Royal Bed combine in his three-year-old season.

They passed Whadaheck on the back stretch, not increasing their own gait any, but making him look like he was standing still. First one of them would get a little ahead, and then the other, but the only thing that mattered was which would have the energy left for a final sprint. "Based on past performance," she said, "Blue Lark didn't have a chance."

Their hoofs sent little scudding clouds of dust out behind them, and their heads were up. You could see they were getting more fun out of the race than any of the people who had bet on them. They left the back stretch and hit an angle where it was hard to see from our location. I glanced around and saw Connie Francis excitedly cheering from within an eager crowd of race fans. I knew LA was essentially a factory town with a dozen large production facilities we called "studios," so it didn't surprise me to encounter someone in the business almost everywhere I went in this town.

Reed's hands grabbed the rail and his face was set. I'd

swear it was because he liked to see the three-year olds run, and not because he had money on it.

They came on down, and now the jockeys were letting them go. A short guy in a brown coat too large for him moved over to stand close to Connie Francis. High Heels' boy was going to the bat, bringing it down on the chest-nut's flank with long, hard blows. But still the horses stayed even. Half the home-stretch was covered now.

High Heels started to gain, and the crowd went nutso. He was the favorite, the money was on him, and there he came, his legs hitting clean and sweet, his nose out. He put his withers opposite Blue Lark's nose, then his girth, and then his haunch. He was going to take it by a full length, which was adding insult to—

Blue Lark's boy turned the reins in his hand, lifting his horse's head by the bit, and his tiny spurs nipped Blue Lark, once. Blue Lark went forward as though he'd been shot from a gun, breaking his stride, leaping like a jack-rabbit, in defiance of all the rules of fast running. But it was too near the finish line and that clumsy rabbit jump carried him over—half a head in front of the favorite.

The little guy in the brown coat grabbed Connie's purse and made a dash in our direction. As my crowd chatted among themselves about the results of the race, I stuck out a leg and tripped up the purse-snatcher. Connie was screaming in the background. The short guy went down hard and I stood on his neck, unable to resist lean-ing down and whispering, "Who's sorry now?" He looked up at me from his big square head, pointy nose, and little eyes, like a guy in a VIP cartoon from *True Magazine*.

The track security officials rushed over with one of the stewards, took the thief in hand, and thanked me for my effort. Everybody in my crowd backed away from the officials, except for Reed and Francesca, who were introduced to Miss Francis. A young, clean-shaven gent who had been with her earlier at the rail also kept back from us, but I knew that if we peeked under his mirrored shades and fawn-colored hat, we'd find a new Hollywood factory worker, Dick Clark.

Out on the track, Blue Lark was brought to the judge's stand for photos and my crowd went under the grandstand to collect our winnings.

"What, pray tell, was the point of that?" Reed asked me, as the teller at the cash window counted out, stacked, and handed me $700.

"Just keeping up my front as a crime fighter," I answered, stuffing the money into my upper coat pocket and wincing as a thick cloud of cigar smoke floated my way.

Reed chuckled deep in his throat. "Crime fighter, indeed." He seemed to like using that last word a lot. "Come back upstairs. I have something to show you."

We all trudged back up to the meeting room at the top of the stadium. Once there, Reed sent Pinky off to bring back an order of drinks. Phil Castle and his Elvis buddy, Sam, also stepped out. Reed put a manicured palm out to me. "Let's see your winnings."

I brought out the stack of thirty-five twenty-dollar bills and shrugged. After all, they had given me the winning tickets. Easy come, easy gone. The Old Duck handed one to Francesca, who held it up to the light and nodded. Then she handed it to me.

"Take a look," Reed said, and I did.

It looked to me like a new twenty. I waved it like a little flag and said, "Nice picture of Andy Jackson—"

Reed bent slightly to stub out his cigar. "US currency contains red and blue fibers."

I looked at the twenty again, to be sure. "So, does this one."

"Indeed, but notice how very few blue fibers are in the bill and you'll see that it is counterfeit."

I looked at the twenty for a third time and saw what Miss Degarre had seen. Or had not seen. While the red fibers were obvious at a glance, far fewer blue ones were visibly trapped in the paper. I got the other bills out from my winnings and compared them to a twenty in my wallet. They all lacked a significant amount of blue fibers compared to the amount in my real bill. They were all sourdough.

Pinky came back with a tray full of drink glasses. Sam and Phil soon followed, nodding to Reed as if to signal that all was well. "It's Sunday, so the bar's closed," Pinky said. "All I could get was this lemonade. Sorry."

"I hate that stuff," Sam said.

Francesca and Wexler agreed. Phil seemed to have no problem with it and sipped lightly through a straw, while Reed explained, "Our organization within the American Workers Alliance is not the only communist cell in operation in Southern California. Even though we here are all working for My Independent America, members of another group are plotting to undermine the country's financial strength with this phony money."

Francesca smiled in a way that made all of the men in the room look at her.

"We just came from a quick meeting with the track paymaster," Sam the Elvis-impersonator said.

"You were right," Phil told Reed, rubbing the knuckles of his right hand. "This is a distribution center for the queer money. The paymaster said that a package of it appears in his office twice a week."

"Wait a minute," I interrupted. "If you think this is being done by another cell, and you obviously don't like it, can't you just take it up at some high-level meeting and work things out together?"

Reed sampled the lemonade and wiped the edges of his mustache on the back of an index finger. "The organization doesn't operate like that, son, and more's the pity. An operation last year inside a Boy Scout troop almost ruined a plan to infiltrate the teachers of Hollywood High School. Nonetheless, it's important for security reasons that each cell within the organization operates independently. In that way, if one group is caught, the other groups can continue on with their plans. And I'm afraid that there is no high-level meeting."

I was pretty sure that that last part was a lie. Hell, the whole thing could have been a lie, too.

Francesca's eyes were as dark and shiny as tar. "As to our not liking this fake money scheme," she said in a voice that oozed easily toward me, "it's sloppy and too easy to be discovered by the police or other authorities. It has to end before it draws too much attention to our other—"

Reed cut her off. "You understand, Comrade Wade, that if we stopped the distribution here, it would merely start up again somewhere else. We need to stop it at the source."

I went, "Hmmm," to show them that I was interested. "I'm guessing that you think the source is somewhere near Marineland."

"How'd he know that?" Wexler said in a voice you could chop wood with. His expression turned even firmer and meaner than usual. "I still don't think we can trust him."

Reed did something that proved he was still elegantly in control. He simply rattled the ice cubes in his glass of lemonade and handed it to Wexler, saying, "I mentioned it to him in Vegas, Eddie. Calm yourself down, or you'll be removed."

Wexler shot a glance at Phil and Sam and then handed

back the glass to Reed with a nod of acceptance.

"So, that's why we need your skills," Reed said, coming back to me. "We need you to locate where the money is coming from and how it's getting here to Santa Anita."

I decided to let them see me as a loyal and understanding Party member. "I get it now. You want to know who's involved, so you, er, we can approach them directly, before undue notice occurs and interferes with our overall operations."

Reed smiled and raised his glass, not noticing that he'd dripped condensation onto my shoe. "A toast to your success, son. And to My Independent America."

The rest of my party, including me, picked up glasses and joined the toast, while Miss Degarre winked a dark eye at me.

ℝ℞

They'd planned to take me back to my boat where they had picked me up earlier that day, but instead I had Sam and Phil drop me at the Brown Derby. The evening dinner crowd packed the place and I had to walk sideways past the waiters and cigarette girl near Larry Welk's booth to get to my office in the back of the building.

The wide and clamorous kitchen in the next room smelled of Italian Wedding Soup, so I slurped a bowl while checking the mail that had been shoved under my office door.

One letter started with the word, "Greetings," but it was from something called Publishers Clearing House, so I shoved it into the trash. There was a perfumed note from a woman in Oxnard, asking me to drive up there for an exclusive interview. Hmmm…

That went into the trash, too. And a bill from the California Department of Private Investigators and Adjusters to renew my license. That one I spilled soap on while stuffing it into a drawer of my desk.

I tried giving Walt another call, but his private line didn't answer. I thought it pretty important to inform him of the funny money floating around Santa Anita, but a girl at the main office said he was over in England, of all places, working with the production staff of something called *Pollyanna*. I thought about calling Lex to see how she was doing, but my heart wasn't in it. Instead, I caught a cab and went back to my cabin cruiser to think things through.

Night had fallen by the time I reached the *Cervantes II* and I went aboard wanting a drink and a cigarette. The sun had gone down quickly for a summer day and the moon was nowhere to be found. I snooped around the boat to be sure I was alone, poured a glass of Jamieson, and caught the tail end of the Johnny Dollar radio program, *A Life at Stake Matter*. I listened without hearing much and finally went back topside to stand at the helm, looking out at the dark waters, as if I were going somewhere. Anywhere. Okay, Mr. Private Investigator and Adjuster—quick review.

First of all, I'd killed someone, on purpose. In a way, I'd been forced into doing it, but there it was still. I had decided, perhaps out of muscle reflex or some other excuse, to intentionally take another person's life.

Yet, in a roundabout way, that violent act had cemented my relationship with the Communists. They now believed that I'd proven my loyalty to the cause and as a result they trusted me to inform to them on the FBI and to use my knowledge and skills as an investigator to identify and possibly root out individuals who interfered with their larger plans against America.

Whew. I took a hefty slug of Irish whiskey. And what were those plans?

As I gazed out over the dark Pacific, it occurred to me that there was nothing out there. Nothing major stood between the coast of Russia and Red China and little old Uncle Sam. In my mind, I pictured the wide expanse of ocean between our shore and theirs, but as wide as the ocean expanse was, nothing much had stopped the Japanese from crossing it less than twenty years ago with explosive weapons and a desire to cripple or even take over parts of our country.

Today, we live in a world of ICBMs loaded with nuclear devices that can destroy a city in a flash. We really weren't that far from the Fall of Rome, or the Fall of Europe, if you thought about it. Only this time, it could happen overnight.

I let my mind wander farther out into the unknown. The Fall of America. The Fall of Democracy. It would be beyond anything we'd ever known. It would be huge, super. It would be the end. Roll credits. That's all, folks.

I took another swig and brought my mind home again. So, they wanted me to stop a measly counterfeiting operation. Why? Because it was somehow interfering with another, bigger operation. Someone was smuggling funny money into the USA for purposes of disrupting our economy. And yet, there was something else, an even bigger threat to the country, that had to be hidden or protected from discovery by official eyes.

Something else, like what? Something else being smuggled in at the same site? What? Animal, vegetable, or mineral? Chemical, physical, or biological?

Maybe Walt would know. Or Max, or someone else at the FBI. But was it even remotely possible that I'd been right when I'd said that the FBI had my parents killed? Were they possibly double agents, like me?

Except I was the double-double agent now. Or was I? There was only one clear way to find the truth—follow through with the investigation that Reed wanted at Marineland and keep an eye out for the "bigger" operation that they hoped to keep hidden.

I chuckled. I'd go there under the guise of a mild-mannered reporter, but I'd need an in. And I'd steel myself against taking another life, if I had to. Even if it meant my own.

Okay. Enough of the quick review already. Any farther and I'd steer off the edge of the world where there be dragons, or just plain madness. I knew one thing for certain: as usual, I was going to have to do a lot of legwork. The only problem was that things were so spread out in the LA environs that I always had to drive, instead of walk, making for long days in heavy traffic—which I hate.

Ah, well. I shook myself in the chilled night air and went below for another drink. I was drinking a lot lately.

# CHAPTER 12

*Abruptly and much too soon:*

I was up and moving again. Barely.

Monday was wash day on the Wade boat. At least the third Monday of every month, and that was today, according to an insurance company calendar I had pinned to the bulkhead over the galley. Usually, I hauled my sheets, towels, and other dirty clothes to the Stumpf coin-operated laundry over in Venice, but today…well, today the little men with jack-hammers were tearing up the dockside of my mind and the sloop in my stomach was pitching and rolling. At least I still had my wits about me…somewhere.

I shook the last of my shot-from-guns Post Toaties into a clean bowl and mixed in a handful of Rice Krisp-ies—snap, crackle, pop—only to find that I was out of milk, so I ate them all dry like candy and brewed a pot of strong coffee in the Silex. Next I stumbled out to the car and got Norman on the line, intending to see if he could relay the call to Suzi so I could find out how Lex was do-ing. Third-hand information is better than no information.

"I'm wearing a new pair of glasses," Norman told me,

as I sat in the driver's seat and gulped coffee from a thermos. "The temples go straight back along the sides of my head and hug my skull, so they don't slide down."

"Must make your head look streamlined," I offered, figuring he would not look anything like Clark Kent. The sky was so overcast this morning that everything appeared to have been shot through a day-for-night lens. Or maybe I was still in a mental fog.

Ironically, Norman said, "I think I can figure a way to treat my glasses so they automatically turn dark in strong sunlight."

Next he'd probably find a way to convert them to X-ray specs. "Listen, Norman, you said you wanted to do more detective work—"

"You mean some spadework?"

"Ah…yeah…or sleuthing. So I was wondering if you could research the background on a guy from Texas named August Reed. He's a high-up mucky-muck in the American Workers Alliance."

"A commie?"

"Ah, yeah—Here's your chance to help stop them. Get back to me with anything you find, but don't let him know you're checking up on him."

"Dangerous?"

"Yeah, could be. So just do the basic research on his past, location, and known associates. Okay?"

"Cool. And then you'll read the new chapters of my Martian novel. Okay?"

I took a deep swallow of hot coffee and said "Yeah" for the fourth time. "Can you patch me through to Suzi now?"

The thermos was empty by the time she came on the crackling line. This car-phone relay thing that Norman had rigged up was a handy, but not always very reliable. I could lose the call at any time, so I talked fast. Suzi said that Lex had checked into a clinic for tests and was scheduled for chemical and radiation therapy later in the week. Time would tell. I then asked her who she knew at Marineland.

"Actually, I used to know the Personnel Manager there. That's how I got Weezie her job. But Matt has since moved on to work at Desilu Studios. I think the Marketing Director there is named Kropp. Yes, Sally Kropp."

I told her that I needed to get behind the scenes at the park and snoop around among the employees there. "I thought I'd tell them I was a reporter for a great metropolitan newspaper back east or maybe *Look Magazine*, working on an in-depth cover story."

"Oh so, your cover story is a cover story for Look, huh?" I dry-washed my face with an open palm, like Edgar Kennedy used to, but said nothing, as Suzi went on: "I seem to recall that the magazine already ran a story on Marineland about a year ago, during the park's expansion. You'd better tell them you're a stringer for Collier's instead. I'll see if I can call Sally Kropp and set something up."

She was right and I knew I could use her help. "How about you coming along? Two heads are better, you know, and it just might pull you out of your—"

"Depression?"

"I was going to say blue funk."

"I told you before that I'm not depressed. I just don't know if I want to continue—like I have been. Sunset Investigations is pretty much down to just me now and I'm tempted not renew my license and just walk away. Start life over somehow. I—I haven't felt myself lately."

I involuntarily snickered at her last comment and tried to cheer her by saying, "Maybe I can help with that."

The phone suddenly felt cold in my hand as she heard

the double meaning. Then she gave a little laugh and I knew, like Pepsi Cola, I'd hit the spot. "Okay, you're right," I said, trying to let her know that I was sympathetic and not a complete jerk. "It's probably just as well that you don't come in on this case. No sweat, my sweet. I'll play it alone."

"I'm sorry, Standy."

I promised to call her again that evening after I got back from scoping the lay of the land around the park and then we played that game to see who would hang up first. She did. So I won—I guess.

The rest of the morning, I spent getting my act together and making the boat…well, shipshape. I thought about taking it down to Palos Verdes near the park, but didn't know where I could moor it. Maybe near Terminal Island. That would be one of the things I'd scope out when I'd driven down there.

By noon, the clouds had burned off and the day had warmed considerably. I took the time to write down the who, what, when, and where of recent events into a little notebook I carried, so I could review the details of the case later and hopefully gain new perspective. I also took a few minutes to make myself more presentable, shining my shoes and getting black polish under the fingernails of my right hand. Then I gassed up the Kaiser, purchased a couple tacos from a stand off Vista Del Mar and headed south on Sepulveda past Redondo Beach. The beef from the tacos was doubly hot and burned the roof of my mouth and tongue, so I killed a bottle of Pepsi on the first one and scarfed down the second one dry. The radio sang Top Forty tunes to me. My favorites were good ol' "Lipstick on Your Collar" and a new one: "Waterlooo-o."

Of all the parks and attractions in the LA area, Marineland was the one that fascinated me the most. There had been seal acts, aquariums, and fish tanks on view for

years in every state of the Union, but Marineland combined and brought it all together into a single Hollywood
performance art form. Hell, one of its sea lions had even
appeared in *Twenty Thousand Leagues Under the Sea* and
they frequently shot scenes for the *Sea Hunt* TV show at
this location.

The site had originally opened before Disneyland and
was probably California's first major theme park. And
they didn't just house exotic fish here and put on shows
for the kiddies. The ninety-acre location captured the natural beauty of the Portuguese Bend area on the blunt peninsula over-looking the Pacific and it contained a top-
flight restaurant and facilities for education and oceanic
research. I pulled off Palos Verdes Drive South, past
what appeared to be a stand of palm trees shaped like a
big W, and drove on a mile or so to the concrete entrance
sign displaying a big blue porpoise. Apparently, the park
was closed to the public on Mondays, so I drove across
the wide empty expanse of the lot. The sea breeze from
the cliffs overlooking the ocean blew cool and sweet. I
finally wheeled to a stop in a slot near the attached restaurant. And there, peacefully and primly, under the open
sunroof of her Renault, sat a cute blonde, fanning herself
with a folded Texaco roadmap.

"What are you doing here?" I asked.

She shielded her eyes from the sun's glare while looking up at me. "You sounded so forlorn on the phone that I
decided to come with."

"I don't know," I told her. "It…it's nice, but…"

"Come on," Suzi said, almost knocking me over as she
opened her car door to get out. "We're late for the staff
meeting. You carry the camera equipment." She straightened her skirt, touched up the back of her hair, and
marched toward the entrance of the administration building.

I found and lugged a late model Hasselblad and a bag full of film and lenses from the back seat of her car. I left the tripod next to a tangle of diving equipment as a mute protest. Nobody makes a pack-mule out of Stan Wade, no matter how prim and cute they are.

⌘⌘⌘

As a professional investigator, I'm trained to keep track of little details, facts, and clues, but there's a limit to everything and that's why I carried a notebook. In the next ten minutes, I was introduced to six separate employees of the theme park and it was all I could do to resist the urge to start scribbling notes about them. I hoped that Suzi could keep track of the details, since the little gray card catalog in my head was spinning out of control.

Inside the park's main building and outside a pair of mahogany doors sculpted with an ornate wave design, we were met by a slim and fit woman in a yellow blouse and tan slacks, thirty or so, with coffee-colored winged glasses. Her blonde hair was unbraided and hung down over her shoulders, feathering across her cheeks in translucent shades of wheat and gold. "So you're the reporter that Weezie mentioned? I'm Sally Kropp, Sales and Marketing."

Before Suzi could speak, I asserted myself, sliding in and saying, "Harvey LaPoka," and accepting her elegant hand. "This is my wife, Harriet. We're from *Collier's Magazine.*"

Suzi shot me a look that could melt steel and settled for clicking her ball-point pen a few times, while the marketing woman looked confused.

Sally Kropp glanced down through her thick glasses. "I—I don't see a wedding ring—on either of you."

"Oh, we're in the middle of a trial separation," I confessed. Sally Kropp was certainly a keen observer. I suddenly noticed the black lines of shoe polish under my fingernails, so I moved my hands away to adjust the camera strap to my other shoulder.

"Yes," Suzi smiled openly. "And it's likely to become a permanent separation, very soon. You can probably imagine why."

Again the Kropp woman seemed slightly flustered. "But I was expecting a Miss Sunset—"

"Sunset is my maiden name," Suzi said.

Kropp paused for a heartbeat and then smiled back at us. "Ah, that explains it. Well then, shall we proceed?"

As we passed through the double doors into the meeting room, somehow Suzi managed to discreetly stomp my foot while jabbing an elbow into my ribs. Kenpo?

A blade of pain shot up my side and my eyes began to water.

"We're meeting today to go over our plans for additional park expansion and new marketing events." Sally Kropp stopped short, seeing the tear that was starting to form above my right cheek.

I shared my pained expression with Suzi, who realized what her playful jab in my injured side had caused. "Oh, Harv," she said. "What is it, dear? Did you bump your sore ribs again?"

I nodded my head up and down, like Francis the talking mule, letting the film case drop to the floor. Suzi appeared genuinely contrite, explaining to the people in the room: "He cracked a rib a few months ago, falling off of—"

"A stack of record albums," I grunted. "I was moving a pile of jazz LPs and tripped."

That got us blank stares from everyone and then, "Are you all right?" and "Can we get you anything?" and "Here, sit down, easy."

I raised an assuring palm, while Suzi helped me into one of the swivel chairs that surrounded the conference table. "I'll be fine," I winced and looked longingly at her. "I'm sure that Harriet can carry all my gear now." That got me another blast of heat vision, while Sally Kropp began introducing us to the three people seated at the table and explaining why we were here.

Chester "Chet" Simonson, the smooth-face operations manager, with a politician's hair-trigger smile that would register on a light meter, listened to Kropp's introduction. The middle-aged man in the lightweight tan Clipper Craft suit with lighter tan Van Heusen tab collar shirt and thin tie, blinked out at the world through glasses as thick as Kropp's, only they had silvery frames.

The park's Business Manager, John Meskin, said that he handled all of the corporation's contracts and should have been advised that we would be joining the meeting. Despite his chilly reception, he seemed a casual sort of guy in brown, pleated slacks, a shirt unbuttoned at the neck, and tasseled brown leather loafers. His grin was more or less visible through his salt-and-vinegar beard and I noticed a gap between his top front teeth. He was about fifty, five ten or so tall, with a modest paunch. His eyes weren't as friendly as the rest of his face.

Then there was Lola McKinley, Chief Financial Officer, or highly-paid bookkeeper, who wore red-tipped hands and dyed red hair. She was strikingly tall, slender, fetchingly sculpted in beige Capri's and matching top. Her jaw moved up and down, chewing gum, as she fussed with the circular carousel of 35-mm slides mounted in a projector at the end of the conference table.

I tried to determine if any of these people were communists, but that's the trouble with communists: they tend to look like any of these people. The same is true for counterfeiters. If I was to locate the source of the phony money, it wouldn't be by the appearance of anyone in this group. It would be by their actions. And that would require a lot of surveillance. Stake out on Crowd Street.

The doors behind Suzi and I swung open and two more meeting attendees entered. Great.

Kropp quickly introduced David Eisner, the park's CEO, and Alan Everetton, Head of Security. "The LaPokas are here from *Collier's Magazine* to do a feature story on the park's forthcoming expansion activities."

Eisner beamed at the news and shook our hands dryly, taking a place near the head of the table close to the movie screen that was descended from the ceiling. He was as handsome as a movie star cast as a judge. The spider-web wrinkles spread out from the corners of his eyes to his receding hairline with its landing-strip of white hair. His eyes were the darkest brown I had ever seen, like leather on a horse saddle soaked in bourbon. He wore a blue plaid Palm Beach sport jacket with pale blue shirt, navy tie and slacks. "Glad you could join us." His smile was genuine, despite one discolored incisor.

"I thought Collier's got bought out by Look magazine," said the head of security, Alan Everetton, from my side. I winced inwardly and not from the pain in my ribs. Here was another sharp-witted and suspicious employee.

True to his profession, Everetton was careful to check every detail he was told. A muscled and uniformed man, his eyes were like charcoal smoke gathered inside blue glass marbles. His face was of a classic Mediterranean mold—petulant mouth given to scorn like a Roman emperor, or Brando, and a very large nose which dominated a closely-shaved jaw. His dark blue shirt and trousers were knife-edged and he looked neat, clean, and competent.

"You're right about that," I grinned, looking back at him with innocent eyes. "Part of the acquisition deal with

Look hasn't completely gone through yet and we're still wrapping up existing projects until they reassign us."

"Sounds good," CEO Eisner pronounced impatiently. "Sally, thanks for setting this up for us."

Everetton still kept his eyes on me. "We'll want to approve anything, of course, before you take it public."

"That's my department," Sally Kropp said, addressing him with a firm voice, while fiddling with the vertical louvered blinds to darken the room. "But if it'll make you happy, Alan, I'll see that you get a copy of what they create before it goes public."

Everetton nodded, looked at everybody in the room like they might bite him if he gave them half a chance, and sat down.

"Now, if we could get started," Lola McKinley said, switching on the slide projector which began to hum and cast a square of light on the movie screen. "Here are the most expensive of our proposed plans for the park's future."

A bright illustration on the screen depicted small cruises in gaily-colored speed boats to Avalon on Catalina Island. Another showed a clear Plexiglas tunnel-like dome with a family of four walking under a school of tuna. There were several more colorful ocean-oriented dreams of the future that would probably cost more to build than the Spruce Goose. I thought that the patriotic theme for the Fourth of July celebration in a few weeks was affordable, but a bit silly. After all, who would really want to see a parade of marines at Marineland? Other marines?

Streamers of blue smoke from the group's cigarettes drifted through the shaft of light from the projector. I felt the urge to sneeze, but I kept it under control while Suzi took notes and asked insightful questions for publication. The team didn't seem prepared to come to a decision today on how best to invest the park's profits. In the end, Sally promised to provide Suzi and me with copies of the appropriate slides, once the final decision was made.

As the meeting began to break up and both the blinds and windows themselves were thankfully cranked open, a willowy blonde of no more than twenty stepped into the room. She patiently waited in a white short-sleeve blouse, blue jeans, and bare feet with hair cut chin-length and just a touch of lipstick.

Sally Kropp finally noticed her. "I'd like you to give our new friends here the grand tour, Weezie." Then, gesturing in our direction, she started introductions. "This is Mr. and Mrs. La—"

"Oh, I already know Suzi Sunset," the girl gushed enthusiastically. She went on to approach me, her face bright with fresh sunburn. "And you must be her boyfriend, Stan Spade."

The room grew quiet. My stomach did a little flip, as I tried to play dumb.

Sally Kropp seemed the most perplexed again. "Whom did you say?"

"Well, you see—" I started to explain.

Suzi moved forward, shaking her head. There was confident assurance and a hint of laughter in her tone. "I'm afraid you have us confused with someone else." She looked straight into Weezie's eyes. "Suzi Sunset is my sister. My name's Harriet and this is my scoundrel husband, Harvey."

Now it was the blonde girl's turn to look slightly perplexed. The rest of the group seemed to be growing impatient, so I added, "A lot of people make that mistake, since Harriet and Suzi are twins."

Everetton's eyes narrowed, but he said nothing. I could almost hear the gears turning in his head.

"Oh..." Weezie swallowed, finally getting it. "Actually, I'm sorry. You—you look so much like her—"

I decided to go farther out on the limb and bluffed with: "Who's this Sam Spade?" I turned to Suzi, "Do we know him?"

"I think he's a character in a movie," Simonson offered in a Midwestern nasal twang.

"No, he was on the radio with…oh, it'll come to me," Meskin said through wide teeth and bristling whiskers. "…Howard Duff."

"Sorry, but you're all wrong," Eisner, ever the executive officer, advised. "He's what you call a private eye in a murder mystery I once read in my youth. Something about a stolen bird…"

Weezie tried to play innocent. "Who would steal a bird?"

"Well." I smiled with relief. "It's a mystery to me." I raised the camera for all to notice. "I'd like to get some shots of each of you for the article. Can we go outside where the light is better?"

Everyone began primping and filing out of the conference room. Suzi took young Weezie's hand and I caught her casually tapping an index finger to her own lips. I think Everetton caught it too, but I bumbled along after, trying to appear harmless and happy. We all came out of the building to stand beside a gurgling fountain in the bright, afternoon air that filled the park. All except Security Chief Everetton, who instead of squinting in the sunlight of Marineland, continued to quietly give me the old fish eye.

# CHAPTER 13

*Later that day*:

Okay, I'll admit it—if I wasn't looking for hidden communists and counterfeit cash, I'd really enjoy wandering around Marineland. It had opened back in 1954, when I was just getting started in the detective business and helping out Mr. P. I'd never been to the park before, although I'd heard all about it in the newspapers and other media. The press had been full of stories about its colorful sea characters. There was Bubbles, the first pilot whale for display; Orky and Corky, the famous killer whales, who performed in the oceanarium; Omar, the giant octopus; Zippy and Smiley, the porpoises; and Captain Winston's educated Sea Lion Show.

It was this assemblage of undersea animals that charmed me the most. I live on a boat in the ocean, but I seldom get to see most of these creatures, and never up close. The ones here at the park didn't just swim around. They performed amazing feats and stunts. Come to think of it, unlike Old Man Walt's theme park with zero animals, here at Marineland everything was live—like a splashing circus. It was as different and exciting as a live

TV show, compared to a canned kinescope. Anything could happen since the performers are live and exotic, and that added an extra thrill to the whole experience. I began to think of Marineland as the Greatest Show NOT On Earth.

While my thoughts literally swam with such fantasies, Suzi and her friend, Louise Parker, consulted quietly together. The girl seemed too young to have spent time as a bargirl, but then I recalled some of the darker fantasies that haunt the fair LA-Land.

Our guise as reporters enabled Suzi and me to go "backstage" and see the great and wonderful operations from an insider's point of view. The largest feature of the park was the Sea Arena dolphin pool next to the main building's large oval tank and circular pilot whale stadium. According to a handy and colorful brochure, The Sea Arena was, "…an aquatic amphitheater housing the amazing educated porpoises and the riotously funny sea lions in watery apartments around a 500,000 gallon tank, which is the third of the three-rings in the Sea Circus. The wondrous Sea Arena opened in July of 1958, seats 3,000 persons, and has a stage as big as the one in the famed Hollywood Bowl." Beyond the park to the south was the Marineland Pier, with opportunities for coastal boat cruises and special tours out into the channel for possible whale watching at certain times of the year.

I shot several rolls of film with the single-lens, reflex camera and even though the park was closed for the day and crews of workmen were busy emptying trashcans and picking up stray cigarette butts, I hoped that Norman would be able to develop good results from my amateur, up-side-down photography, because I truly thought the view of the place from the cliff overlooking the ocean was postcard perfect.

While I was focusing on a group of porpoises rehearsing their Marineland Globetrotters routine, someone stepped in front of the camera's view screen. "I did some quick checking up on you. Nobody at *Look* knows anything about you or any cover story for the magazine."

I looked up into Everetton's smoky eyes and sighed. "I've already explained that. We're still on the payroll for the magazine that they acquired. And nobody ever said that it was a cover story. The editors decide that. Sometimes based on the quality and content of the photos I shoot."

He grunted and stood his ground while the girls started wandering back in our direction. "Just remember—" He smiled thinly. "—I'll be carefully reviewing those photos and keeping a close eye on you two while you're on the premises."

I wondered why this guy was so tightly wound. Was he the one involved with the counterfeiting? He didn't seem like a commie. Was he undercover like me, or just a hardboiled, hardheaded hard-ass? The situation was getting too complex again and I needed to make it simple, if I could.

"Look, Chief," I said, "can we agree on at least one thing?"

His eyes tightened, as if preparing to send or receive a punch. "What?"

I tried to de-fuse things by saying casually, "Simplify."

He must have misunderstood me, because his face relaxed a little and he spoke two words back to me: "Semper fi." Then he pointed down to where both his shoes and mine gleamed blackly in the high sunlight. I realized he erroneously thought that we were brothers in arms and members of the Order of the Kiwi Polish. Which was a good thing. Wasn't it?

Suzi and her friend arrived, expectantly.

Everetton let a slight smile curl the right side of his mouth and he rotated away. "I may be the head of security here, but you're only a visitor, so don't call me chief."

We watched him move away and then Suzi used one of my lines: "What did I miss?"

"I—I think we just silently sang the Marine Hymn together."

She looked at me with a blank expression and shrugged. "Could have been worse. He could have shot you."

ↄ⃝ↄ

"So you guys are actually here for what exactly?" the young blonde girl asked, nibbling a fat French fry. Weezie had put on shoes and come with us to talk over dinner.

We were seated at a chrome and Formica table in a restaurant that was celebrating its grand opening about a mile north of Marineland. According to the history illustrated on our paper placemats, Hegenburgers was a new branch of a successful Oakland eating establishment that cleverly took its name from its location on the main access road to the airport: Hegenberger Road. Of course, they specialized in hamburgers, but that didn't stop Suzi from ordering a tuna sandwich and ice tea. Weezie had a Hegenchicken sandwich with cheese. I settled for a double cheeseburger dripping with guacamole and mushrooms.

The place was moderately crowed and smelled of delicious bacon and grilled beef. A jukebox near our table crooned popular love ballads like, "Lonely Boy," "See You in September," and "A Teenager in Love."

Weezie struggled to be heard over the forlorn libido tunes. "What the hell is actually going on with you two? And can I help?"

Her choice of words surprised me. "We really don't need any—"

Suzi interrupted me. "It could be dangerous."

The girl blinked and smiled widely. "Shit. That sounds great!"

"I mean it," Suzi retorted.

"Have you seen anything funny or unusual at the park?" I asked, squeezing ketchup on my cheeseburger, trying not to spurt it loudly.

"Everything there is funny and unusual. Do you mean suspicious?"

I nodded since my mouth was busy navigating around the red, cellophane-flagged toothpick that barely held my burger together.

"Well, actually, I don't think you'll have any more trouble from that tight ass Everetton for a while," she went on, "but that could change any day, once he finds out the truth about you two."

"Then we need to move fast," I said, swallowing mostly greasy meat and bun. "What happens to the money when people buy tickets to the park?"

Weezie shrugged. "Hey, I'm just a lowly employee working her way through college. The money goes to Lola McKinley, I guess, then on to the bank. We all get paychecks at the end of the week."

"So, the cash gets counted and shipped to the bank?" Suzi asked, sipping tea through a stripped straw.

"I guess. Has there been a robbery, or something?"

People seated a few tables away started giving us *The Look*. They might have been the King family, with their boy Stevie whom I'd met briefly in Vegas. Had they followed me, or were they simply an average American family on a summer's vacation out West? I took a slug of Coke—they didn't serve Pepsi here—and tried a different tactic on the girl.

"Are the park employees part of a union?"

She shook her head. "Ah, no. Management won't allow it."

"Have you noticed any communist talk or literature circulating there?" Suzi asked, changing tactics.

"At the park?" Weezie's eyes expanded. She put down her burger and swore again like a pirate. "Are you fucking kidding me? Soviets? Clandestine operations? It's a goddamn theme park. A research center. We're the farthest thing from Siberia."

I shot another look over at the nearby family and leaned forward to Weezie with a lowered voice and a new idea. "What do you research?"

"Me? I'm studying undersea archeology. My dad used to do it, before he passed away, years ago. Ever since Suzi got me this job here, I've decided to follow my roots back to the sea."

Not fully understanding most of that, I said, "If you're lucky, maybe you'll discover sunken treasure."

"Don't laugh. It's possible with all the old smuggler's caves and ancient coves nearby, but the real reason I'm employed there is to learn more about the tides and groundswell that alter the coast line. Parts of the Southern California coast around the park have been eroded over the centuries by the constant battering of the waves, taking away the indigenous people's culture and livelihood."

I noticed that the girl kept control of her mouth when she was at work or talking about it. "It's too deep for me," I quipped, wiping mustard from my fingers with a paper napkin.

"And too far off the track," Suzi added. "Any other research?"

"Something about dolphin echolocation, actually. They received a large grant from the government for that program."

"This is getting us nowhere," I sighed. "I need to talk to the CFO and cherchez la buck. Follow the money." I looked up and felt my face and heart tighten. I gripped the edge of the table.

"Standy, what is it?" Suzi asked, turning to spy over her shoulder in the direction I was staring.

Eddie Wexler and Sam the Elvis Impersonator had just walked into the restaurant.

I ducked my head, pretending to massage away a sudden ache from my brow.

"Do you know them?" Suzi whispered.

"Uh-huh." I dug some cash out and slide it under my plate. "That should cover the check. I want to get you girls out of here right away."

Weezie the Mouth kept her head still, but scanned the room suspiciously with her eyes. "Who the hell are those guys?"

"Let's go," I said, drawing the girl up from her chair and guiding her toward the front entrance. Suzi positioned herself to block us from the view of the undercover commies who were being lead to a far table by the hostess. They seemed to have missed seeing me, but this couldn't be a coincidence. It was clear that I was being followed, possibly on general principle, but of all the members of August Reed's friendly little group, these two were the least friendly. As Weezie would say, "What the fuck? Actually."

∽∾∽

I drove my Kaiser with the three of us back to Marineland through the gathering dusk. Weezie lived in one of the small motel rooms attached to the park. Suzi and I dropped her there, promising to be back in the morning, and then took our separate cars to the County General Hospital on Mission Road near Lincoln Park.

Lex did not look good. In fact, she looked down-right lousy. "You look great!" I said, entering the semi-private room. The other bed was empty, except where Suzi sat on it, her feet primly together, and arms resting in her lap. Lex lay in her own rumpled and cranked-up bed, anything but prim and nothing near to resting.

"My doc's the same guy that treated Bogart for esophageal cancer in 1956," she wheezed. "Thought ya'd want to know that, squirrel."

I arched an eyebrow. "I'm sure he must have improved his technique since then."

She lifted a plastic cup of water. "Here's hoping." She took a sip from a bent straw.

Suzi glanced at me with worry and doubt. She had added a scarf with a large print of a pink dahlia, tied loosely around her neck and left shoulder.

"After this is over, we all should go bowling," Lex grunted. "There's a new alley opened up on Pico, where they got them automatic pin setter-upper machines on every lane." She adjusted her hospital gown around her wide torso and tried to appear as tough as a fifty-cent steak.

"Sure, Lex," I said, easing my butt into a stiff chair and wishing I had a stiff drink. "What did the doctor say about your condition?"

She cleared her throat and smiled. "Too early to tell."

Suzi leaned in and patted the back of Lex's left hand. "I'm sure it'll all be fine soon."

"Yeah, I got radiation treatments and have to wear this dosimeter doo-dad." She pronounced it dose-o-meter. "If it turns from gray to blue, I'll know that I got enough doses of radioactivity and either the cancer is done for or I am."

"Oh shush," I said. "We'll be back drinking at the Blue Phrog before you know it."

"No more drinking."

An elderly nurse-volunteer came in, leading a gawky lad we all knew. She smiled like Gwanny in a Warner's cartoon. "This is Mrs. Iglesias's room and, oh my, these must be some of her guests."

Lex said her favorite phrase, "Shit fire," and looked delighted.

I came to my feet and gave Norman's hand a hardy shake. "Hiya, kid. Hey, I've got one for you."

"Okay," he said, shifting his weight. "I'm ready."

"A lot of kisses at the bottom," I quoted.

He thought for a second and then answered, "I'll be glad I got 'em. It's from 'I'm Going to Sit Right Down and Write Myself a Letter.'"

"Damn. You win again." I tussled his hair.

The frames of his new glasses where solid black and lacked any tape. His shirt, pants, and vest seemed rumpled, but comfortable. He carried a brown paper grocery bag rolled at the top and an inquisitive expression. "Don't they give you a TV in your room?"

"I asked the same thing about an hour ago," Lex answered grumpily. "You'd think they could wheel one in on a cart or something."

"I'll just go check on that for you," the little nurse lady said. Then she advised before leaving the room, "But there won't be any remote control."

Lex coughed and gargled that we'd rough it until Norman could build us one. Suzi handed her a tissue and a cup of water. Norman reached into his paper bag to bring out a couple of books and a copy of *TV Guide Magazine* with Robert Young on the cover. Lex took a moment before accepting the gift of reading material and looked at the cover of one of the books.

"Who's this Ray Raspberry guy and why would I want to read him?"

"Bradbury," Norman corrected. "He's a local writer who's made it big." He taped the cover of the hardback. "I thought you'd like his new book, *A Medicine for Melancholy*. The title seemed like ironic destiny for your situation."

Lex grimaced.

"Let's call it kismet," Suzi said, as if thinking out loud.

"Nah." Lex shook her head and set the books on a night stand beside her bed. "It's caramel, or something." Then she winked at me.

I could never tell about Lex. Sometimes she was genuinely dense and other times she was the smartest person in the room.

Suzi adjusted the pink scarf on her shoulder. "It's so good to see you holding up your spirits."

"That reminds me. The doc says I can't drink anything during my treatment."

Suzi thought aloud that that might be a good thing.

Norman asked about the badge on Lex's hospital gown and we went through the dosimeter discussion again. Norman wanted to know if he could have one, too.

"You'll all get one, if you hang around me much longer."

An intern in crisp whites wheeled in a small TV on a stand and fussed with the rabbit ears until he could get a clear view of *What's My Line?* on the screen. The mystery guest was Jack Benny and he went over to kiss a blindfolded Jayne Meadows.

"Not him again," Lex said.

While I explained how Benny had Lex and me thrown out of the CBS studios a few months earlier, Norm shook out a small black box, about the size of a deck of playing cards, from his grocery bag and handed it to me. "I'll bet you can use this." The box was heavy and had a silver toggle switch on one side. "It's a TTB. I made it from a miniature Japanese radio."

I flipped the switch, which I probably shouldn't have, because with Norm you never knew and the thing just might have blown up in my hand. However, nothing happened. "All right, I'll bite. What's a TTB?"

He pushed up his glasses even though they didn't need it. "It's a transistorized tracker beeper. I got the plans from an issue of *Science Illustrated*. It transmits way up at 1690 Kilohertz where there's hardly any signal. You can hear it as an intermittent beep on any AM radio."

I switched it off. "Thanks, Norman. How long does it operate?"

"About four hours. Then the batteries are drained. I can make more of them easy."

"Can I get one?" Suzi asked.

"I'll take a dozen, if you please," Lex chimed in.

I hefted it. "It would be good if there was a magnet on the case, so you could stick it on the underside of a car or something."

Norm snatched it back and dropped it into his bag. "I should have thought of that. Sorry."

Lex caught the embarrassed tone. "Hey, your beeper tracker thingy is a great idea, kid."

"You just need to develop it more," Suzi added.

"It's a prototype," Norm admitted.

"There, you see?" I said to Lex and Suzi. "It's a prototype."

Lex blinked openly. "Is that the same as a dummy?"

Suzi and I both threw her a look that could have won a game of darts.

"He'll develop it further and get it back to us," Suzi said. "Right?"

Norm slowly nodded agreement.

"Hey, this is great teamwork, huh?" I offered.

"Cut it out," Lex said, "or I'll start bawling."

An oriental man, wearing a stethoscope and doctor's smock came into the room and must have caught the tail end of Lex's comment. "It will be several months before you'll be healthy enough to go bowling," he said, consulting the chart at the foot of the bed. "Why is that so funny, please?"

We all tried to explain at once, but ended up being told firmly that visiting hours were over. On the way out, Norm filled me in on what little he'd learned of August Reed's background. There wasn't much that I didn't already know, except that Reed had a low-level security clearance during World War II and that he'd contributed heavily over the years to a research facility near the Berkley campus.

As it turned out, Norman had arrived by bus, so Suzi volunteered to take him back home. Actually, I nudged her in that direction, because I was slightly suspicious that I'd been followed on the way to the hospital. Regardless of how she might have appeared, I knew that she was still feeling down. Her denials of being depressed were betrayed by the look on her face when Lex had told us that the hospital bills were already starting to pile up. Suzi just cared too much about people and their troubles to ever be a true success in this hard-nosed profession in the land of the fruits and nuts.

I was right about my being followed. Whoever it was, they drove a late-model Oldsmobile Rocket 88 with no front license plate. I circled around while listening to a re-broadcast of Yours Truly, Johnny Dollar on the radio, *A Life at Stake Matter,* and searching for that new bowling alley. A weather forecast said there'd be a cold front moving in tomorrow with possible coastal fog. I finally gave up the exploration and headed home to the *Cervantes II* with the Olds still in tow.

There was a new song playing, when I parked in the gravel near my gangway. It was a peppy number where a black lead singer and chorus kept moaning and repeating, "Tell me what'd I say." I shut off the sound and engine and waited for the other car to grind to a stop next to mine.

Eddie Wexler rolled down his passenger window and I could see that Sam the Elvis had been driving.

I cranked my own window open. "Tell me, what'd I say?"

Just like in the movies, Wexler tried to look his toughest. "Who's the dame?"

I chewed on a bitter thought for a moment and then let it go. "She's my cover for investigating the park, like the boss asked me."

He gave me a lopsided grin. If I'd been a dame, I would have called it a lopsided leer. Who knows? Maybe it was.

"So how much does she know?" Sam called from the driver's seat.

I got out of the Kaiser. "She's just someone who knows someone at Marineland, okay? She doesn't know anything else."

Sam leaned forward, concerned. "I don't know—"

"And why am I not surprised by that?" I headed up the gangway. "Go home and get some sleep. Maybe it'll come to you."

"We're watching you, Wade," Wexler shouted at my back. "Don't louse this up, shit face."

I turned. "What are we? In the school yard, Eddie? You trying to pick a fight, comrade?"

Sam reached over and kept Wexler from getting out and coming at me. "You aren't fooling me with that comrade stuff, Wade. I know you. And the first time you louse up, you're dead."

"The cheaper the crook, the gaudy—" I mumbled.

"What's that?"

The guy was a serious threat. Stupid, but serious. Which made him even more of a threat. I decided that there was no advantage in provoking him further and bounced the rest of the way up the gangway.

Sam put the Olds into gear and began backing the car out of the small lot. I watched Wexler point his right forefinger at me and cock his thumb. Then they were just a couple of dwindling taillights and a faint cloud of exhaust.

A life at stake matter, indeed.

# CHAPTER 14

*Long ago and far away*:

Lex floated before me like a dead fish. She reached under her throat and yanked up, pulling off a skin-tight mask to reveal Suzi's expressionless face.

I couldn't move.

Suzi's eyes rolled up until they were completely white and her hands clawed at her neck to strip away skin and expose the glaring features of Naomi.

I couldn't breathe.

The dead FBI agent glided directly toward me, gun blazing.

My gun jumped. I watched the bullet tear into her forehead, yanking apart her right eye while she screamed, "Let's not be so damn haaasty!"

*I'm a self-absorbed idiot.* It never occurred to me until I woke up in my tangled bunk on my creaking boat that Lex might in fact die from her throat cancer, or that my friends might be in serious danger from Wexler and company.

I was wet from sweat. I needed a shower, but I pulled myself topside into the night air. Just like everyone else on this spinning planet, I'd had my share of dreams. But the one tonight really shook me and my muscles still ached from the tension. We all liked to think that there's a point to our dreams. We imagined that they had some profound meaning.

Out in the dark Pacific channel, a freighter slowly moved south, blinking a small light like something out of the final scene of *The Great Gatsby*. I wondered why I did what I did. Why me?

There were plenty of cops, PIs, and insurance investigators. So why did I feel the need to put myself at risk and possibly others as well? In my gut, it felt like the right thing to do, what I was supposed to do, even though I didn't know why. Hell, I'd probably die before I ever really knew the true reason why.

It came to me slowly, as I stared out at the black void and that single point of light. Everybody eventually realized they didn't know why. No matter how unique or special we tried to be, we all shared the same sense of drifting in the unknown. Then once in a long while, we dreamed of something better than what we were and we determined to make that dream come true. So to that extent, our dreams did have meaning.

I rubbed goose flesh from my arms and went below for a hit off the bottle I kept in a footlocker. The twenty-year-old Scotch burned going down.

"This has got to stop," someone said as I stretched out on the bunk again for only a few seconds.

Two hours later, I was awake again and scraping the stubble from my chin. The day had warmed only slightly. I caught the dull haze of the eastern sun through a porthole and heard the faint screeching of sea gulls searching for their breakfast.

I put the night behind me and the bottle back into the footlocker under my old Boy Scout uniform and next to a broken-framed photo of my gridiron team at USC.

The bottom of the sky looked green out over the ocean, as I drove down the coast behind a couple of vooming Harleys. I went straight to Marineland alone, without even calling Suzi, stopping only for French toast and coffee at some new pancake house that claimed to be "international." Everyone needed a gimmick to make it in Hollywood, the land of 10,000 swimming pools.

While there, I fed a dime into payphone and listened to it bong before I spun the dial. Cindy at the Brown Derby said that my mail was piling up, but there were no phone messages that she knew of. I thanked her and caught myself staring longingly at the bright and cheerful cigarette machine next to the pay phone. Oh well.

At ten a.m., the attractions at Marineland had opened to the public. Already there was a line of tour buses spaced out along the outer rim of the parking lot. Crowds of hyped and inquisitive visitors were filling the stands of the Sea Arena. A blaring PA system invited them to see a special surprise guest at the eleven o'clock show. Weezie met me in the small lobby off the administration building and lead me around to the rear of the facility, where she left me to pretend I was snapping arty photos among massive tanks of sea water and the marine life therein. The room connected to the underside of the vast arena tank and was enclosed by a massive sheet of clear Plex. Several other open-top tanks gurgled around me. Sunlight from the staging area above wobbled bluely in the chamber as twin porpoises glided by in the main tank. They seemed to hang in the dull blue water, their eyes inquisitive. I was standing next to a giant fishbowl where the sea life could almost touch my palm.

The lone detective was beginning to feel like his old self again, though I regretted not calling or bringing Suzi along. A huge manta ray sailed past the other side of the thick glass beside my right shoulder. The enormous thing swooped gracefully by like a ballerina trailing a billowing cape. I yelped a little and the Hasselblad slipped from my fingers, the strap jerking at my neck.

"Oh, there you are." Simonson came around the edge of a doorway with Lola McKinley behind him. He wore a gray suit and bright blue tie covered with tropical fish. McKinley was still in Capri's, still snapping her gum, and still smiling under russet locks. They walked up together and Simonson put a finger next to his nose. "Give us a minute, won't you, Lola?"

She seemed mildly surprised, saying, "Ah, okay," and exited back around the edge of the room's entrance.

The operations manager waited. I fiddled with the viewfinder. "It's only fair to tell you," he said, "I've spoken about you with one of the park's major investors."

So, that was it. "Is he an elderly gent from Texas?"

"Uh-huh." Simonson's eyes were red, like he'd been swimming in chlorinated water. "I know now that you're a private copper here to investigate the…money issue."

"Yeah, that funny little money issue. I already have a few definite ideas about that."

"Good. Comrade Reed wants you to report your findings to him tonight out on the Waves."

I drew a blank. "The Waves?"

The gray eyes behind his glasses met mine and held them. "The gambling boat. Out in the channel."

I tried to recall what Reed had said regarding a gambling boat. I was pretty sure he'd been against the idea of a casino operating twelve miles out of shore in international waters. But he certainly did like to gamble, so…

A quiet "floating" game for the upper class of Southern California sort of made sense and it would turn a handy profit for the Cause. "How do I get out there?"

"A launch usually leaves the park pier around 8:30

each night. Just tell them that Miss Fortune sent you."

Francesca Fortuna Degarre?

The black shadow of the stingray swooped near us, quietly brushing the glass wall.

I ducked slightly, clutching the camera. "Do you mind if we get the hell out of here?"

Simonson chuckled knowingly. "Manny is harmless. It's the sharks and barracuda that you have to watch out for."

We walked out of the room together and up the stairs. "Thanks for the tip. You've got barracuda here?"

As we stepped back into the crowded sunlight, Simonson smiled, teeth gleaming. "Of course not. Marineland is for children." He gestured to the fish pictures on his tie. "That's Orky and that's Corky, the performing whales. It's all for the kiddies." He strolled away into the passing school of tourists, just as I remembered what type of whales Orky and Corky were: killer.

I rotated the crank on the camera to feed in more film, snapping shots of a trained seal act, fluttering flags, soft-drink stands, garbage trucks, a crowded fishing pond, and a couple hundred people in sunglasses, sandals, and colorful stretched shorts. I wandered to the south end of the complex and peered down from a chest-high stone wall over the high cliff to the pier below. Runabouts and whale-watcher boats were docked in the early afternoon light.

Happy music blared around me as an echoing voice announced from elevated speakers that the "Three-ring Sea Circus" would begin in ten minutes. A small boy, perhaps eleven or twelve years old, in glasses, t-shirt and shorts, was searching the milling mob in earnest and running his fingers through his curly blond hair. He was obviously lost and I felt the urge to help him. It only took a few minutes to signal one of the park's uniformed pages and confirm that David was indeed looking for his mother. The boy was vacationing from Indiana and talked a nervous blue streak with a mid-western twang.

While I bought him a spearmint snow cone, an announcement went out over the public address system, and soon mother and son were united. The boy gave both me and the page a gap-toothed smile and a hugging handshake. Mrs. Letterman watched this carefully and then everyone went back to their normal lives, as if the event had never happened. Just another forgotten episode of Stan Dalmas Wade, the clueless and caring detective.

I shrugged and glimpsed, upside down in the viewfinder, Eddie Wexler wearing an open-neck polo shirt and smoking a panatela. I didn't want any more of his grief, so I turned, bought a fried fish sandwich, and went back down below the arena again to sit and sort things through my muddled mind. My thoughts went back to Suzi again and I had a sort of epiphany. What if I proposed to her? Yeah, that would lift her spirits and dispel her despair, wouldn't it? Certainly lift mine, too. But it would also likely put her in more danger, as well.

I was still sorting deep thoughts and life options, when I succeeded in getting tartar sauce on my pant leg. I dipped my handkerchief into a secondary tank filled with sunfish and brightly-colored coral and was dabbing at the stain, when I heard a cracking sound and something scrape the concrete behind me . Then I felt the something slam the concrete of my cranium and my world went black.

I came back to consciousness slowly, dazed and disoriented, as if someone were gradually turning up the brightness in the sub-basement fall-out shelter of my mind. I felt a tugging and twisting at my hands. I felt a turning and twisting at my hips. I felt a lifting and a shock of cold all over my body as I dropped into water over my head. My wrists were held by heavy wire tied tightly to a cinder block. It took me down into the blurry coral bed where I'd soon sleep forever.

A gray eel watched with unblinking eyes. Maybe I could get his needle teeth to bite through the thick wired around my hands. I kicked and tried to get my head to the surface and the eel swam away among the blue and green coral. I looked up at the rippling daylight and started seeing green and orange spots. I screamed deep in my throat, sucked water through my nose, and involuntarily coughed out what little air I had left. The colors began to bleed together. Red flecks floated among the pale greens and yellows. Black spots blossomed, as I forced my eyes as wide as possible to capture the light that quickly faded to total and complete darkness.

❧❧

Someone jumped on my chest. Someone pinched my nose and held my tongue. Someone blew into my mouth and pounded on me again and again. I coughed up a gallon of seawater, gasped enough air to fill a weather balloon, and dimly saw that someone was Lloyd Bridges in his "Sea Hunt" wet suit.

My head cleared as I retched, coughing up more oceans. The rubber skin-diving outfit had been an illusion, but it was straight-up Bridges who'd been jumping, pinching, and pounding.

His tan, blond face dripped down at me with concern. "Who did this to you?" he asked, while someone else unwound the wire from my wrists. The other someone was young and lean. I saw then that both men wore wet swimming trunks and canvas shoes.

"That's my question," I said, unsteadily. "Also, where'd you two come from?"

"Hey, fella," the other guy said, shaking water from his dark hair. "Are you okay?"

Bridges leaned back as I tried to sit up—and failed. He showed me his palms. "Take it easy. I'll get us some help."

"Wait," I coughed. "Don't leave me. What happened?"

"Good question," the actor said, rising. "I was coming down here for a smoke before the show and heard a splash and someone running."

The base of my head began to throb. I felt at the back of my neck and found a sensitive knob that wasn't there that morning. "Are—are you really Lloyd Bridges? I'm not dead or dreaming this?"

The actor nodded and grinned shyly. "And this is Captain Nemo," he said in the flat voice I recognized from his TV narration.

The lean man arched an eyebrow and grinned. "It's Nimoy, not Nemo."

"We call him that because he has a natural talent for ships and diving," Bridges said. "We use Lenny in a lot of episodes."

My head and stomach were still reeling, so without thinking, I said, "I read the trades."

Nimoy looked concerned again. "Let's get him to the medical station."

"Right," Bridges said and they helped me to my feet.

The lifeguard at the park turned out to be a registered lifeguard, after all. Seemed that occasionally, visitors to Marineland would tumble into the water, but usually not with a cinderblock wired to their arms. The guard led me to a small room that functioned as a medical station, where an old guy smoking a cigar told me to lay down on a cot while he checked me over.

Weezie heard about my "accident" and brought me a

set of dry clothes borrowed from one of the maintenance men. They were baggy and displayed the park's logo on the back, but I didn't complain. I was damn happy about a lot of things, considering the alternative.

The old doctor kept flicking ashes from his cigar and holding my eyes open to peer into them as if examining my brain. He grunted a few times, tilted his head, and pronounced me healthy enough to get dressed and go. I gathered my wet wallet, keys, lighter, and camera. Wrung out my coat, shirt, and socks, and checked my dead brother's watch, seeing with a shrug that it was still ticking. USN aviator chronometers are hard to stop. My ruined notebook went into a handy Reliance Waste Management trashcan.

While I finished toweling down and heaving up, I thought of what I hadn't seen of my assailant. Something dangled and drifted out of focus in my soggy memory.

I told Bridges and his buddy to let me handle explaining everything to the park officials. He told me that would be a good idea, since he and Lenny were here at the park doing a personal appearance for a "Sea Serpent" episode of his ZIV-produced TV show. In the middle of our discussion, Suzi showed up, punched me in the shoulder and conferred with Weezie. The two actors went out to meet their audience, while I lay back thinking about eel teeth, colored coral, and fading light.

The crowds hadn't thinned any when the two girls and I made our way back out to the parking lot in the brisk air. The lifeguard didn't know all the details of my situation and seemed eager to allow us to "go home and get some rest." The tender spot at the back of my head felt better, but water still sloshed in my left ear.

"I'll drive," Suzi said. "You can sit in the back with my diving gear."

"Aw, come on," I said. "I almost died in there."

She glared. "And if I'd been with you, it might not have happened. How'd you let anyone sneak up on you like that, anyway?"

"I was thinking about…" I stopped before I said too much concerning our relationship and meekly climbed into the back seat. "Where are we going?"

"I'm hungry," she addressed Weezie as if I wasn't there.

"I'm thirsty," Weezie replied. "And I know a damn good place for a drink."

"Lead me to it," I moaned from my cramped position in the back of the Renault. Weezie gave directions down Tucker road past the Hegenburgers' restaurant to a small and weather-worn shack called the Rusty Scupper.

# CHAPTER 15

*Once inside*:

So, let me understand this shit." Weezie pulled her hair back into two pony tails and tied them off with rubber braids from the pockets of her jeans. "You live on a boat, but you don't know the first thing about diving?"

I was trying to be reasonable. "Most people who live near the water aren't skilled as frogmen."

"Yeah, but you actually live on the water. And today you were in over your goddam head, man."

Suzi jumped in. "Good time to learn how to dive."

"I know how to dive."

"But not deep. God, I'll bet you can't even snorkel."

"Can too! I can spit and blow through my nose to clear my mask like a pro."

We were seated at a wobbly table, surrounded by working-class people, mostly men. The walls were decorated clumsily with fishnets, shells, and sponges. Twin ceiling fans circulated the blue haze of tobacco and bar-b-cue smoke above our heads. Suzi giggled and leaned back, making her chair creak. "Standy here went swimming in an ocean of mud a couple of months ago."

"What—" Weezie said, "—the hell?"

"Long story." I took a pull off my beer bottle. "Look, I'm willing to learn to skin dive, just not now. Too busy."

"We could teach you." Weezie wiggled her pencil-thin brows. "Lloyd could help, too."

I was stumped. "Why would Lloyd help?"

"Actually, we're kinda going together. I think he's handsome."

"You had a crush on Lloyd Bridges?" Suzi gushed.

"He looks just like he does on TV," I said, "and all this time I've been blaming my set."

Suzi punched my right arm. Weezie punched my left. I looked around the noisy bar to see if we were being watched. As it happened, we were.

Sam the Elvis impersonator sat nursing a green bottle of beer at another small table near a couple of buzzing and bonging pinball machines. I'd missed noticing him when we'd first come into the dark interior, but now I saw him get up and come our way. Spent peanut shells crunched under his feet. Before he got to our table, the barkeep laid another platter of bar-b-cued stingray before us and I nudged the greasy mess away with the sleeve of my workman's uniform.

Sam politely nodded his dark pompadour to the ladies. "Ladies." Then he stared intently at me. "We need to talk."

"Where's Heckle, Jekyll?"

"That's what we need to talk about." He turned back to Suzi and Weezie. "Ladies?"

Suzi tightened her jaw and sharpened her own stare. "We're not going anywhere, buddy."

Weezie nodded, seemed less certain, but nonetheless mimed, "Screw you."

"That's my cue," I said, coming off my chair. "The ladies have joined the party, comrade. At least, as far as you're concerned."

He looked the two women over yet again. I think he had a "crush" on them. My right fist was clinching to crush his chin, when he whispered, "I'm not a member of the party. I'm part of the agency where we keep all the intelligence centralized."

While I processed this absurdity, Suzi said, "You mean the…Oh, that agency."

Sam nodded. "That's all right, baby,' he said in his best Elvis voice. "That's all right, momma."

The two women glanced at each other as if they'd just heard a hound-dog crying.

I checked to make sure that the bartender wasn't near and listening. Then I said, "Bullshit."

The impersonator shrugged. "Then I'll just have to tell your uncle."

"Uncle Sam?" Weezie said.

The man shook his head and looked directly into my eyes. Maybe he had a crush on me now. "Walt."

The last of the sea water cleared from my head. "Ladies," I said and took a step away from them. "I hope you don't mind." I pulled at Sam's sleeve, so we could quietly conspire. "I need a minute to think this through."

He showed me his even teeth. "I fully understand. But don't take too long. The Agency and the Bureau are connected, albeit loosely—"

"Albeit, yet," I hissed. "I'll bet."

Sam hesitated. "Anybody ever tell you that you talk funny?"

"All the time. Now, you talk."

He kept his voice down and scanned the room without moving his head. "We sometimes share intel and operatives. When a case is big enough, we occasionally work together. But from opposite ends."

"So you're saying that you and I are both communists working undercover to infiltrate the organization."

He snorted. "Not quite. We're both undercover, all right, but we're first infiltrating the communists, who are—"

"Infiltrating the organization. Okay. See? That's the part I have to think through."

"Look at it this way," he offered. "I'm an Elvis impersonator who is pretending to be a communist, but who really is an officer of the CIA."

"Sounds simple, when you put it that way."

"We're more than halfway through the twentieth century, Wade. You need to keep up with the times. I'm attached to Wexler to keep him off your back, so you can get a lead on what Reed is really up to. This nonsense about counterfeit money at Marineland is nothing, compared to what the commies are really planning."

"Which is?"

"What you're supposed to find out. Walt, Hoover, and our new director Dulles, all want to know the details and I'm here to see that you live to get them the answers."

You simply couldn't make this stuff up. "Well, you weren't here this afternoon," I exclaimed, "when someone tied me to a block of concrete and tossed me into—"

The noise level in the bar seemed to lower. Suzi and Weezie gestured for me to quiet down.

"It wasn't Wexler," Sam assured me calmly. "He's back at his office, meeting Reed."

I took a breath and eased it out. "And supposing I believe you. Then what?"

"Then we both wrap up this phony money deal and find out what the commies are really up to here. Can I count on you?"

Another good question. The air was full of them lately. Sam's story was loony-tunes crazy. Crazy enough not to be something made up. Maybe part of it was true. The guy seemed earnest enough and, as I thought back, he'd never done anything I could feel was a genuine threat. Beating up the guy at Santa Anita could have just been the work of Phil alone. And Sam had never echoed any of Wexler's threats.

And who could seriously worry about a guy who dressed up like Elvis Presley? The real Elvis would never offer his services to the FBI or CIA, would he? I needed to get back to basics. I needed to find out who'd tried to kill me, and why, where the phony money was coming from, and how it got to the racetrack. I needed to find out why the commies were trying to take over the west coast mob. And I needed to find another drink.

I wondered what Mr. P would do in this situation. Probably take the doggedly direct but surprising route. Well enough, then. "Bartender," I shouted. "Drinks on the house."

While everybody rushed the bar, I pulled Suzi and Weezie over to where Elvis of the CIA stood. "Suzi," I ordered, "You contact the security office at Santa Anita and find out if Reliance Management handles their trash."

"Reliance? But they're—"

I stopped her with a wave of my hand and turned to Weezie. "I want you to check something for me at the park. Something I saw deep in the fish tanks."

The girl nodded, enthused. "This is so damn actually super, man."

"You said it." I clasped Sam on the shoulder and felt the strap of the holster and gun he wore. "I'm going to need some of your armament, Sammy, because you and I are going to catch the queer at the pier. Pay the man and let's fly."

ΣΩΣ

I was not nearly as confident as I appeared. Stranger still, everyone accepted my direction and followed my lead.

In fact, I was still confused about a lot of things, but it stood to reason that the funny money passing through the realm of Corky and Orky would first likely come via a boat and that idea lead directly to the pier.

The girls took off on their individual assignments, while I rode south of the park in the gathering twilight with Sam the CIA Elvis. "What's your real name, anyway?"

"Ellery, but keep calling me Sam." He steered us down a blacktop two-lane off Palos Verdes South to the shoreline. The car radio said that the coast guard had issued a warning of a large cold front coming in and a good chance for heavy fog.

I had Ellery the Elvis's snub-nose .38 in the pocket of my maintenance man outfit, but was still hesitant to fire it at anyone, which put me in a dangerous position. I kept this thought to myself and forged doggedly ahead— which was also dangerous. Sam had his back-up piece from his glove box. I still felt that I should have had a few more beers.

There were three boats tied up at the pier, all dark. A small skiff, another sailboat partly hoisted out of the water, and a white-hulled cabin cruiser, at least forty-eight feet long.

We approached the cruiser's stern. She had pretty lines and a sharp bow to slice through chop, yet she was wide enough to provide room to stretch. Sam and I quietly climbed on board and stepped into the roomy cockpit. The wooden cover was in place on the hatch leading below. I pushed it up and slid it off. The cabin was empty, but bathed in faint florescent light. It was a roomy living space with cushioned seats that could be made into bunks, a kitchenette/galley, table, and sink, much like my boat, only cleaner.

I descended into the cabin with Sam behind me and went over to the louvered door leading to the head and forward bunk. I pulled it open and the light from the cabin fell on a large gun in the right hand of Dandy Phil Castle.

"Hello, Sam," he said around me, showing his natural, well-polished teeth. "What are you doing here—with him?"

I was the monkey in the middle of them, so I leaned to one side on the bulkhead.

Sam Ellery eased out a reply. "Hello, partner. Thought I'd find you here, fouling up Reed's operation again."

Dandy Phil didn't like that. He brushed back his dark hair and motioned with the gun for us to raise our hands. He wore jeans, deck shoes, a tan jacket half-zipped, and a yellow polo shirt.

"That's a nice purple polo," I said. "Mind telling me where you bought it?"

His chin dipped slightly and his eyes flicked down to check the color.

Sam and I moved in.

Phil fired in the confined cabin. I heard Sam cry out and his gun strike the deck. Phil's gun moved straight back to me. I felt the weight of the .38 in my pocket, but left it there.

"Get above deck," Phil ordered. "Both of you."

As we went up the ladder, I saw Phil pick up a square package wrapped in thick waxed paper and black tape. Then the night and fog moved around us. Sam held his hand, dripping blood. Phil came topside and told us both to turn around. The sea breeze cooled my hot face. I heard a dull thump and glimpsed Sam's body falling into a net and almost over the side. I knew I was next and I already had a swell lump at the back of my head.

My hands were raised. I took a breath and let half of it out. I spun around and caught his arm with my left as he started to bring the gun down to bash me. I knocked the weapon aside and swung my right fist at his face.

He took the weak punch on the side of his head, but it was enough to knock the gun from his hand.

He threw a punch back and connected with my sore ribs.

I ignored the pain and threw another punch.

He threw a punch and my teeth clicked.

I threw a kick.

He jumped back.

I jumped forward and threw a punch.

He threw a punch.

I thought about my gun.

He threw a punch.

He threw another punch.

I went down, tasting blood.

He pulled a switchblade knife.

Sam moaned and staggered to his feet behind us.

I scrambled away from the knife that gleamed in the mist.

Phil reached down and yanked at the net under Sam's feet.

That's when I should have brought out my gun—but I didn't. I hesitated and Sam went down again, hitting his head hard on the boat's brass fittings.

"Enough," I gasped.

"You've had enough?" Phil asked, waving the knife before him.

"Enough," I said again, "of this bullshit!" I came at him in a red haze.

The knife came up. I blocked it and caught enough of his arm to twist the blade from his hand.

The knife rattled on the deck. He clamped my right arm like a Stilson wrench and pounded my ribs again. A lightning bolt of pain shot through me. I went down with him on top, strangling my throat and hissing in my face.

I stretched my left hand to reach the knife, but it was inches away from my fingertips, at the foot of Sam's prone body. I started seeing black spots and screamed.

Phil screamed back, in defiance and triumph.

Sam's body jerked. His feet kicked out, sending the knife spinning across the deck. I clutched it and drove it into the meaty side of Phil's right thigh. His scream increased and his weight left my throat and chest.

The fog and pain blinded me. I shook my head to clear it and it made me even groggier. I couldn't locate Phil, but in the dim light I saw Sam struggle again to his feet, tangle himself in the fishing net, and go down for the third time. I groaned and pulled myself into a wicker chair, thinking, "Suffering Succotash."

The lights of the distant park glowed through the mist. Flashlight beams probed the night as people gathered along the pier, drawn by sounds of the struggle.

"Call an ambulance," I yelled and staggered over to support Sam.

# CHAPTER 16

*A little later*:

The same old doc at the park's med station checked my head again and wrapped my ribs. He gave me some Darvon pills and told me to stay out of trouble. I think he was getting sick of meeting and treating me. I shared the opinion. He also told me that he thought one of my back teeth had been knocked loose. He patched Sam's hand and had him hauled off to a Long Beach hospital for further treatment. I pressed a crunching bag of ice alternating between my jaw to the back of my scalp and wondered where Phil had gone.

Even though the sun was down and the fog was in, the park was still bright and busy. Attendees and spectators seemed to prefer the cooler night air and thronged the various water shows like pilot fish on sharks. From somewhere a calliope played "Popeye the Sailor," but it might have just been in my head.

I suddenly realized that I'd been winding my watch while thinking things through before confronting Eisner and his staff.

When I entered the CEO's office, Lola McKinley was

already seated in a cushioned chair, filing her short, ruby fingernails and popping her gum. Both activities unlikely for a Financial Officer, but I let it pass. I had asked Weezie and Suzi to follow me in and we all stood there waiting until Eisner hung up the phone. He stabbed out a filtered cigarette in a large clamshell next to a grenade setting upright on his desk. "I've instructed our security chief to work with the police and keep a tight lid on this evening's violence," Eisner said.

I had forgotten his first name—Dick or Dave—and my notebook was now just so much soggy trash. So I couldn't check it to be sure.

He yanked a pack of Tareytons from the inside breast pocket of his olive sport coat, nudged a couple of cigarettes out with a tap of a finger, and pulled one free with his lips. The grenade on his desk turned out to be a lighter.

Lola McKinley must have seen this act before, because she went right on filing and chewing.

Eisner scowled at us. "I've asked Everetton to join us here, so we all can get our stories straight."

Lola said, "We're concerned about managing the company's image." Her voice was calm and official. "Any bad publicity would significantly affect our bottom line."

I glanced at Suzi, who had settled into another of the room's comfortable chairs. Weezie rubbernecked the room as if she'd never been here before, which was entirely possible given her low position on the park's org chart.

The main door to the office opened and Everetton strode in followed by the business manager, John Meskin, and our friend from the advertising and sales department, Sally Kropp.

There wasn't enough seating to accommodate all these

people, so I suggested that we adjourn to the conference room.

"No, we'll handle this right here," Eisner said. He rolled the chair out from behind his desk, so Sally could sit down. "Go ahead, Alan. Tell them what you found out."

Everetton shot me a measured glance and moved to the center of the crowded room. "I've got a contact in the Bureau of Motor Vehicles, as some of you know. So I ran this guy's plates." He jerked a thumb in my direction, hitchhiking. "He's not a photographer and he's not a marine." He gave me a glare. "He's a private dick, named Stan Wade." His voice sounded as though it came out of a cave and no one responded, except Weezie, who said, "Sonofabitch," and then she covered her mouth with a hand and looked down.

Eisner leaned back, resting his weight on the front of the desk, cigarette smoke trailing to the ceiling.

I figured it was better to let Everetton get it all out, before I started spilling what I'd learned and suspected.

The security officer came up to me, the corner of one eye wrinkled with fury. "I gave you a break, mister, and you took advantage."

A clock ticked somewhere near us.

"Hey, Alan," I breathed, "I thought we were brothers or comrades in arms. But you couldn't stop yourself and checked up on me anyway, didn't you? How do I know you're not the person who tried to drown me?"

"What are you talking about?"

I had intentionally dangled the loaded word, "comrade," but he hadn't risen to the bait. It occurred to me to cast deeper.

"I'm talking about the inferior level of security you run here at the park. Not only can I stroll in under a phony identity, but someone can even try to kick me here, all without your awareness. Or maybe you were involved."

"You bastard. I'll—"

I charged on. "Then there's the matter of this evening's fight at the pier. Where were you when that little event took place?"

"I don't have to justify myself to you." He reached behind his back and brought up a pair of silvery handcuffs. "I'm officially taking you—"

"Now hold on, Chief," Eisner said, mashing out his smoke. "First, I want to hear what this whole thing is all about." His off-color tooth caught the light.

Everetton almost growled like a wolf, but he took a step back and cocked his head, listening for a lie.

I didn't give him one. Instead, I took a deep breath to control my own anger. "I have to admit, Chief. You're a pretty good investigator, after all. Yes, you're right about my identity, and this is my, uh…partner, Suzi Sunset. But apparently, you missed the fact that counterfeit money has been flowing into the country through the park you're supposed to be guarding."

That got arise out of almost everyone in the room, including Suzi, who said, "Are you sure that you should be telling—"

"It's all right. I think I've got this doped out now."

Sally Kropp coughed. Lola McKinley put her file away and leaned forward with interest. Meskin seemed totally confused and cracked his knuckles. Eisner…first name David, it finally came to me…was as imperial as ever.

I mentally reviewed all I'd learned, fitting the facts together like pieces from multiple jigsaw puzzles. Something still didn't click—still didn't snap, crackle, or pop.

And then it did.

"Okay," I began. "You all know about the fight at the pier. The guy there was smuggling phony bills in from a boat off-shore and, unfortunately, got away tonight before he could be stopped. But he's like a wounded tiger now and we know who he is."

"Who?" Eisner and Everetton asked at the same time.

"Do any of you know a man called Phil Castle? He's from out of town, stocky, about five foot two. Dark hair and complexion."

Sally Kropp raised her hand, as if to be allowed to leave. "I've seen a man like that meeting with John about some vendor contracts or other."

"That's right," Everetton agreed. "I escorted that gentleman to Meskin's office just last week."

"What? Wait." The little business manager raised his hands as if to surrender. "He's a financier from New York. Said he was thinking of investing in the park's expansion. I only met him that once."

"So when the money comes in at the pier," I mused, "what do you do with it?"

"Nothing," Meskin squawked. "I don't know anything about it."

"I do," Suzi said. "You were right, Standy. I checked and Reliance Management handles the trash pick-up both here and at Santa Anita. By the way, the track officials said to thank you for spotting and stopping that low-life pickpocket, Chuck Manson."

I conjured the name and finally said, "Never heard of him. So the counterfeit is probably transported to the track for distribution by one of the corporation's garbage trucks."

"Shit," Everetton said.

"Standy?" Sally said,

"First name, middle initial," I said and blew Suzi a kiss before realizing how it must have looked.

"So, who tried to drown you?" Weezie asked.

"That depends," I answered. "Did you find red flecks

in the coral bed of the tank where I was dumped?"

"Yes," Weezie said. "Actually, they looked like—"

One of the chairs seemed to have grown less comfortable, as its occupant moved to hide her shortened fingernails.

The clock ticked. Everyone slowly came to gaze at the CFO.

"You know," Meskin offered. "I was going to ask why my accounts seemed slightly off, ever since you instituted that new billing system."

"Lola?" Sally said.

"You heard me talking to Simonson this afternoon about a money issue," I said, taking a step toward McKinley, "and you mistakenly assumed I'd discovered your cooked books. That's why you hit me from behind and busted up your nail polish, wiring me to that cinder block."

"Lola!" Sally said.

The red-haired CFO scrunched up her face like she was going to scream. Everetton moved on her, rattling his handcuffs, and she burst out crying like lost child.

Eisner told the security chief to put the cuffs away, but to find someplace to hold McKinley, until she could be officially dealt with.

We watched the two exit the room, the door closing behind them with a "shush."

Sally slumped. "Lola…"

"But she didn't act alone," I announced. "I have a tough time believing that Lola would attempt murder simply because she thought I knew about the accounts being off. And she could never have lifted me into that tank without help. Where is Simonson, anyway?"

"I sent him on a business trip to Catalina," Eisner said, lighting another cigarette. "He's setting up a sea cruise attraction from Avalon to the park."

Meskin cracked his knuckles. "I've always suspected they were in bed together."

"Literally?" Eisner asked, setting his grenade-lighter down.

Meskin nodded.

"Oh, Lola," Weezie said.

Eisner started for the door. "Wait here. I want to check Chet's office."

"Hold it," I called, moving in behind him. "I'll go with you. Suzi, keep an eye on things here." And I kept my eye on the man in front of me, as we hurried down the hall. Sam's gun was still in my pocket.

As it happened, I didn't need it. Once we were in Simonson's office, it was pretty clear from the blood and body on the floor, that Chet hadn't made it to Catalina Island. He'd gone somewhere else beyond Avalon and beyond the sea.

⇛

The phone was off the hook and beeping for attention.

Eisner nudged the door shut behind us as we both leaned down to inspect the knife sticking out of the operations manager's neck.

I used the baggy sleeve of my maintenance outfit to hang up the receiver and immediately heard a clock ticking here in this room, too. Time flies when you're having…fun?

Twenty-dollar bills were scattered about like giant confetti. Several drawers hung open from a row of file cabinets along one wall. On the floor next to the leg of an overturned chair, lay a wad of waxed paper and black tape. I'd seen it and the knife before, less than an hour earlier.

A faint trail of bloody footprints stained some of the

papers and the short shag carpet between the limp body and the office door.

"Castle," Eisner said.

"He couldn't have gotten far with that hole I put in his leg."

"He damn well got this far with it."

"True." I gritted my teeth and felt a sharp pain in my jaw. "We should check the med station, assuming he knows about it."

Eisner ground out his cigarette in an empty ashtray on a credenza next to the disordered desk. "I'll handle this, comrade," he said. "Reed's expecting a full report from you on his gambling yacht. I'll try and reach him on the ship-to-shore and bring him up to date."

"You know, comrade," I said. "There's an even chance that the money comes in from his own boat."

Eisner nodded. "He'll love hearing that. When you tell him, let him know that we can plug the pipeline from here to the race track."

"But we still don't know where to find Dandy Phil."

"I said I'd handle it, dammit," the commie CEO roared. "You're going out to the Waves."

I decided not to fight with him, assuming I could first confer with Suzi—and one other thing. I pulled at the sagging hips of my outfit. "Can I get out of this clown suit and into a decent change of clothes?"

# CHAPTER 17

*Later that night*:

The speedboat bounced and porpoised, making my left back molar throb. I stood holding onto railing damp with spindrift, watching the waves in the searchlight. Most of the time, I don't know what's going on, which is probably why I work at being a detective. But occasionally, I don't know what I'm getting into either and this was one of those times.

I could only imagine why Dandy Phil had killed Simonson. He'd had enough time and proximity to the operations manager's office. There had been a fight involving money, evidenced by the scattered twenties. But as to the specific details, I may never know.

Earlier that evening, I'd called Phil the Knife a wounded tiger. Now he was presumably on the prowl among the park attendees. He could have left with any of them, during the last hour. Or he still could be hiding, waiting to pounce from just down the hall.

Eisner and I headed back to his office. Everetton hadn't returned, but the CEO got him on the phone, instructing that he stay close to Lola. There didn't seem to be any good reason to advise the rest of the people in the room about our gruesome discovery. The meeting broke up and I took Suzi aside, telling her to not let Weezie spend the night alone.

Eisner pulled a gray seersucker suit from his office closet and I put it on with a clean shirt and thin black tie. It hung reasonably well, but didn't match my scuffed and still-damp shoes. Not to worry. Like a true executive, the CEO had one of those upright polish and buff machines. Minutes later, I looked ready to accept an Emmy.

But the pain in my jaw wouldn't go away. It was 9:45 when the motor launch pulled alongside the refurbished freighter. Canned music played and a string of outdoor lights made the tarnished exterior appear not just bright, but gay. This was the Waves, probably named such to emulate the successful desert casino, the Sands.

I looked up and saw Pinky waiting at the top of the ladder. He was eating a sandwich and used it to gesture me aboard. He led me down the starboard companionway which ended at a flight of metal stairs going up. At the top was a hatch and beyond that a narrow deck above the boat-deck. The music was louder here accompanied by the rattling sound of slot machines. There were wide windows rather than portholes, all of them curtained from the inside, except the one most forward.

Pinky finished his sandwich and ushered me into the wheelhouse. "Wait right here."

I listened to the ship's throbbing engines resonate with the throbbing in my jaw. A blue-chinned character in a fake captain's uniform stood at the controls next to a chart table. He squinted at me but didn't say a word. Then he shifted his gaze back out to the dark sea. Maybe he thought we were going somewhere.

I waited right there, putting my hands in my pockets and feeling strangely elegant. Back when I was about seventeen, I thought owning a floating casino would be one of the greatest things in the world. I also thought that it would be cool to have my own theme song. The tune I'd made up for myself came back to me now and I whistled it quietly while looking around the cabin.

The lights were dim to cut down glare on the window glass, but I could see a chart rolled out on the table, indicating our position halfway between the shore and Catalina. I recognized the ragged shape of Long Beach on the chart and was just wondering why someone had penciled in what looked like a propeller near Terminal Island, when August Reed stepped over the transom, accompanied by the stunningly coiffed Miss Francesca Degarre. She was dressed to the earlobes in diamonds and a moonlit gown.

The Old Duck wore a blue blazer with gold buttons, gray flannel slacks, and a white yachting cap. No cigar, thank god.

"Mister Wade," he said, raising his arms as if to hug me. "Delighted to see you. What have you to report?"

"I see your point now about how hard it would be to re-float an oil platform and turn it into a gambling casino," I said. "This converted freighter is much more practical and a little nostalgic, too."

Degarre's cat's-eyes sparkled in the subdued light. A corner of her mouth curled coyly. "You like? The last ship like this was shut down in the 1930s by the municipal authorities. We have a special permit to operate our yacht outside the twelve-mile limit."

Reed stroked his beard and brushed one side of his mustache. "The thirties were a long time ago, Fortuna. Let's talk about current events. Your report, son?"

I briefed him on how the funny money came to the racetrack via the garbage trucks and how I figured that Simonson was using his operations-manager position to get it from the Marineland pier to the trucks. "Now that he's dead, it will likely stop."

Miss Degarre shivered, "Did you kill him?"

I didn't like her interest, or her assumption of my nature. "No," I answered. "He was knifed by our own Dandy Phil Castle."

"Careful what you say, comrade," Reed counseled. "Castle is a trusted Party member."

"Well, I've got news for you: he nearly killed me, too. And now he's out there on the loose."

Reed seemed troubled. "I always suspected someone of running the counterfeit through the park and interfering with our bigger operation. I didn't expect it to be Castle."

"I've got more bad news for you. It comes to the pier wrapped in waterproof packaging, possibly from this very boat." I decided to press my luck and reach for the brass ring on this merry-go-round, by asking, "What's this bigger operation, anyway? Is it that 'My Independent America' thing you mentioned? Some sort of immediate communist takeover?"

"Not quite immediate," Reed said, looking over my shoulder to the man at the ship's controls. "All I'll say is that your present government wants you to think the threat of communism is greater than it really is. That way, they can justify the military budget and make people believe they should trust anything the government says or does, since the alternative would lead to defeat."

He cleared his throat and brought out a cigar from inside his blazer, unwrapping the cellophane. "It's a classic 'war-scare' tactic used to keep the public in line, but it won't work in the long run, son. Mark my word, the younger generation will not fall for it much longer." His eyes caught and held the middle distance. "In a few years there will be a cultural shift; a revolution for peace that will change everything. In the meantime, the Communist Party will be waiting. Waiting to—" He snipped off the tip of the cigar with a small, sharp tool.

The head of the AWA was almost making sense, but it also sounded too much like a stump speech. The pain in my jaw had spread to my neck and forehead. Even my eyeballs ached. All I could muster was, "If you say so."

"How does the counterfeit money get here?" asked Francesca. "How did it get to the yacht?"

"I don't know…yet. But I'll deal with that tomorrow. Right now, I'm still recovering from a hell of a fight I had earlier."

Degarre sucked in a little air and widened her eyes slightly. Reed noticed her reaction and guided me out of the cabin, leaving her behind the closed hatch. "Sorry to lecture there, son. Go get some rest. You've earned it. I'll look into what you've told me. But I want you here again tomorrow night, dressed more appropriately for the stylish occasion. Your assignment will be to locate how and who is smuggling the money to and from the yacht. Get me?"

I dared not even shake my head. "Got you."

He opened his mouth and started to follow my lead, but then only gestured to Pinky who had been waiting farther down the rail.

As I boarded the motor launch back to shore, I thought, well then I'll say it: "Good."

I swallowed a couple of Darvon capsules dry to deaden the pain and got the hell out of there.

☙❧

The pain in my head traveled with me all the way back to Weezie's room at Marineland. Suzi said that there had been no sign of Phil and that Eisner had taken control of cleaning up of Simonson's office and body.

I wasn't fully focused and slumped a little in a chair by the bed while Weezie and Suzi chatted on and on about a galleon that had run aground and sank in the sixteenth century and someone called Doctor Quentin Zircon. With a name like that, he'd be a whiz at Scrabble.

I glanced over to the nightstand and noticed a hardback copy of *The Doomsters*. When I idly picked it up, Weezie noticed. "Now there's a damn good private eye."

I turned slightly to look behind me.

"Not you." She came over and took the book from my hands. "In here. Lew Archer."

I yawned. "Who?"

Both women directed sighs at me.

"Is he actually worth all this shit and trouble?" Weezie said.

"Hmm," Suzi said. "Shit and trouble are his business."

My body was so fatigued that I didn't argue and I didn't think I could get out of the chair without help. "Come on, Standy. We can't stay here all night."

Since I was just a wee-mite dippy from Darvon and a whole-lot sore all over, I left my car in the parking lot and let my sidekick drive us. We got behind a broad Pontiac on the 405 and cruised in its wake all the way past Inglewood. There was a colored kid lying in the Pontiac's rear window-well in front of us and he waved as we peeled off to go east on Santa Monica Boulevard. The gas gauge on Suzi's Renault was nearing "E," so she stopped at a friendly Texaco for a fill up and a free set of steak knives. Even a conflict from something as silly as a gas war made me uncomfortable and cautious.

"We need to spend the night somewhere secluded," I told Suzi. "Somewhere unsuspected."

"I know a place over on the Strip," she nodded. Hardly anyone ever goes there anymore."

A three-quarter moon had come out from a bank of soft gray clouds and the neon of Hollywood was fully aglow as we parked outside a Spanish estate on the corner of Sunset Boulevard and Crescent Heights. The mellow light filled the courtyard, illuminating a swimming pool surrounded by a rambling set of bungalows. I knew this place, but had never stayed here. It had once been owned and named after the luminous silent-screen star Nazimova. An "h" had been added to her first name, Alla, to give the residence its current title: the Garden of Allah. Famous writers such as Dorothy Parker and Bob Benchley had frequented the bar and briefly called the place home back in the '30s. Since then, the exotic hotel had fallen on hard times and now was what you might fondly call a "joint." There was even word that it would be torn down in a few months, replaced by an S&L or a carry-out. But that hadn't stopped a few Hollywood notables from maintaining a "Hernando hideaway" down among the drooping palms, peeling paint, and chipping stucco.

"No one will think to look for us here," Suzi assured me, as we climbed the tile stairs. "I have a key to a small suite of rooms on the second floor, overlooking Crescent."

This was all news to me. "Where'd you get it? The key?"

"Errol Flynn."

I stopped in mid-step. "You are such a wicked, wicked name-dropper, I swear."

"Ha. You should talk."

"What?" I protested, dragging my tired body up the stairs by leaning most of my weight on the twisted iron banister.

"I heard you boasting about that case you took last year with Vincent Price," she said, turning the key and opening the door. "Something about a stolen painting while he was making *The Fly*."

"Wait. I never bragged about that to you. I didn't even want to take the case, but he damn-near begged me."

"Thou dost protest too much, kind sir."

"It's true. He kept pleading, 'Help me. Help me.' How did you know about it, anyway?"

Suzi snorted, switching on the lights. "Ha. My spies are everywhere."

"Under the circumstances, that's not funny."

"Anyway, Errol begged me, too. So we're even."

"I don't want to know any more, thanks."

"It's perfectly harmless."

It was my turn to say, "Ha. And I suppose Flynn just gave you that key as a professional courtesy."

She shook her head. "Let's not fight. Okay?"

"You're right. I'm too tired. And hungry."

It had been a long and busy day. My body could take only so much more of this professional investigation business. While Suzi drove a block up Sunset to Schwab's to buy us BLTs and paper-cups of tomato soup, I took advantage of the room's bar for a double shot of Dewars and claw-footed bath tub for a hot soaking of my weary bones and achy muscles.

She also returned with a late addition of the Times. We sat and ate together on a floral and somewhat saggy couch, watching the end of the 1934 movie, *Twentieth Century*. I chewed on the right side of my mouth, as Lombard was conned over and over again by Barrymore on the suite's console TV. Suzi seemed to love it. John Barrymore and Errol Flynn were two of a kind—both dashing drunkards who'd paid for their sins by falling hard at the end of their careers. Barrymore had seemed immortal until he surprised everyone by finally dying. Flynn seemed immortal too, but his day would eventually come, probably sooner than anyone expected. I raised my glass and silently toasted the two Don Juans.

Suzi clicked the remote and Groucho's duck came down. I missed hearing the secret word, because I'd gone back to scanning the headlines.

Liberace had won a case in court against a columnist who intimated the pianist was a homosexual. RCA announced that it was developing a home TV taping system called, "Hear-See." Klaus Fuchs, who had given America's atomic and hydrogen bomb secrets to the Soviet Union, was quietly released from a British prison after serving nine years.

But no mention at all of a dead operations manager at a local theme park. It might have been too early yet for the story to hit the newspapers. Or Reed's comrades might keep it silent forever.

I was wondering again about his big operation, when I spotted an unexpected news item that I hadn't expected: the mother of George Reeves was arriving tomorrow by train to view her son's body and the site of his death. I grunted, thinking that I'd like to be a fly on that morgue wall.

"You worked a case for Reeves a couple of months ago, didn't you?" Suzi's blue eyes moved from the paper to me.

I nodded, but said, "Can't talk about it. Hush-hush confidential."

She pulled her legs under her on the couch and turned to confront me directly. "You can't keep secrets from me, Standy."

I laughed. "You have *nooo* idea, sweetheart."

"After all we've been through? After all these years?"

"Confidential means confidential."

"I've known you since we were—"

I'd been bashed and beaten all day and now simply ran

out of patience. I raised my voice without realizing it. "Enough is enough, all ready."

She backed away a couple of inches. "I—I thought we weren't going to fight." A casual lock of blonde hair fell across her right eye and cheek.

"That was the pain in my head talking. You're right. Not fight."

She clicked the off button on the remote and ran her hand slowly along my arm, letting it slide behind my neck. Our faces were only inches apart.

I put my arm around her slim waist and we kissed like thirsty school kids at a drinking fountain. I lifted her and carried her to the bed. Within minutes, we had slipped beneath the sheets and were both on the edge of that wonderful cliff, falling all the way off together.

Later, with her naked body next to mine, our thighs intertwined, the soft warmth of her breasts against my chest, I thought again about proposing to this woman. Maybe in the morning.

# CHAPTER 18

*Suddenly, from out of nowhere*:

Sharp pain.

Pain like a hot needle. Pain like a fishhook in the side of my mouth. Throbbing pain like I wanted to carve away the left side of my face from ear to chin with a frigging Bowie knife.

I stumbled into the bathroom and saw that my cheek had swollen. I touched the tender curve of my jaw and muttered, "Squirrel." All that Dewars and Darvon and I still had the worst toothache in my life.

The pain and the bright morning sunlight were blinding splinters of glass in my eyes, as we drove to Suzi's dentist, Dr. Wang. Forms were filled out, papers were signed, and the next thing I knew, a technician with minty breath was draping a lead apron over me and telling me to bite down on what felt like a plastic spatula. An eternity later, the doctor came in, studied the X-rays, and said, "Oh, that will have to come out."

I'd never had a tooth pulled before and immediately down-shifted into denial. Besides, there was the fact that Dr. Wang was young, female, Chinese, and hadn't even looked inside my mouth yet. I tried to be casual and introduced myself. I watched her mull over my name and thought she was going to question it, but instead, she said, "You think you funny man. Let me look." She pushed me back with a tiny hand, cranked my chair down with a stomping foot, and swiveled an intense spotlight into my face.

I sat there tense with only a paper napkin as a shield, while she washed her hands. Then she poked a mirror and pointy-thing into my mouth and ignited my head.

"Tooth wiggles. Must come out."

My ass tried to grow legs and climb up out of the chair. "Okay," I swallowed, catching my breath. "Let's get it out."

She backed away a step. "You mean right now?"

"I'm here. Let's do it. Right now."

So she gave me a couple of shots of Novocain and minutes later started probing, digging, and yanking, all without any pain whatsoever. It felt almost heavenly compared to what I'd been through all morning. I was a passenger on a slow pack mule ride down the Grand Canyon. I bounced along under the bright light, occasionally spitting red tobacco juice into the water swirling below.

Finally, I heard snap-crackle-pop, and she stuffed a wad of gauze in the left side of my mouth, telling me to bite down.

My curved-rooted molar lay dead on its side in a porcelain bowl, like a pale and pink guppy.

"You want?"

I shook my head.

"You do what I say. And you do very well. I give you a 'scription for Darvon."

I tried to talk with my mouth stiff and closed. "Full of Darvon. Got anything else?"

"Morphine or Codeine."

I breathed deeply and let it out slowly through my nose. "Darvon, it is then."

"Okay. No smoke. No drink alcohol. Three days." She showed me three fingers. One wore a jade ring. "Erythromycin or Tetracycline?"

I went, "Huh?"

"Antibiotics."

I just shrugged.

She tilted her head slightly. "Okay. You see me again in three days."

Suzi met me in the waiting room. We paid the bill, drove to a pharmacy, and picked up my 'scriptions—all with very little drooling and not the slightest hint of pain—yet.

Back at the bungalow, I spit out the bloody gauze and tried to inspect the damage. It was wet, red, and dark. My tongue touched the tiny crater, but nothing came out. Good.

I lay down, hoping to sleep, but could hear Suzi in the other room on the phone. She called Weezie and they talked some more about gold doubloons. She called Lex and promised to come visit her tomorrow, if possible. She called someone about looking after Phooey. I finally drifted off to a dead sleep and woke up hours later to get up and take pills.

Coming out of the bathroom, still holding a glass of water, I said, "Who's Phooey?"

She was working the cross-word puzzle in the newspaper. "The cat."

I came over to the couch and sat beside her, still a little groggy. "You named the cat Phooy?"

"That's her attitude about a lot of things."

"Of course, it is," I gently pushed at the side of my jaw. "He's a cat."

"She. And my neighbor will see that she's taken care of while I take care of you, partner."

"Ahwww, shucks, ma'am…" I stretched, discovering that my shoulder felt better than either the front or back of my head. "That reminds me. How's Lex doing?"

"She scheduled for surgery soon. We need to get to the hospital, if you can make it."

"Well, you and I are scheduled to go back onto the yacht tonight," I informed her. "And I need to make a few calls, if you can let me."

She handed me the phone and took my water-glass back to the bathroom, saying, "If we're going to your fancy floating casino, we'll have to buy some new clothes."

I didn't answer, concentrating instead on calling Cindy's number at the Derby and waited for her to pick up. She said that my uncle had called from Europe, but he'd call back later. I could leave word at his office, if it was urgent. Someone named Max had called too, but he didn't leave any message. Since I didn't have a direct number for Max at the FBI, I couldn't easily return that call either.

"Oh, and Mr. Cobb said you better get your hind-end in here soon," Cindy related. "A security agent needs to show up at least once a week, he said, if you expect to get paid."

"Okay, thanks. Do me a favor, tell him I just had oral surgery, plus I'll be sitting up with a sick friend for a while."

I heard her breath in. "Is everything okay, Stan?"

"Things are fine for now. I should be back on the job early next week."

We wished each other well and good-bye. I sat there for a few seconds winding my watch and wanting Walt back in the country.

⌘

The high-end men's and ladies wear shops in LA don't close at sundown. For all I know, they never close, giving high-class patrons maximum opportunity to purchase high-cost haberdashery and gowns day or night.

I hate shopping for clothes and refuse to buy or wear anything resembling a tuxedo. In my line of work, I never need one and it would just hang somewhere on my boat, growing mold.

"There are tux rental services, you know," Suzi said.

"Let's just get me a simple fresh set of clothes," I said. "That way, you can afford a pretty new dress."

We finally settled on a light-weight dark sport jacket and slacks for me from Michael's, where Mickey Cohen used to run book, and sleeveless saffron gown with long white gloves for my lady from an expensive shop in Beverly Hills. Our excursion this evening to the yacht was supposed to appear as a social affair—a reward for faithful service to the party, so neither Suzi nor I wore a gun.

We risked stopping briefly by her apartment to clean up, change into our new duds, and add jewelry to Suzi's ensemble. She put her hair up in a way I'd never seen before and I commented that she ought to always wear it that way.

"Too much trouble," she said, straightening my tie. "Stop fidgeting."

"Sorry."

That got me a peck on my not-sore cheek.

She wiped away any lipstick traces and said, "Ready, set, go."

The bright orange sun was sinking into a familiar cloudless western sky when we boarded the motor-launch back to the Waves.

Suzi shivered under my arm as we neared the yacht,

and I didn't think it was from the chilling air. "You didn't have to come, you know," I said. "I appreciate it, but I don't like putting you in danger."

"Oh, I'm over my fear of being shot again." She looked up at me with deep blue eyes under Maybelline lashes. "Now I'm mostly afraid of being alone."

I held her closer and had a little trouble swallowing.

As we stepped up the ladder on the side of the yacht, we were greeted again by rosy-faced Pinky. "Welcome aboard."

"What's your real, full name?"

He laughed, patting his gut with both hands. "H. Casper Petrovich."

"Sure it is," I said. "In spades."

He laughed again, deeply this time, and watched us stroll along the gangway.

The raucous metal clanking din of the slot machine payouts seemed louder and more frequent than I remembered.

The games were in full swing. The gambling area was decked out in purple and green, with matching outfits worn by the dealers and leggy cocktail waitresses. No roulette or crap tables, since the boat pitches slightly from the waves, but plenty of poker games and lots of slots.

I was surprised to see Lloyd Bridges seated forward at a blackjack table. The guy next to him had a healthy stack of chips and won several hands while we watched. I was pretty sure I saw him palming cards but nobody stopped him.

I moved over to stand near Bridges and said, "They ought to make it illegal for players to use both hands during the game."

He looked up and shrugged. "Then some poor soul will simply learn how to pull the switch with one hand."

The guy next to him suddenly picked up his winnings

and departed our company. Suzi went off to powder her nose, while I wandered over to watch a poker game between Chico Marx, Peter Lorre, and a slouching James Durante.

The Schnoz pulled in a pile of chips and said, "I love that kind of carryings on." I lighted Lorre's cigarette with my courtesy lighter and he offered me one in return from a gold cigarette case.

"Thank you, but I don't smoke.

"Oh, of course not," he said. "I'm delighted to hear it. Filthy, filthy habit."

"This is the luckiest casino I've ever played in," Chico told the dealer. "I almost always win."

"That goes double for me, too," Durante wheezed.

The dealer riffled the deck, but said nothing.

"Which is part of the reason why the local officials are slow to close this place down," Lorre advised around a dangling butt. "When everybody wins almost every time, they just let it ride."

If everybody wins, I thought, then the house loses. So, why do Miss Francesca Fortuna Degarre and Mr. August Reed operate a gambling yacht in the first place?

Suzi came back to whisper in my ear. "I slipped below deck and saw someone pulling in a small net in from an open port hole."

We carefully scanned the room to ensure we were not being noticed. I followed her out and down a ladder. We wandered the less-active compartments of the ship, hearing the constant hum of the engines. Near a dogged hatch marked *Off Limits to Guest and Crew*, we eased along a dimly lit passageway. Suzi indicated a small puddle and train of seawater on the deck under a closed porthole. We followed the wet trail and I saw a man closing a locker with a quiet clang. It was the blue-chinned steersman that I'd seen on the bridge the night before.

"Belay that sailor," I called and he dashed down a companionway into the shadows. We thumped along the steel deck behind him, past a rack of scuba gear. We lost him around a corner, until he lunged at us from behind a massive air duct, the subdued light gleaming off the blade of a knife in his fist.

His face gleamed as well from stress and sweat as he moved to the right and came within striking distance of Suzi. Before I could block him, Suzi gave a yell and jabbed a stiff hand palm-up into his stomach and another into his forearm forcing the knife to clatter to the deck. I gave him an uppercut that should have knocked him out of his socks.

"Let me guess," I said, catching my breath. "Kenpo."

Suzi touched up the hair at the nap of her neck and nodded. "Classic hand-sword strike."

⌘⌘⌘

Reed and Miss Degarre were delighted at the results of our escapade. The locker was opened and the waterproof packet of cash was confirmed to be phony.

"The case of the counterfeit currency is officially closed, son. Congratulations. I knew I could rely on your investigative skills."

"And the wonderful skills of your beautiful woman," Francesca said, handing a champagne glass to Suzi and pouting her lips. Miss Degarre proposed a toast and swiveled inside one of those tight pantsuits I'd seen in photos of Ida Lupino.

We drank and drank again, discussing how the money possibly came from Avalon by way of a speedboat that docked briefly alongside the floating casino at night.

"I think I can manage the situation from this point on," Reed said. "You've provided a great service. One might even say that you performed—" He clicked his heels and touched the bill of his cap. "—admirably."

We chuckled politely at his lame joke. Francesca moved her left hip until it was touching Suzi, who gave her a stare.

"In that case," I said, "how about paying me for my services?"

Francesca began stroking Suzi's right shoulder.

Suzi handed her the champagne glass and barked, "Stop it."

"Name it," Reed beamed beneath his mustache and enveloped the catty woman beneath his right arm.

"You wouldn't happen to have a certain bullet taken from the body of a certain FBI agent, would you? It sort of belongs to me and I'd feel better if I had it back."

Reed made a face that said Not Bad. "Well, well. Assuming that I did, I don't think it would be wise to share it with you at this time." He set his own glass down. "Let me instead share some important insight into your parents' past," he volunteered.

"Go ahead."

"They were extremely loyal to the Party for many years. Their main assignment was to acquire blueprints for a mini-avionics project at Lockheed. They were successful in this endeavor before their unfortunate deaths. It was a great sacrifice for the cause. You should be proud, son."

"Assuming what you say is true," I countered. "How did they die?"

"I've already told you. By the hands of the federal government."

I tried to remain expressionless.

"You're thinking that I'm a lying fool," he said. "If I were you—" He tightened his grip on the woman. "...I wouldn't."

Suzi came to my side. We entwined hands and she asked, "What ever became of the plans?"

"Inoperable, back then. But we've continued to work on them and someday soon they will bear fruit for the Party."

Francesca snickered.

I felt sour bile building in my stomach. My thoughts were trapped between hate and vengeance. I had killed before. It had been a terrible weight. But strangely, now it seemed like the right thing. Like a good reason.

Suzi probably recognized the look that my face suppressed. "I think that it's time we were going," she said.

Reed seemed slightly relieved. He accepted her suggestion, saying offhandedly, "Leave as you came aboard, comrades—loyal to the Party."

On the way back to shore, Suzi stopped for a second and rubbed her shoulders. "What a leech."

"They both are." I concentrated on where my missing molar had been until my temper cooled. "I don't know if I can do this anymore."

"Don't lose hope, Standy."

"How can you say that?" There was no despair in my voice, just ignorance.

"We have a saying at Sunset Investigations," she told me as we made our way back to the Marineland pier. "Keep calm, but keep looking."

❦

Weezie welcomed us into her room at the park. It was after hours and the night air had settled into the quieted arenas where the big and little fishes were asleep in their tanks until show time tomorrow. The young woman had just hung up from talking with her curator friend, Zircon, at a maritime museum up the coast. She was excited about a freighter that had gone down on the reef before the war and babbled on about it being right on top of an earlier wreck from 1582.

"Quentin says that the Santa Marta ran aground off Santa Catalina with an estimated 200 friggin' tons of gold from the Philippines." Her eyes shone from both the yarn she was spinning and the rum we were drinking. "A salvage expedition was dispatched from Acapulco the following year, but the damn galleon must have slipped off the reef."

My jaw began to throb again, insisting on attention.

"Why hasn't anyone found it during this century?" Suzi asked.

"Oh, they've looked," Weezie answered. "Jesus, they've looked. But the bitch just seems to've disappeared, until now."

Suzi was beginning to catch the treasure fever. She sipped her drink and said, "Do you honestly think that the old freighter went down on top of the site where the galleon sank? What are the odds of that happening?"

"Damn good," Weezie laughed. "No wonder it's never been found. But now we have the ocho real coin that I located during a dive near the hulk of the freighter."

I couldn't get my mind off Reed. I'd succeeding in crimping the counterfeiting pipeline, but I still wondered about his bigger operation.

"Ocho real are better known to most people as pieces of eight," Weezie explained. "Eight bits to a coin."

I refilled my glass, took another Darvon to deaden the pain in my head.

"Oh, I see," Suzi answered. "And two bits are a quarter—of a Spanish doubloon."

"Two bits, four bits, six bits, a dollar. All for treasure stand up and holler!"

They giggled together, hearts and heads full of golden dreams.

My own head was full of booze, pills, and general pain. I left them there in the kitchenette, scheming like pirates, while I glided into the darkened bedroom.

What was Reed up to?

Must come out

Phooy.

Dull pain.

# CHAPTER 19

*The next day*:

I came to my senses again in the morning, half out of bed and half dressed. I remembered being sick in a lime green tile bathroom. The socket in my jaw only ached moderately, but the rest of my body felt as if I'd gone three rounds against Sugar Ray Robinson and Floyd Patterson, put together.

It was after 10:30 when I found the notes. Suzi's said: "Went home to sleep in my own bed. You should try it sometime." Weezie's tiny handwriting added: "Gotta go to work. Don't worry. I slept on the couch."

My throat was as dry as a tennis ball. I was eighty percent ashamed and seventy percent angry. Nearly half a day gone and I didn't know what happened to Phil, what the full story was with my parents, and what my next move would be as a double-double agent for Walt. At the moment, I really didn't want to go on with any of that. But I knew I would. I found a bottle of Bufferin and ate four of them with about a gallon of cold water. I washed up, locked up, and went out to wrestle up my faithful Kaiser from the Marineland parking lot.

Coffee at the burger joint sobered me a little. I vaguely recalled something about a treasure hunt, and decided that I'd dreamt it.

Driving north, I called Norman on the car-phone. He wanted to play. "'Wait for the mail. I'll never fail.'"

"Just a second," I said, steering between a Volkswagen bus and a truck stacked full of old tires. "'If you don't get a letter, then you know I'm in jail.' It's from Toot Toot Tootsie."

Crackle of static. "Right enough. Your turn."

I tried to think straight and drive straight, cradling the phone on my sore shoulder. "Okay. 'Bet your bottom dollar, you and I are through.'"

"Why? Whadido?"

"No. That's the lyric. 'Bet your bottom dollar, you and I are through.'"

"I've got no idea. Can I get a clue?"

"Wrong. It's 'Lipstick on your collar told a tale on you.'"

"Yeah?" he said, enthusiastically. "Told a tale on you?"

I said, "Yeaaah," and felt much better. "I'll be coming over in about an hour to pick you up, so we can visit Lex."

❧❧❧

When we got to her hospital room, Lex was getting her ears pierced. Suzi stood by the bed, comforting her. A pudgy lady in a candy-striped gown dabbed Lex's earlobes with a topical anesthetic and dug at them with a sterile needle.

"Jeeez…" Norman said and looked away.

Lex waved and hand and gargled, "Getting' dolled up."

I questioned Suzi with my eyebrows.

"The doctor was here and said she should avoid talking as much as possible."

"I know," I said. "But, what…?"

"She always wanted pierced ears," Suzi shrugged. "This seemed like a good time."

I looked at Norman, who said, "Don't look at me."

A short, bifocaled man came in the room, humming to himself. His thin dark hair was combed straight back and he wore a white gown, stethoscope, and name tag that read, Dr. Noom, Ear, Nose, Throat. He tapped a clipboard on his right thigh. "Ah, Mrs. Iglesia, you are more beautiful than ever."

I swear that Lex blushed a little as she held a square of gauze to each ear. "Folks, meet is my Burmese wonder doctor."

We went round the room with quick introductions and then the girl in the stripped dress gathered her equipment on a tray and left with a smile, while Dr. Noom began explaining Lex's treatment plan.

"Esophageal cancer is a malignancy of the esophagus." Dr. Noom gestured at his broad upper chest area, as if we were all dumb. He said that the hospital had biopsied a small localized tumor from Lex's throat, and she was responding well to radiotherapy. But she would still need surgery and then chemotherapy treatments every three weeks. After surgery, she would not be able to speak for some time and would need to use pen and paper to communicate.

Suzi asked the big question. "Will she recover okay?"

Dr. Noom flipped a page on his clipboard and studied it before answering. "The prognosis depends on the extent of the disease, you understand. A successful recovery will involve substantial weight loss from reduced appetite, coughing, and a heartburn-like sensation. The main thing is that we want to be sure that the cancer does not spread elsewhere, such as to her lungs or liver."

I nodded and noticed that Suzi and Norm did too.

Lex groaned and said, "Got to avoid eternal bleeding."

Dr. Noom did the smallest double-take I'd ever seen and started to go on, but Lex quickly added, "Can you all leave me have a minute here? I need to talk with the squirrel."

Suzi, Norm, and Noom hesitated, finally making their way together out of the room.

Lex waited until the door fully closed and then looked at me under tight brows. "I'm scared brown."

"Hey," I said, "it's going to be—"

"If anything happens to me, I want ya to have all my stuff, but promise you'll look after Alex."

"Okay."

She thumbed the soft flesh under her chin and looked away. "If I don't make it, I just want ya to know that Toby once told me ya were—the best hope for the future. We kidded ya a lot, Stanley, but we both—love ya—like a—son."

I came around and sat by her side on the hospital bed. "Easy now. The doc says you shouldn't talk."

She took slow ragged breath. "Do me one favor."

"Sure. Sure. Anything."

She picked at a thread of her hospital gown. "Stop drinkin'."

"What?"

She looked up at me with wet eyes. "I may need you.

"Yeah, but—"

"Do or die."

Before I could respond, there was a knock at the door. Dr. Noom and the gang came back in. "We need a second series of X-rays now to see if the lumen isn't badly obstructed."

"I just had X-rays myself yesterday," I offered, while Lex dabbed at her eyes.

"Oh?" Dr. Noom said.

I pointed at my left cheek. "Tooth extraction."

"Hmm, in that case…" He reached into the pocket of his gown and brought out a handful of metal clips, smaller than fifty-cent pieces. "Each of you should have a dosimeter, especially when we go down for radiation treatment."

"Don't want to get too many roaches," Lex croaked.

The doctor shook his head and pinned one of the clips to the edge of her gown.

Norman said, "Roentgens. The film in dosimeter will turn dark when developed, if we get too much exposure. Right, doctor?"

"Correct. It's merely a safety precaution."

Lex went over and sat in a wheelchair that had been tucked behind the other bed.

Suzi and Norm took turns wheeling her down the hall to the elevators. While we rode to the first floor, Norman commented that this must all cost a lot of money.

"We'll burn that bridge when we come to it," I said as we passed the Information desk. "You guys go on ahead. I want to check on something."

Minutes later, I was in the billing office, getting and giving details. Norm had been right, the treatment was going to cost a lot of money and I wondered how I was going to help pay for it. I assumed, like everything else, I'd figure it out eventually.

Back at the Information desk, I was told to follow the radiation signs in order to catch up with my friends. Once the X-rays were complete, Suzi, Norm, and I went to the cafeteria for hot roast-beef sandwiches. Later, Dr. Noom scanned the X-ray film and informed us that he'd schedule surgery for tomorrow. "I know you all want to be here then, but the patient will need utmost rest during recovery. You can call in to the hospital after two p.m. and check on her condition, but I wouldn't plan a visit for several days. Not until, say, Monday, the twenty-ninth, at the earliest."

We hung around a while longer, playing checkers, watching daytime game shows on the little TV, and making small talk. Norm had brought along the manuscript for his new novel and wanted to "treat" Lex by reading it aloud, but I suddenly remembered that we needed to get back to the boat, Suzi said we were supposed to meet with Weezie to talk to Professor Zircon, and Lex allowed that she was kinda tired, so we said our goodbyes and good lucks.

The last thing Lex said to me as I was leaving was, "Do or die."

I really didn't like that. I wanted a drink, and suddenly didn't like that either.

෴

Out in the warm sunlight of the parking lot, Norm, Suzi and I stood around for perhaps twenty minutes commiserating and discussing Lex's condition.

"There's not much we can do at this point," Suzi concluded.

I agreed that we should remain patient, but stay busy with other things to keep our mind off the worst-case scenario.

Suzi and Weezie were going to meet up with Lloyd Bridges that afternoon and dive off the side of his boat, hoping to discover signs of their sunken treasure. The corroding freighter's engines had blown during a storm decades earlier and the hulk sat in sixty feet of water on a reef not from where the Waves lay anchored.

Norman had something called a parabolic microphone that could pick up distant conversations from other boats across a calm sea, or so he claimed. He also claimed that he could build a remote-controlled underwater movie camera, but I had serious doubts about that, even for Norman.

"Look," I said. "You wanted to be more involved with my investigations, right?"

"Yeah, shamus. Mystery is my meat. Crime is my bread and butter."

I winced, but soldiered on. "So we'll take my boat out to assist with Suzi's dives, while keeping an eye and ear on the Redskies' yacht."

"Red skies in the morning," he quoted, "sailor takes warning."

"Don't worry. We'll be fine. I'll teach you some seamanship, too."

"Have you still got your eye-patch and maybe a spyglass?"

"We'll use binoculars. I threw the eye-patch overboard months ago. You may be next."

"Aye, aye."

We swung by Weirdo Weirick's apartment so he could stuff his stuff into a couple of gym bags and cardboard cartons.

He had a lot of stuff, but an hour and a half later, we were casting off from my slip at the dock. I'd switched to a tan oxford shirt with button-down collar, a pair of jeans, and dark topsiders. Norm wore a checkered blue shirt, a fisherman's vest with bulging pockets, and red high-top Keds. As I revved the engines past the furthest channel marker, he started turning green and soon gave up his roast beef to Poseidon.

"That reminds me," I said. "Can you do anything to repair a soggy Hasselblad?"

He took his time concluding his business over the side and almost losing his glasses. I fiddled with the radio to find a weather report and steered farther south along the channel to where the Waves stood moored. We came nearer and I could see a trim thirty-foot cruiser on the other side of the yacht. Figures with tanks and flippers were already rolling and jumping over the side into the ocean. I gave a blast on the horn and saw a guy up top at the controls wave back with his cap.

Norman came forward still clutching his stomach. "Okay, here's one for you," he said in a voice as sad a bagpipes. "Why didn't the chicken cross the road?"

I was glad to see that he was holding his own, but I had no idea what he was asking. He stared at me and repeated, "Why didn't the chicken cross the road?"

"Ah, is that a song lyric?"

He plunked down in a seat next to the wheel. "He wanted to lay it on the line. Get it?"

"That's definitely not a lyric from a song," I protested. "How're you feeling?"

The sea breeze played with his hair, but his completion looked good now. Normal Norman. "Okay, how about this? 'Mr. purple people eater, what is your line?'"

I immediately came back with: "'Eating purple people and it's mighty fine.' And that's not an old band tune. That's more of your science fictiony stuff."

He belched loudly and I thought he was going to head for the rail again, but he took a deep breath of ocean air and replied, "I have a friend who says she was abducted by a UFO."

"Don't start with that crazy stuff."

He waggled his fingers at me. "She claims they did some stuff to her."

I felt like I'd taken one step beyond into the twilight zone. "I'm giving you fair warning, Norman."

"And people think I'm the one who's weird—"

"No. You're despicable." I resigned myself to ignore him. We came alongside the cabin cruiser just as Weezie and Suzi popped to the surface. Lloyd Bridges helped haul them back on board, while I dropped anchor and secured the engines.

"There's a forest of kelp down there," Weezie said, wringing water from her hair. "Did you see those sea lions?"

"They won't bother you," Lloyd said, "unless you bother them."

"Where's the gold?" Norman shouted.

The girls were shucking off their tanks and flippers. Lloyd hung a couple of bumpers over the side of his boat as it neared mine. All I had were a couple of blown-out tires to hang on my craft.

"Didn't see any," Weezie answered.

Suzi came over and leaned toward me on the rail. "But we saw something that will interest you, Standy."

I reached out and helped her up to the deck of my boat. "Not sharks, I hope."

"No, we saw a couple of other frogmen at the far end of the sunken iron ship." She lowered her voice. "They were moving large cases from inside the wreck, hauling them up to Reed's yacht."

# CHAPTER 20

*And so*:

I came back on board around four in the afternoon that Friday to find Norm seated on the stern with his legs on the rail and wearing earphones, an LA Dodgers ball cap, and plenty of suntan lotion.

When I tapped him on the shoulder, he jumped a little and removed the earphones. "They're talking about a union committee meeting tonight on the yacht," he said gesturing with the contraption he'd built from an umbrella, microphone, and what appeared to be the handle of a paint roller. He'd been pointing it across the water to the upper deck of the Waves starboard side, where I now trained my binoculars to see Reed and someone else chatting and smoking.

Norman adjusted the headset back on his ears and brought the "dish" of the umbrella up in the direction of the other boat. I watched Reed toss his cigar over the side, but couldn't see who the other guy was since he was hidden by a shadow from the overhead.

I'd spent the morning and the better part of the afternoon over on Lloyd's cruiser, helping Suzi and Weezie

with their dives. My sinuses and missing tooth made it impossible for me to go down, even if I'd been fully trained and qualified. They hadn't found anything more of value near the old wreck and there hadn't been any further sign of other divers all day.

Nonetheless, this was exciting stuff for Norman, who'd started taking notes for a new book he planned to write. "It's mystery novel," he said, when I asked about the three-ring binder and its scribbled pages on the deck beside him. "A mystery at sea. I'm calling it 'The Fin Man.'"

I immediately felt the call of the scotch bottle in my footlocker, but resisted it on account of my promise to Lex. I had an idea of what they were bringing onboard the Waves from the wreaked freighter below, but I needed to get back aboard the yacht to confirm my suspicions. The AWA meeting there tonight might be my best opportunity.

I left Norman at his listening post and went below for the last of my antibiotics and pain pills. I tweaked the dial on the ship's radio and caught a news report while I shaved and tried to trim my shaggy mop. The white streak that ran from forehead to the top of my scalp seemed to be growing wider.

Robert Kennedy was grilling Jimmy Hoffa in Washington about teamster racketeering. The President was meeting Queen Elizabeth in Canada for the official opening of the Saint Lawrence Seaway. A strong storm was forming out in the Pacific and would make landfall here in the next twenty-four hours. Voters in Hawaii were going to the polls tomorrow on the question of whether to become the fiftieth state. I made a mental note to call Mr. P first chance and nervously rattled the change and dosimeter badge in my trouser pocket with my left hand.

As I came back topside, I carried the bottle of scotch

in my other hand. I heaved it into the eternal sea where it sank with a plop to rest somewhere down next to Lex's cigars.

"What was that?" Norman called.

"Another mystery of the sea."

He stood up and stretched. Norman was becoming a pretty good swabby. "I'll bet scuba diving feels a lot like flying underwater."

"Probably."

He headed below deck, adding, "Down, down and away."

I chuckled and looked up into the blue sky. A small propeller plane buzzed the beach, leaving skywriting that read, *Plan 9*. It made me think about my own plans. Was I wrong to assume that proposing to Suzi would lift her spirits? She already seemed pretty upbeat lately. Was I paranoid to think that Reed might have the incriminating bullet from Naomi's body?

I looked up again as the letters above me began to smear.

Or was this message from on high quite simply just another advertisement for some new movie? One thing I knew for sure: It didn't represent any impending danger from a UFO, or outer space. No, the real danger was always much nearer.

ℰℐℰℐ

A small group of neatly-dressed men assembled in the dark paneled officer's mess room aboard the Waves that night. I'd been granted entrance to describe the successful conclusion of my latest investigation for the Cause. I had the feeling that most of the individuals in this room weren't giving their proper names and telling all they knew, but then again neither was I.

I tried not to appear too interested as I listened to everyone relate their Party operations and programs. The editor of a small suburban newspaper described his success of inserting subversive stories among the local news. Another guy had access to personal information from people who filed for hunting and dog licenses. A bubble-cheeked dude in a felt Stetson ran a movie theater and bragged about subliminal cuts. No one seemed to mind when I left to find the head.

While the AWA meeting droned on, I quietly roamed a companionway and climbed down a ladder to be nearer the ship's center. I received sympathetic directions from the single crew members I passed. After all, this was a sporting yacht and a few of the crew had seen me before, conferring with Reed and Degarre. Standing outside the "off limits" area of the ship, I pulled the dosimeter from my pocket and wondered if the filmstrip in its little window would turn a black from radiation exposure. I was proud of myself at this discovery and began humming, "Who's Sorry Now."

Over the constant vibration of the ship's engines, I thought I heard faint female voices calling back to me, like sirens of the sea. I located a hatch about ten feet from the off-limits sign and heard a thumping knock from behind it. I tapped a knuckle on the undogged hatch and a man's voice cried out. Glancing first up and down the deserted passageway, I opened the compartment.

Dandy Phil Castle was a mess. His clothes were foul. His eyes were wild. His hair limp and damp. They had him tied down with cord on a bare bunk. He screamed terror when he saw me, spraying spittle and blood. His leg where I'd stabbed him was swollen, red, and tightly wrapped with a tourniquet made from the belt of his trousers. His eyes bulged in my direction, delirious with pain, infection from knife wound, and something else—fear.

Reed's cultured drawl boomed from behind me. "He came back to us in order to cover his tracks and to show how he was loyal to other Party members."

I tried to hide my surprise. "The guy's a murderer. Why are you taking care of him?"

Eddie Wexler stood beside the Old Duck. "Don't worry," he said, gesturing with a small automatic. "Dandy Phil will survive, but probably in hell."

Reed closed the hatch, dampening but not cutting off the screams. I raised my fists in a sign of surrender, hoping Wexler would put away the gun. No such luck.

Wexler's eyes were like steel marbles. "What are you doing here?"

I shrugged, keeping my fists above my head. "I was looking to play Keno."

"There's no Keno on this ship."

"I was misinformed."

"What are you, a wise guy?"

"No. That would be our gang-green friend from Vegas in there."

"Comrade Castle has always been very ambitious," Reed explained while pressing me along until we were back on the upper deck. "And rest assured, son, he'll be taken care of." As we reached starboard rail and the stiff breeze from the impending storm, I thought of the other comrade whom Reed had taken care of a week earlier at the warehouse.

"I told you I'd kill you, shit face," Wexler added and cuffed me at the back of my head where I'd already grown a serious bruise. Pain lanced through my entire body.

Reed moved in, saying, "Now, hold on a min—" and then he saw the dosimeter that fell from my fist and clattered to the deck.

That was all the bad luck and distraction I needed to

head for my second natural element: the water. I leapt feet-first over the rail and hit the dark ocean, already kicking off my shoes. I took deep strokes pulling myself as far from the yacht as I could before coming up for air. When I broke the surface, I inhaled like a beached sheepshead and dove down again.

It had started to rain fat drops, which helped to hide me from their weak search light. I didn't think they fired shots at me, but I couldn't be sure. In fact, I couldn't be sure about a lot of things in this case, but I promised myself that I'd bill Walt five times—no, ten times my normal fee as I swam hand-over-hand through the cold choppy sea, aiming for the twin lights of the *Cervantes II*.

৩৩৩

I made it to my boat and hollered for Norman to toss me a line. We hauled up the anchor and I fired up the engines, taking my boat to other side of Catalina Island, where I didn't think they'd find us right away.

In the morning, wearing an old pair of oxblood loafers, I greeted Suzi and Weezie as they came on board from Lloyd's cruiser. Wet clouds still hung low on the horizon, like torn black cotton as we drank coffee and compare notes.

I now understood why Reed had wanted the counterfeit operation shut down. He had said, "It's interfering with another important operation that we do control."

"I'm almost certain that they've been smuggling radioactive material from somewhere and hiding it underwater in the iron wreck to weaken the exposure and escape detection."

Weezie was the first to respond and it was extremely colorful.

"U235 or U238?" Norman asked.

"How should I know? U2…whatever…would make your skin glow or turn the badge black."

Suzi studied the brim of her coffee mug. "Where would they get radioactive material?"

I told them about seeing the propeller drawing on the chart near the Navy yard at Long Beach. "It wasn't a propeller at all. I'm sure it was a scribbled version of the radiation symbol I saw when I got my X-ray's at the dentist's office and we all saw at the hospital."

"But there's not supposed to be any nuclear vessels at Terminal Island," Norm said, wiping his glasses on his handkerchief.

The radio across the cabin squawked, issuing storm warnings. The boat rocked deeply on its keel.

"The key word there is 'supposed'" Lloyd said. "Look, I have a contact at the naval facility. I'll see what I can find out, but it'll take time to get a confirmation if any radioactive materials are missing. In the meantime, we should alert the federal authorities about this."

The rain was thundering harder now on the deck above our heads.

"In the meantime, we should get the hell out of this storm," Weezie advised.

"We don't have any direct proof, Standy, just suspicions."

The boat was beginning to pitch and roll. Water seeped in through a porthole I'd intended to repair. I knew the old girl couldn't take much more and I had to get her to calmer water. Maybe then I could contact Max at the Fat Butt Idiots. But first we had to get out of these rough seas to safe moorings.

The sky became lavender and black and the sea full of frothy white caps, as we slid to safe harbor.

We split into teams. Lloyd and Weezie left in his newer, bigger boat for Terminal Island where he could consult with his friend. Norm and I dropped Suzi off near the park, so she could drive to the hospital and check on Lex. Then we rode the *Cervantes II* through blowing sheets of rain to its normal dockage where my car was parked. The tides were shifting from the heavy weather and the boat was in danger of being beaten by the increasing swells. I brought it inland along the channel where the new Marina del Rey was being dredged and secure it there with additional spring lines. We remained onboard most of the day restocking provisions and patching small leaks.

"I'm learning more about seamanship than I am about detective work," Norman complained.

I promised to teach him all I knew—which didn't feel like much.

That night, the water turned dark green, dented with rain. The full howling force of the storm hit, blowing patches from the boat's paint and causing us to employ all three anchors. The Coast Guard issued repeated alerts. I finally switched off the radio around three a.m., as the storm passed over the coast and we got some sleep.

The morning came with a welcome supply of sunlight, fresh air, and a receding tide. I had to concentrate attention now on moving the *Cervantes II* out of the channel and into the open sea, or we'd get stuck in the muck.

As I brought the boat back into open water, I saw that the Waves was no longer afloat out beyond Marineland. I didn't think the storm had been strong enough to sink the converted freighter, so where had it gone with its strange cargo?

# CHAPTER 21

*All that morning*:

We cruised around Catalina, but found no sign of them. They must have sailed either north or south after the storm had passed. East would have put them in one of the larger harbors where we could have found them and west would have sailed them far out into the Pacific.

I chose south, figuring that since I now knew what the big operation was, they would try to escape to Mexican waters, like the cowards Norman said they were. My snooping on board the yacht had probably caused them to up their schedule, whatever it was.

We searched along the coast for the better part of a day and a half, but found nothing before turning back into U.S. waters. As we passed San Diego headed for home, I had to admit that we'd lost them for good. They could be anywhere now.

Norman had taken vacation time from his job at the electronics repair store. Suzi had kept close to Lex while she recovered from surgery. Weezie said that Lloyd had confirmed "something of grave value" was missing from the naval facilities, but his source gave no specific details.

I brought the *Cervantes II* in for re-fueling and tried to work the phones for further information or a sympathetic ear. I left word for Walt to call me and had no luck at all trying to contact Sam Ellery at the CIA. No one there claimed to have ever heard of him, naturally.

By Tuesday, I had almost reconciled myself to walking into FBI headquarters to try and locate Max with my fool story, when Norman and I decided to first check in on Lex at the hospital. We stopped by my office, where Cindy gave me a message that Walt was still in the UK overseeing pre-production of another film there, *Pollyanna*.

"Is Walt Disney your client?" Suzi asked. "Do you think you could arrange for Jimmy to meet Mickey Mouse?"

"I'll see what I can do," I told her, pointing at myself over and over. "He's already met Dopey, Goofy, and Dumbo."

During the drive to the hospital, Norman tried to keep my spirits up by asking about my Superman case. "I always thought it would be great if they teamed up Superman more," he said, slathering on sun lotion onto his nose and forehead. "Not just with Batman, but with Green Arrow, Aquaman, and even Wonder Woman."

Superman and Wonder Woman, huh?"

"Now that would be a major league comic book everybody would want to buy."

"Sort of a Super Justice Agency, huh?"

"Yeah, the SJA…or something. Just imagine!"

I kept thinking of Reed's slogan for Party activities: *My Independent America*.

Lex's throat operation was a guarded success. "Too soon to tell," Dr. Noom said. "We're unable to detect if the cancer has been completely stopped. It will depend on the results of further tests. But America has much better medical treatment than Asian countries like my native Burma. There her prognosis would not be so promising," he assured us. "Here there is some degree of hope."

I'd heard that sort of comment about America before from another man. Walt had once told me that the future would be controlled by China, if and when they marshal their population and computing machines. When I mentioned it to Norman, he said, "Oh, yeah, computers will take over mankind someday. It's in all the science fiction novels. Robots, androids, and massive underground calculators that can control all the other machines. Someday, there'll be a computer in everyone's car and pocket, telling you where to go, what to buy, and who should be their best friend."

"I think you've been reading too many stories by your buddy, Philip Dick." But I wasn't entirely sure.

Returning to *Cervantes II*, under a pleasant late-June sky, Norman went below decks while I studied coastal charts north of LA, hoping to spark an idea of where the Waves had gone. He was only gone for a minute. He came back topside with a curious look. "The door to the forward cabin compartment is locked, from the inside."

We went below, moving slowly and listening to every creak the old boat offered.

Norm was right. The door had one of those locks with a button on the inside of the compartment that you pushed to secure it from the inside. Somehow it had been locked while we were gone.

I got my gun out, motioned Norman back, and stood off to one side, calling, "Is someone in there?"

Nothing.

I called again and took a chance of wrapping on the paneled door.

Still nothing.

"Well, we'll have to force it," I said. I counted to three loudly and threw a football block with my good shoulder.

The frame split at the lock and the door flew partway open. It would have opened all the way, except for Dandy Phil's body. He still wore the yellow polo shirt, but it was soiled now with sweat and blood. The cabin stank of putrefaction.

I lowered a hand, placed two fingers along his neck, and avoided the ivory grin of his rectus. I felt the unnatural coolness of the post mortem flesh, but no pulse. His still eyes stared at the color pinup on the bulkhead of a very young Miss April.

Norman said, "He was as dead as big money quiz shows on TV."

I sighed. "Everybody hates cheaters, but this is over kill."

Norm burped. "I was going to say nauseating. I think I saw something like this once on *You Asked For It*. It's a locked-cabin mystery."

"I don't think so," I said. "Not on an old wooden boat like this." I showed him how on an old boat like this, someone could apply pressure to the wooden door frame while holding in the button on the lock. "They could set the lock and ease the door closed while carefully releasing pressure on the frame and the bolt would drop into place."

"I gotta write that down. It's like being in a living detective story."

"Only for some of us," I mused, know that Reed had tried to set me up with another homicide. I hadn't been able to find them, but they had obviously found me. And they could still be nearby right now watching to see what I did about the dead body.

What I did was drive to a payphone and called the operator, asking her to connect me with the LAPD.

∽∾∽∾

The police arrived and started searching for clues. I drove downtown in the Kaiser with Norman, following a black-and-white. We parked behind Parker Center headquarters and were escorted inside without handcuffs.

The chief investigator of the homicide bureau was a dark-skinned man with a diamond-tipped stare that bore down on Norman and me. I couldn't remember seeing a Negro cop before. "Do you realize that if you were like me and you were involved with something like this—you'd be inside the slammer for life?"

It was hard to tell what to tell and who to tell it to. There had been too many homicides. The tout in the warehouse, Simonson at Marineland, and now Phil Castle on my boat. Then there was the one I'd committed in Vegas.

I let him rant, complain, and blow smoke at me. Norman was shaken by the intimidation, but knew practically nothing about the case. I reminded myself again that it was a bad idea to involve my friends in my crazy profession.

My old pal, Captain Steve Seidman, finally joined the conversation.

"I can't help you. It looks like you did it."

"Who? Not me. I only wounded him."

"Then who killed him?" Steve asked.

"Them."

"Them, who?"

Pronoun trouble.

"I'm not asking you to break the law," I said, "just bend it a little, can't you?"

He leaned back in a swivel chair. "Look, kid, the Lord knows that I owe you one, but my hands are tied."

"It doesn't matter who did it," the dark homicide investigator said. "You're taking the fall."

"Maybe not, Harold," Seidman announced. "We got a call a few minutes before I came in. A federal agent said the dead body on Stan's boat was part of an ongoing FBI case. Something about the security of the nation being involved."

The homicide cop swore mightily, as if it were his super-power.

Apparently, Max had been keeping an eye on me, probably on relayed orders from Walt. So I hadn't been operating all alone in the cold, after all.

"How did the FBI know about this?" the investigator growled.

"How should I know?" Seidman answered. "Maybe that's why they call them spooks."

"Hey, now," the other cop bleated, "who you calling a spook?"

"Don't be so sensitive, Harold. You know what I mean."

"Uh-huh." His bloodshot attention rolled back to me. "What's the story, Wade?"

They made me go through it all a couple more times, giving me a poker face and shifting back and forth from one Oxford to the other. Finally, they let the two of us go, but they pulled my PI license, revoked my gun permit, and confiscated my .38, mostly out of spite. Maybe I could operate as an ordinary citizen working for Suzi's agency.

After we left Parker Center, I planned to try and contact Max, but a news bulletin on the car radio stopped me. The report stated that a female FBI agent had been recently killed in Vegas. An un-named source there had provided details, as well as a bullet which would be sent to the LAPD for analysis. I knew that Reed was the source and that the bullet would match my gun.

I'd just escaped being arrested by the police because of one dead body, but now they'd be back after me again because of another, along with the FBI. I was on the run from commies and had no clear idea how to contact Sam at the CIA.

I could think of only one guy to contact, but I first had to get Norman somewhere safe before I called Mickey Cohen.

# CHAPTER 22

*That same day*:

So, after the brief police station break, we returned to our regularly-scheduled program of what the hell do we do now? We needed to lay low to figure a way to counter the commies and avoid the cops.

Norm and I discussed it and finally decided it would be best if we split up. I dropped him off at the apartment of his UFO girlfriend in Inglewood between a Putt-Putt course and the Hollywood Turf Club. Sports, girls, and horses—it seemed like the very last place anyone would look for him.

Me? I drove over to the Blue Phrog, thoughts swarming like bees in my head, gradually becoming more and more convinced that, in my line of work, I should not have any friends at all, because eventually I got them all into some kind of god-damn trouble. Maybe I should forget about proposing to Suzi. Maybe I should give up puzzling other-people's problems altogether and concentrate on solving my own.

The clouds were marbling in the orange evening light as I stomped up the wooden gangway to the slanting boat that housed my favorite bar. The soft sky was drifting into night and that helped to calm my buzzing introspection. Quiet piano jazz sifted from behind the doors of the Blue Phrog. Two men stepped toward me from the shadows. The one with big ears said, "There he is."

I tried to avoid them by jumping down to the beach, but they had me before I could climb the railing. Big Ears clamped a strong hand on my forearm, squeezing and saying, "Where's the Moroccan Globe?"

His partner stared intently into my eyes, over a nose that would have impressed Cyrano. He clutched the collar of my jacket and gave a slow growl through onion breath. "Give it up, smart guy."

I had absolutely no idea who they were, or what they meant.

Big Ears shook my shoulder.

I smiled and decided to try a bluff. "Sorry guys. Ah, that case wrapped up in February. By now, the cops must have it all."

The guy with the nose backed up a step. "The cops?" He looked at his partner. "Then the General will have it by this time."

I felt the grip on my arm weaken. Big Ears said, "Shit. That means we're going to have to deal with the dame again."

"You can talk to Carmelita," Big Nose said. "I don't want anything more to do with her."

"I talked to her last time."

"But she likes you, Jeff. I can see it in her eyes. They flash like Sylvania Blue Tip bulbs."

"Well I have a flash for you, junior. It's not going to happen."

They argued and walked together down the gangway to the gravel parking lot and the road beyond.

Big Nose's voice drifted back to me as the two men

melded into the blue of the night. "You never want to have any fun."

I watched them fade out and then noticed that the music from inside the Phrog had shifted to a show-tune from The King And I: "Shall We Dance?"

As I took a stool at the leveled bar, people were already stomping their feet one-two-three to the modified waltz. As usual, the place was rocking with enthusiasm. So much so, that I had trouble hearing Mickey Cohen say, "What?" in my ear from the phone at the end of the bar. I palmed the receiver and shouted a request to Sonny to turn down the juke. Several patrons grumbled as the volume dropped enough for me to inform Mickey that the commies were trying to infiltrate his west coast organization.

If the Reds were going to tell the cops what I'd been up to, it was only fair that I tell the Mob what the Reds had been up to. Maybe he could apply pressure enough that it might take some of the heat off me. Maybe I could force a standoff, or what the newspapers lately called "détente."

"Thanks for the tip, kiddo," Mickey said. "I'll keep my eye peeled."

That was a gruesome image. "You should also know that the main guy behind it all is named August Reed. He heads up the American Workers Alliance and has something to do with the gambling yacht, the Waves." I looked up and mouthed the word, "coffee" to Sonny.

"Yeah, I know the guy," Mickey said. "White hair and beard with the South in his mouth."

"That's him. The yacht was in the channel off San Pedro the other night before the storm, but it's since sailed away to parts unknown."

"Yeah, well, if it's anywhere around these parts," he said in a voice that sounded like he was moving a cigar from one side of his mouth to the other with his tongue, "it won't be unknown for long."

I popped my last Darvon capsules into my mouth and got them down with a gulp of coffee. "Can you let me know, if you find it?"

"What do you mean, 'if I find it'? I'll find it all right and when I do I'll tell you. I owe you that much."

I rang off and sat there studying how my right eye reflected back from the surface of the black coffee in my mug. I'd always envisioned a detective to be a sort of flashlight, bringing dark things to the light, and exposing the truth. It hadn't occurred to me that it also attracted insects. I mused about how the case had gone and how my life had gone. I'd expected that being a PI would be as poetic as a Chandler story without the noir. I would have to read a couple of his books again to figure out what went wrong.

The music swelled in the background while I blew on another cup of steaming brew, thinking again how this all had fallen on me like a curse because of my willful killing. Sonny tried talking to me once, but I didn't care to listen. I had fallen into a funk and was just beginning to make eyes at an attractive amber bottle of Chivas Regal on the shelf behind the bar, when someone plunked a handbag down next to my right elbow.

Suzi's cold voice said, "Sonny called me."

I glanced at the fat barkeep squeaking a towel inside a highball glass. "Of all the gin joints in all the cities, I had to come into yours."

"City of angles," he said. "I'm putting the coffee on your tab and the phone calls, too."

Suzi urged me up and steered me toward the tilted door.

I sighed.

Sonny called after us, "See you at Kenpo, Suzi."

I gave her a question mark expression.

"He's in my class," she said, directing me to her little car.

"Wish I was."

"You're in my pants," she whispered.

Oh, boy. "Your place or your place?"

Naturally, we ended up at Flynn's place.

❦

An hour or so later, back at the Garden of Allah apartments, I buttoned up my shirt and placed a follow-up call to Mickey. He said that he had connections with the Maritime Union and there was a good chance that the Waves lay anchored on the Pacific side of the Channel Islands ninety miles north of LA near Santa Barbara. I remembered from Norman's report on Reed's background that the oilman once had property on one of the islands.

It was a long shot and a long way off. It would eat up a day just driving up there to check out the lead. But it was the best lead I had and it would be a good idea to get the hell out of LA, before the cops and FBI agents landed on me with big flat feet. Even though it made sense to get out of town to avoid capture, all I really had were hunches and suspicions. All the time and effort I'd spent on the case had amounted to the deaths of at least three people. Who would be next? Why bother continuing to put my friends at risk?

I tried to express some of this to Suzi while we sat in Flynn's ornate suite and ate baloney and brie sandwiches. I held back telling her that I'd deliberately killed Naomi. I couldn't bring myself to admit that the death had been intentional. I told her it was justified and an accident. She seemed to buy it, attempting to lift my mood by saying she understood, and that any guilt I felt was to be expected and that the sandwiches were the yuckiest ever.

Still, I struggled. "But you told me that you were thinking of quitting," I said. "So why can't I?"

She placed a cool hand on my sore cheek and bore into me with her ice blues. "Because you're good at it, Standy. And frankly, you're not that good at anything else. It's what you do."

"It's what I don't do well."

She sighed. "Then you should keep trying, until you get it right."

"That's a lousy argument."

She raised her hands as if to push me away. "All right. I give up trying to get you to not give up."

"That's even lousier."

She reached over and handed me the phone, stretching out the cord so I could hold the whole instrument in my lap. "Call Mr. P, your old boss. See what he has to say about it."

What the hell. Why not?

She left the room, so I could concentrate. After I'd dialed the long-distance operator and gotten a connection to my party, I greeted Mr. P and broke the ice by asking about the referendum vote there that has made Hawaii the fiftieth state. I was surprised to find that he thought it a farce.

"The hell of it is, Stan," the old man said, "only the American residents here on the islands were counted in the vote; not the natives. The true Hawaiians didn't get to vote on US statehood."

"That wasn't reported here in the news."

His voice was thin on the extended phone line. "It puts something official between the west coast and the Russian shoreline, but I can't help feeling like I'm on ground zero here in paradise."

I told him that I sympathized about the Russian threat and went on to explain what had been happening to me in general and how I felt about the mess I was in. It all came out in a rush, like the rattling of an alarm clock.

He listened and waited until I wound down. "Do you know why I took you on as an operative back at the beginning?"

"Because you were broke and I was willing to work cheap?"

"Not at all, Stan." There was a flare of static. "It was because you were and are a fighter. And I've seen you fight again and again to help other people—especially those who can't help themselves."

"You mean like God or something?"

"Stop with the jokes already," the old man ordered. "Nobody likes an educated donkey. You're a fighter and you need something to fight for and to fight against, or else you'll go..."

The word hung there until I finally said it: "Nuts."

"That's it, Stan. That's it! Do something crazy. They expect you to run and hide. Do something nuts. They'll never suspect you to run toward them. Go to Santa Barbara. In fact, I know a guy there from a case I worked back in the late '40s. He was starting to write mystery novels and I still get letters from him from time to time. He's a deep thinker and can help you focus on both your case and your emotions."

"I don't know, Mr. P. Why should I bother to go to Santa Barbara? It all sounds too much like psycho therapy."

Suzi came back in and sat next to me. "And what's wrong with therapy?"

I ignored her.

"Listen, kid," the old man said. "You go up there. And face your feelings. At the same time, you'll be under cover and fighting to help people. It's perfect."

More under cover. I was beginning to feel like a used mattress.

Suzi said, "My family is from Santa Barbara, Standy."

What the hell. Do or die.

"I can drive you there," she went on. "Weezie and Lloyd can look after your boat while we're gone."

I slumped like an empty hammock and asked Mr. P, "Who's this writer friend of yours?"

"His name is Ken Millar. Damn good writer. Goes under the pen-name of Ross MacDonald.

Oh, what the hell.

# CHAPTER 23

*One day later*:

By Thursday, the craziness of my life seemed to have calmed and my mood had improved. I walked through the cool morning air, up Camino de la Luz in Santa Barbara to a rambling house with green shingle walls which stood on a dusty cliff-side road. Beside the home sat a worn wooden stairway that lead down to the beach. A lighthouse loomed about a couple of hundred feet to the left, ready to ward off danger and welcome newcomers like me.

As a boy, I'd hiked in scrub woods like these, near the dude ranch where I'd first met Suzi. It'd been a different world than the one I inhabited now down in the land of 100,000 swimming pools. A brighter, quieter world.

A woman of about forty answered the door. She had blonde-and-gray hair and a look on her face of someone who studied and accepted what the world gave her.

"Yes?"

"I'd like to see Mr. Millar. It's about someone he knows."

Her eyes imagined who I might have meant. "Do you mean our daughter?"

I scuffed the sole of my shoe against the concrete step, not sure how to answer. "No. I'm here because of another young woman named Sunset. Her maiden name was Evans."

The lines of her face softened. "He's back in the garden. I'll let him know you're here." She left me in a small office with a large window where blue jays squawked and dive-bombed from the branches outside.

As it turned out, Santa Barbara was mostly a small college town and Suzi's family had known the Millar's years earlier. She had dropped me off here and then gone across town to visit with her sister. I'd gotten the Millar's address from Mr. P and had the idea now that he'd called ahead to advise them of my coming to this quiet, out-of-the-way home overlooking the sea.

The room I was ushered into was like a preserve from pre-WWII days with plenty of bookcases along the walls and old roll-top desk. The cracked leather furniture had been comfortably molded by years of use. A set of old chessmen laid out on a board stood like miniature armies stalled on a small table in the sunlight that slanted from the window.

Millar came in and shook hands with me. He was a medium-height, high-shouldered man of forty to forty-five. Graying brows hung above his noncommittal eyes. He lowered himself into the chair behind his desk and typewriter. His head was partly bald. A few strands of hair lay across the top of his scalp. There was a crisp, clean smell about him that I couldn't place.

"You mentioned to my wife, knowing Suzanne?"

"Yes, I was told to look you up for a number of reasons, the least of which being your knowledge of the area around Santa Barbara. I'm from down Los Angeles way."

"I somewhat assumed that you're not from around here," the man said. "How is Suzanne and what is your relationship to her?"

I cleared my throat. "She's fine. And I'm her boy-friend, sort of."

He nodded while a jay swooped down outside his window to steal something from the sill.

"What can I do for you, Mr…"

"Wade." I took pains to spell it. "Do you mind if I sit down?"

He indicated one of the heavy chairs between the desk and chess table.

"Like Suzi," I began, "I'm a private investigator. We've run into a little trouble with the case we're working together and thought you might be able to help."

"Where is Suzi?"

I looked at the battered crystal of my watch. "She should be along very shortly."

He grunted deep in his throat. "Tell me, Mr. Wade, do you play chess?"

"Call me Stan, please. And I used to play back in col-lege, but I'm sure I'm not as good at it as you are."

"At the moment, I'm a little distracted by events in my own life and can hardly spare time. But since you are, as you say, a detective, perhaps you could suggest some-thing that would help me with my daughter, Lin." He emphasized the last words with skepticism.

"All right." I leaned forward, curious. "What can you tell me, then, about your daughter's situation?"

"She's missing. Again. Has been for several days. We think she's somewhere in Nevada, possibly."

Unconsciously rubbing my right temple, I realized I already had more on my plate than I could handle. But since I needed Millar's help, I nodded for him to feel comfortable going on.

"She's done it before. The last time was in May for several weeks. We finally located her in a bar in Reno."

There was something about this man that made me feel reverent. I knew he was a writer, but I hadn't read any of his books. As I sat there in the coolness of his office, I saw several volumes of his work on shaded book shelves, next to those of my favorite author. The titles of his novels were darker than those of Chandler: *Meet Me in the Morgue*, *Find a Victim*, and the one Weezie was reading, *The Doomsters*.

"Perhaps Suzi—Suzanne—and I can help you," I said. "And perhaps you can help us, in return."

He looked at me with sad eyes, as if he'd been down too many mean streets already. "What exactly do you need?"

I asked him if he'd heard of August Reed.

Millar leaned back. "An interesting individual," he said. "I researched him once as a character for one of my novels. I was taken by his confident, yet conflicted personality. He struck me as another one of those people haunted by the events of his ancestors."

"Excuse me?"

Millar tapped his chin with the fingertips of his right hand. "Oh, that's right. You didn't know, did you?"

"Know what?"

"His grandfather seems to have been the famous newspaperman, John Reed. The 'sins of the father' is a theme I lately find fascinating. The son is constantly acting out desires and edicts from the previous generation. It's somewhat oedipal."

"That's a little deep for me," I admitted.

"Excuse me if I doubt you." He dipped his head almost shyly. "Take your own parents as an example. I know nothing of them, but I'm willing to bet that aspects and conditions of their lives continue to resonate in your own. You're either predestined to resist it or unconsciously driven to carry portions of it all forward, perhaps into your own next generation."

"Ah…" He certainly liked to lecture.

"My own father, for example, was a sea captain." He gestured out the window to the blue expanse of ocean that stretched beneath a bright sky. "And there it is. I love to sail."

I suddenly recognized the smell of Old Spice on him.

"You see, it's like Daedalus and Icarus. Something from the father causes the son to fall. And when the hero falls to earth, it's an uber-fall, hidden by time and beyond the control of the individual. I've used it several times to establish the deep motivation within many of my characters."

My chair was becoming uncomfortable and I began thinking again about my own parents. He had a way of acting as though he knew me more than he should and I didn't like it.

Fortunately, his wife came in with a tray of coffee service and we soon were sipping a strong chicory blend from painted china cups and saucers.

I politely cleared my throat. "So who was this John Reed that you mentioned?"

He fingered a bishop on the chessboard. "As I said, he was a reporter stationed in Moscow, famous for having written *Ten Days That Shook the World*, an accounting of the Russian Revolution."

Coffee went down my throat the wrong way, but I contained it graciously, I thought.

Millar gave me a thumbnail sketch of John Reed's history. How he'd helped found the American Communist Labor party. How he'd fled the US in 1917 to become an active communist in Russia. How he'd died in 1920, the only American to have been buried in the Kremlin. Evidently, the elder Reed had been a true idealist dedicated to a popular cause of his day. There was an open question about whether he had sired any illegitimate children. August Reed's claim to be the grandson of the famous American Red seemed as likely and sound as any.

"In a way," Millar said, "it really doesn't matter as long as the oilman believes it to be true. The 'sins of the father,' you see?"

I wanted to say, "Not really," but instead asked, "Do you know anything about a mansion Reed is supposed to have on Santa Cruz Island?"

Millar set his cup down. "You can never hit a distant target by aiming at it directly."

I didn't see how I was ever going to understand this guy, so I decided to level with him. "Look, Mr. Millar, this could be very important. Maybe more so than your missing daughter. Maybe a lot more. Any help you can give…"

He looked away, out the window, to the edge of something I couldn't see and slowly said, "He bought the island place from Leslie Charteris years back. It's on the north side near Cueva Valdez where ancient Indians once gathered to worship the sea and sunset. The property is a single-story stone building on wooded cliff near a popular diving spot, called the Painted Cave."

Hmmm.

જ⊙જ

About an hour later, around 11:30 that morning, Suzi returned and we all spoke further of how we might help the Millar's locate their daughter, Linda. Suzi took to the task more than I. Many of her past cases involved missing persons and she had a personal interest in helping "Ken and Maggie." They gave her a recent photo of Linda and described in detail how she had run off from college months earlier. Maggie, whom I learned was also a writer having authored a dozen books I'd never heard of, served a light lunch of cold-cuts, cheese, and fresh limeade from a cut-glass pitcher.

Ken Millar went on about how the ancient Indians had decorated the area with their rock carvings and stylized glyphs like the ones found in caves on southern France. He seemed to want to share every fascinating detail on the subject. It was all I could do to keep from probing the socket at the back of my mouth. I think he figured I was stifling a yawn, so he switched the subject to how he, Mr. P, and a twenty-two year old Lauren Bacall were involved with an investigation into the death of Elizabeth Short in 1947.

Suzi took this as an opportunity to bring the conversation back to the question of their missing daughter, pledging to make some calls to get a lead on the girl's whereabouts. Feeling slightly disappointed, I of course promised to help.

Soon, we were turning down an offer for an early dinner and thanking the couple for their time and hospitality. Suzi drove with the windows rolled down a couple of miles to the center of town, where we checked into a Holiday Inn as Mr. and Mrs. South. The desk clerk had heard that one before, but let it go for a ten-spot. Once in our room, she sat on the queen-sized bed and placed a call to Weezie.

"Any news from Lloyd about U2-plutonia-stuff missing from the Terminal Island naval base?" I asked.

She shook her head. "But they've found a few more gold coins at the wreck and notified the authorities."

"That doesn't help us," I replied, feeling a strong urge to confess my ill feelings.

"Patience, Standy. Keep looking."

And she began making calls about Millar's daughter.

I was suddenly glad she was working on their case, instead of mine. It seemed safer for her. I wandered out to the parking lot and located a payphone near the highway.

"The word on the street is," Mickey Cohen told me, "your guy, Reed, is running white slave traffic from Mexico on that gambling yacht."

"You sure about that?" I remembered hearing faint voices below decks near the "off limits" section of the Waves.

"Are you questioning my integrity?" Mickey growled.

"Not at all."

"This Red rat bastard stinks on ice," he announced. "And you are very, very correcto, kiddo. He's trying to turn the Organization into a commie underground. When I catch the prick, I'm going to cut his balls off and serve 'em to him one at a time, roasted." He chuckled.

Roast duck. Yum and yuck. "Well, I'm still trying to get a line on his location."

"You find him, you let me know, you know?"

I told him that I knew, I knew, and ended the call.

When I got back to the motel room, Suzi was on the phone with Millar. While they continued the Q and A, I switched on the TV set keeping the sound down and caught the CBS evening news. Douglas Edwards rolled and flipped as he reported a huge fire at the Pentagon where $30 million worth of computers were destroyed. The population of California had topped fifteen million. Mourners, including Gig Young, solemnly gathered at the funeral of George Reeves. Whoever was in the coffin wore a wax life-mask of the actor and I knew why.

"He wants to talk to you," Suzi said.

"What?" I turned from the TV in confusion.

She held the phone out to me. "It's Ken."

"Right." I put the receiver to my ear and said hello.

"I hope you've got your sea legs," he said. "We're going sailing in the morning."

# CHAPTER 24

*Sixteen hours later:*

"Helm's alee," Millar called from under a straw-braid Panama hat, seated in the stern of the rented sloop. For the umpteenth time, I stood in the bow, legs wide, and ducked as the mainsail of the eighteen-footer came over my head and the direction of the wind shifted on my salted face. Soon, he was calling, "Readee a-booout," and I handled the line again as we prepared to tack, streaming through the harsh sun, stiff breeze, and low waves near the north coast of Santa Cruz Island. Millar held his head high, his nose pointed into the wind like a compass needle. For a writer of crime novels, this guy sure loved to sail and to give orders.

"Helllm's aleee."

The bow lifted and we flew out of the channel toward the open ocean, before steering to the northerly side of the island, with only a few years scared off my life.

The sky was bright, clear and blue, containing high above us a faint caulk streak of an intercontinental jet trial and the faded thumbprint of a full moon. I thought about what had happened in the last few weeks and how insignificant I'd been during it all. Very little of it had to do with me. It had been about Naomi, Max, and George Reeves. Walt, Norm, and Lex. Dandy Phil, Weezie, and Lloyd. And Suzi. I had been a Hollywood extra—visitor.

So, what had kept me going? Why did I keep moving forward? Revenge against Reed for his casual and cruel murders? Mr. P's urgings and inspiration? The nagging suspicion of a radioactive threat? Or the guilt I felt for having shot someone on purpose, cold-bloodedly, in the eye? Guilt compounded by shame from having hidden the truth from Suzi? To that extent, I guess, it was all about me after all. Now the only question that mattered was what would I do about it all?

"Helllm's alee! Dammit!"

I ducked barely in time to avoid the swinging boom from smacking the side of my skull. I'd been through more than enough head-cracking already, thank you.

As we dipped through the rolling waves, I scanned the horizon for the silhouette of a ninety-foot gambling yacht. I also kept a weather eye out for migrating whales. You never know.

The air near the island smelled of fish and kelp. About ten minutes later, we pulled neatly into a tiny inlet, near Cueva Valdez, where Millar claimed I could climb a trail up the cliff to Reed's mansion.

"Thanks for bringing me over, Skipper," I told him. "I'll make a point of reading one of your books."

"Do it soon," he said. "Before we both forget."

I shook his hand, shrugged out of my lifejacket and jumped to a rock. After catching my balance, I leaped to a half-submerged log and another, larger rock at the shoreline. A wave flopped against a tiny beach, as I turned and called to Millar in the bobbing boat. "Can you get back to the coast alone, Skipper?"

He lifted a hatch at the stern of the sloop to expose a

fifty-horsepower outboard that had been hidden there the whole time. "Good luck, Icarus," he said, waving his hat to me. The engine started with a low mutter. "I'll be back before sunset to pick you up."

৩৩৩

So, now I was snooping again, this time through heavy brush and an inhospitable tangle of briars. I climbed along the gully of a thin creek-bed between a stand of pitch pine and scrub oak. The thickly grown boughs blocked the sun and kept the breeze out. Clouds of thirsty gnats dove at my hands and head. Sweat began pouring off my face, as I stumbled upon a path, probably carved out through the years by the boots of intrepid fishermen.

I came out on the soft, sun-dappled, reddish pine-needle carpeting near the estate. Below, through the trees, sunlight glinted off a wrinkled blue metal ocean.

The creek beside me gurgled and pooled under a short, flat bridge. A gust of wind caused the pines to sway, granting me a little white noise like three-a.m. TV static.

I slowly inspected the grounds of the estate, wondering and watching for any sign of a guard on patrol. There was an off-center front entrance and a side door that opened from what I took to be the kitchen to a wide terrace. A fenced-in tennis court was connected by fresh concrete to the flag-stone terrace at the back of the residence.

Hunkered down, I made a noise like a duck that wouldn't have fooled Mel Blanc, but it was enough to see if anyone responded. No one did.

If I had a cowboy hat, I could wave it on a stick.

A narrow flight of stairs ran from the stone mansion to a boathouse far below sheathed in weathered gray planking and tar paper. The wide front doors were open and when I leaned over to my left, I caught a glimpse of what looked like a small amphibious plane inside. In front of the boathouse was a ramp that extended around thirty feet off the point of the land.

It occurred to me that I would need some sort of distraction, in order to get inside the mansion. I got out my courtesy lighter and gathered a small pile of leaves and pine needles. Before I could set the pile a fire, a stern voice said, "Hold it!"

I automatically pulled my gun from the pocket of my jacket and performed a somersault roll that surely would have impressed Ed Sullivan. But it was in the wrong direction.

As I came up, the barrel of a rifle smacked the gun from my hand and launched it into the pooled water of the trickling creek. "Aw, shit..." I said, watching the weapon sink from view.

A guy with teeth whiter than whipped cream smiled, leveling the M14 at my chest. He shook his head back and forth like an oscillating fan. Hummed like one, too. "I'm sorry," he grinned. "Was that your favorite gun?"

"It was my only gun." I immediately regretted the statement. When, dear lord, was I going to learn to keep my big trap shut?

"Glad to hear it," he said and swung the walnut stock of his rifle into the side of my head.

I sort of anticipated the blow, but it still knocked me to my knees. I covered my face with my hands and bleated, "I think you broke my nose. Is it bleeding?"

He leaned in to see and I walloped him up side his head with a mossy rock.

Someone else yelled, "Hold it."

I slumped, seeing Eddie Wexler only a few feet away with yet another gun pointed at my chest.

So, this time, I held it high.

They patted me down and shoved me toward the manor house. In a way, it was what I wanted. Just not under these circumstances.

Once inside, I saw the Old Duck, August Reed, wearing an open-neck, white silk shirt and—believe it or not—duck trousers. I heard the sound of a refrigerator door slamming in the kitchen and in strolled Miss Francesca Fortuna, naked, sucking on a cherry Popsicle.

"Ding. Dong," I said. "Avon calling."

She took the frozen treat from her mouth and held it out.

"It's a bit early for me, thanks," I said, hands still raised, shoulders starting to ache.

She batted her fake eyelashes. "I think, you're begging for trouble." She stepped closer, never taking her eyes off me. "And I'm the girl who can give it to you." She shoved the dripping Popsicle into my crotch where it crumpled to soggy pieces and dropped to the linoleum.

I instinctively pulled back. Wexler belted me in the back of my head and I almost saw Tweetie Bird.

Reed put his arm around Francesca's shoulder, cupping one of her breasts. "No time for that, my dear. The ship will be returning soon and you have to get the girls ready."

The girls. The voices.

Wexler opened a thick wooden door off the kitchen pantry and gestured me down a flight of stairs.

"The former owner was a bit of a romantic, son," Reed spoke from behind me. "He built this entrance connecting to where pirates were supposed to have hidden their loot back in the last century."

The steps descended along rough walls with caged light bulbs hanging about every twenty feet. There was a sharp turn to the left halfway down and I smelled the dank odor of seaweed and felt the creeping chill of the underground. They forced me at gunpoint into a large chamber that opened up and probably lead somehow to the boathouse.

The cavern had been fitted out as a workshop and storage area with jumbles of radio equipment, scuba gear, diesel engine parts, and a large crane, presumably for lifting a boat or other heavy equipment from a tide pool that gathered and flowed under one wall of the cave. A sequence of faded cave paintings ran along another mildewed granite wall. One of the stick figures reminded me of the sign of the Saint.

The sound of dripping water echoed around the clammy chamber, while Wexler motioned me over to stand by the pool. I glanced down, wondering how deep it was. If they killed me and threw my body into this dark water, it would probably never be found.

Reed was saying something like, "I'm worried about you, son."

I tried to present a confident front. Do or die. "Well, gee, thanks, dad."

"No, I'm worried about your son."

This time I heard him right. "My son? I—I don't have a son."

"That you know of."

Fierce rage jumped out of me. "Stop trying to mess with my mind."

Wexler laughed. "What? And give up show business?"

Everybody was having a sweet time—at my expense.

"We found the radiation detector you dropped on the yacht, Mr. Wade," Reed said, "So I'm sure you've pieced together the Party's ultimate plan for the state of California." He patted the front of his shirt, feeling for a cigar and finding none. He shrugged.

I remembered the large model airplane docked in the boathouse. "Holy shit! A mini-ICBM?" I guessed.

"You've attached a radioactive bomb to a guided missile?"

Wexler stood over to one side, eight or nine feet away, near a pile of iron canisters, a nickel-plated revolver trained on the red stain at the front of my trousers. "More like a guided airplane, a deadly drone bee controlled remotely by the queen there." He pointed to some sort of control panel on a workbench near the stairs.

"Didn't I see that in an old Republic serial?"

"Serials are for children, son," Reed smirked. "This is a mature weapon with a deadly kick, a conventional explosive which will detonate and spread radiation more than ten miles in all directions. It's our little present on your country's capitalistic birthday."

I got it now and it clinched my entire body. "My Independent America," I said. "Happy Fourth of July."

Reed reached beside him to switch on power to the control box. "A small gas engine gives our little bee a range of ninety miles, depending on prevailing winds. From its nest here on the island, it can sting either downtown LA or Edwards Air Base." He turned to me and smiled through his beard and mustache. "Your choice, son."

I could almost hear Weezie saying, "Fuck me!" I swallowed and tried to reason with these mad men. "But if it flies to the air force base, they'll shoot it down." What was I saying? That sounded like I wanted them to blow up LA.

"No," Wexler said, "it'll fly too low for the military to track it on their radar."

"This is crazy. You're both nuts. Insane."

Wexler stepped around a stack of air tanks, spear guns, and weight belts, zeroing in on me with his shiny gun. "Nobody here is insane. Insane doesn't enter into it, smart ass. It's just business."

"Now, Eddie," Reed counseled. "Calm yourself. Remember that our cause is just."

"Gambling, prostitution, and murder." I directed my words at Wexler. "You don't want to infiltrate the Mob. You want to own the Mob."

Reed began to form a response, but before he could, I told him, "Wexler's nothing like a loyal communist. He's an investment manager. He's been using your operation as a front to expand his position and increase his control within organized crime. I'll bet you skillets to skyscrapers that he's already sold you out for something as capitalistic as real estate contracts."

Wexler laughed and pulled at his long jaw. Reed looked at him and then joined in the laughter.

I struggled to keep my voice calm and even. "If you launch that bomb, you know that America will be forced to retaliate. It's pointless. It could provoke an all-out war. Thousands will die and your cause will be hated forever."

Reed stopped, perhaps realizing for the first time the long-range results of his plans.

"Is that what your grandfather would want?" I asked him. "Mass destruction that would shake the world?"

Reed blinked and reached for something hidden under a rag on the workbench.

"Don't listen to him," Wexler warned, licking his lips.

The Old Duck brought up an automatic and, without pause, fired at Wexler, who took a step back into the jumbled stack of scuba gear. He took another step farther back and fell, firing his own nickel-plated gun twice wildly in Reed's direction.

I ducked behind the cement base of the crane. One of the bullets struck an oxygen cylinder, rocketing it into Reed and the table full of electrical controls. Something there exploded with a deafening concussion, blowing scraps and shards of metal in all directions.

A cloud of dust, dirt, and grit flew up, and when it began to clear, I could see that the supports for the stairway had been blown away and chunks of brutish rock and concrete had fallen, burying Reed in still-cascading debris.

The good news was that the controls to the mini-bomb had to have been shattered and ruined. The bad news was that there was no longer any way out of the cavern.

My ears were ringing like a distant alarm clock. I yawned, trying to hear clearly again. Something in the pile of smoking rubble began to move, heaving up. An arm encased in soiled silk rose from the dirt and muck, with grave determination.

Wexler didn't wait. He fired his pistol again and again into the shifting mound of broken earth.

I had a glowworm of an idea and maneuvered over to where Eddie crouched. Reed's body, now nearly completely buried, slumped and a low death rattle moaned out from under the dirt. I came close enough to Wexler to see the pain and grime on his face and the wildness that danced in his close-set eyes. I reached carefully down into the pile of scuba gear, as he pointed his gun at my head.

"I'll kill you," he screamed. "Kill you! You son of—"

I ducked as he fired and felt a slug burn and tear along the meaty part of my left forearm. In almost the same instant, my right hand came up gripping a spear gun and pressing the trigger. I heard a sound like a strand of broken piano wire whiz through the air. The bolt flew directly into his right eye, as I yelled, "Let's not be. So. Damn. Hasty."

Both of his hands clutched at the aluminum shaft protruding from his head. The end of the spear vibrated for a second and I thought he was going to pull it out. His shoulders bunched as he screeched through the clots of blood that streamed down his face. I watched his body go as limp as a shower curtain and drop to the ground. It spasmed once and came to a final rest near the surface of the tide pool.

I looked over to where Reed had been and saw no movement there. I took a deep breath and glanced back at Wexler's fallen form. Finally, I stood fully erect and stared at the pile of rubble where the stairs and entrance to the cave had been.

Somehow the lights still illuminated the gloom, but the exit was totally sealed under a massive mound of fallen boulders and clotted earth.

My hands shook and I dropped the spear gun. This time, killing someone didn't feel so bad—and that bothered me even more.

I coughed and rubbed filth from my eyes. I stumbled over to verify that the control panel had been fully destroyed. Bits of wire and relays were scattered in the debris. A disconnected dial and broken switch lay within inches of Reed's dead hand.

I guess it was at that moment I realized the air would eventually run out, probably before anyone could dig through the mound of rubble. If I'd had Norman's two-way radio, I could have called for help, assuming that it would work in a cave miles from the populated coastline. I hadn't just fallen to earth, I'd fallen under it.

"Okay," I said, pressing a scrap of cloth against the cut on my arm. My shaky voice echoed in the enclosed space. "So now I'm screwed."

I caught movement out of the corner of my eye and jumped back. A two-foot-long snake slithered out from under the scuba gear. I watched it slide past Wexler's inert body and drop quickly into the tide pool three feet away. Then I got the absolutely worst idea of my life and said, "That's all, folks."

⌒⌒⌒

I would have to swim for it, diving into the inky water of the cave in the hopes of escaping to freedom. I found a flashlight with a ring at its base that I could attach to my wrist with a piece of loose wire. I didn't think the device was waterproof, so I wound some strips of plastic tape around it, to create a make-shift seal.

Not knowing a hell of a lot about skin-diving, I connected the regulator to one of the aqualung tanks and stuffed the mouthpiece between my lips. Nothing. I twisted the valve on the tank and tasted a rush of stale air. I had no way of knowing for sure how full the tank was, or how long the underwater passage might be, so I strapped a second tank onto the first, using the belt from my trousers. I would drag it along behind me, in case of emergencies.

Blood oozed from the wound in my left arm. I tied the wrapping tighter around it, using one of my shoe laces to hold it in place. Then I focused attention on getting the face mask cleared and tight along my brow and nose. I took a tentative breath and sank below the surface. The water was incredibly cold and full of things, like refrigerated chicken soup. Salty, too. Where the hell had that snake gotten to?

Already, I felt a chill in arms and legs. The gleam from my flashlight reached less than three feet ahead through the wet gloom. I blew bubbles and heard them gurgle past my ears.

Fully submerged, I dove straight down and forward through the blackness to where I thought there might be an opening to the sea. The flashlight's narrow cone of light extended before me, but only illuminated a rocky wall covered with barnacles and swaying sea grass.

The heavy scuba tanks seemed to weigh only a few

pounds in the water. I had discarded my pants, shoes, socks, and shirt, setting out now wearing only my skivvies.

The light blinked out and I shook the flashlight to get it going again. In the process, I almost lost the air hose from my mouth. The coldness kept creeping deeper into my flesh. My tooth socket began to ache with a mild throbbing and I tasted the iron tang of blood.

I wore no weight belt or flippers. The walls of the cave seemed to want to jab and hug me in a rough embrace. My ears pinged, probably due to my sinus condition. My teeth locked on the rubber mouthpiece to keep them from chattering. I swam straight into a soggy overhead and banged a shoulder into something sharp enough to tear the skin.

The glow from my flashlight was almost completely dimmed now, but I thought I saw a wobbling gleam far ahead. I discarded the flashlight and pushed off with all my strength toward the gleam.

I stroked hard, bubbles streaming in my wake, and rammed directly into a tight crevasse between two jutting rocks. I heard the crunch from all sides and felt the pinch as I wedged myself tightly into the thin crack that seemed to lead to open water.

A wave of panic shot through me. I tried to back up, but couldn't get clear. Another panic wave hit me and I began thinking that this couldn't possibly be the end.

I groaned and shook my body and head, cracking the face mask on something and knocking it askew. Water poured into the mask, blinding me further. My breathing increased and there were bubbles everywhere. I kicked, pushed, and thrashed to get past this tight restriction. The water clouded with silt and muck. I thought I felt the rock above me move, but I wasn't sure.

The spare tank banged against my hip, and I realized

that I could get free if I left the air-tanks behind.

I twisted my shoulders and slid out of the straps. Sucking in one last breath of oxygen, I eased nimbly through the gap and swam for the faint, flickering light far beyond. The bandage had fallen or been torn away from my forearm.

The cave widened and I held to the right-hand wall still underwater, slithering as fast as I could past spiny urchins, scallops, and frightened lobsters. My heart kicked around in my chest like a trout in a trap and blood from my out-stretched arm trailed faintly behind me. Even though I was approaching the light, the shadows around me began to darken and my lungs began to ache. My diaphragm heaved, demanding that I breathe.

For a second, I thought I saw my parents holding hands, swimming and gesturing for me to hurry and catch up to them. Then I broke the surface into glorious, life-giving air. I gasped and coughed and spat out a mouthful of blood and gulped and said, "Arggh," like a drenched pirate parrot. I was exhausted, but alive. I discovered that I was also naked, except for my brother's wristwatch, which was water resistant and shock resistant. I envied the thing.

I saw that I was floating in a long tunnel cave, with at least a two-thousand-foot swim still ahead to reach the entrance and the open sea. I couldn't feel my arms or legs. I dog-paddled on instinct to keep my head above water, hoping to catch my breath.

The dark, sooty walls of the cave went straight up. I couldn't pull myself up out of the freezing water. I caught a handhold to an outcropping, teeth chattering, head thumping. Clots of seaweed floated on the surface of the dark blue water, tempting me to climb aboard, only to sink beneath my weight.

I swam toward the brilliant light of the cave entrance,

seeing purple and green splotches on the ceiling and reddish-orange patches on the cave walls, probably from mineral deposits within the rocks, or lichen and ocean mold. Farther along, the cavern widened and its steep sides became dotted by starfish and sharp barnacles. The echoing roar of sea lions bounced throughout the cave, like a passing freight train.

Near the entrance, I found a dead seal tangled among a mass of kelp, eyes glazed. But there was no beach or rock shelf I could use to rest and recover my strength.

The one time I tried to pull myself up out of the water to rest, a bull seal with a broken tooth bellowed and charged. I lost my grip on the slippery purchase and fell back into a swift current that pulled me past the entrance. I saw a slight waterfall cascading down from the top of the arch that formed the mouth of the cavern. The fresh water taunted me. The tide relentlessly dragged me farther into the open sea.

I sank under the surface, using what little strength I had left to kick myself back up once more. I was several hundred feet beyond the ragged slopping shore now with no hope of swimming back.

I swiveled around, hoping to find a boat anchored nearby, but all I could see far in the distance was the shape of the gambling yacht nearing the island. I knew I could never swim far enough to be seen by it and I didn't want it to be the last thing I saw before drowning. I turned my back on it and through my feverish mind thought I saw a trimmer boat speeding toward the yacht and heard the bellowing bullhorn sound of a siren calling whoop, whoop.

Struggling to wave my arms above my head, I made a last feeble attempt to be noticed and heard another whooping noise from overhead. A shadow passed over me and a wind buffeted down, churning the water around my head into an attack of small violent waves.

A helicopter hovered above, turning slowly. I caught a mouthful of water and began to choke. Someone leaned out of the side of the chopper, frantically tugging at a strap or cable. He stretched an arm, lost his balance, and came free of the circling aircraft. His body sailed out into the air, tumbling slightly, but arcing straight in my direction, seeming to sail to me on a powerful wind.

I fell below the surface, weak, faint, numb—lost. Someone hit the water next to me and yanked me into the sunlight, pulling me to an orange ring that hung on a line from the chopper. "Hold on, chum. I've got you." I stared uncomprehendingly at the wide grin under the beard of George Reeves.

"Bomb," I sputtered at him. "Bomb in the boathouse. Be careful."

Reeves face filled with sudden alarm. "Bullshit."

# CHAPTER 25

*Within a couple of hours*:

I didn't even know I was carrying a bomb in that suitcase, until I read a report a week later in the newspaper," George said. "That's when I first put together what had happened at the Vegas Convention Center after I left town."

It felt as if we were onboard a ship at sea, probably the Coast Guard cutter. I lay in a bunk under a pile of blankets. A corpsman in whites mentioned that I'd lost a lot of blood and stuck an IV into my right arm. "That's an interesting white streak in your hair, Mr. Wade," he said, starting to drip something down a tube from a plastic bag to my arm. "Is it real?"

"Yes," I said. "I got it while…" Everything blinked out.

George kept talking at me. "You probably want…but I didn't know…then when I heard a couple of days ago that you were accused of Naomi's death…contacted the FBI to get hold of that Othello agent, Max. I was pretty upset, but he explained about her mental problems."

My eyes had trouble focusing. They kept wandering

over in the direction of a closed porthole.

"We were sure you'd been provoked…started hunting for you to set the record straight."

Despite the drip of the IV and the gallons of sea water I'd swallowed, my mouth was bone dry. "Did they find the bomb?"

Somebody in an official military uniform stepped into view. "Yes, sir. The navy's working with us to dismantle the thing. And we just talked to the team that's commandeered the yacht and released the girls there."

I yearned for a Pepsi with ice. "There are more women held at the mansion."

The official snapped to and turned. "A frogman at the collapsed cavern reported finding two dead bodies and your clothes and wallet. I'll check on the women there."

Something in the IV drip was making me dumber than usual. I felt a tugging at my arm, and looked over to see the corpsman painlessly sewing me up. He did a fine job.

George floated in and out, telling me something about his own surgery, and how he'd soon be pumping gas back home in Woolstock, or Iowa, or both. I finally let him drift away.

Sam the Elvis impersonator was dressed in the black-and-white clown outfit and balancing an M14 on his nose. Naomi spanked Miss Fortuna and laughed. I yelled, "Cut. Print. Somebody bury that dead seal."

*Just when we start making sense of the world, it changes on us.*

When I came back to awareness, I was in a wider hospital bed. The porthole had changed into a curtained window and George had switched identities.

"There's a call for you," the corpsman said. "Do you want to take it?"

I lifted my body higher in the bed and reached for the receiver. "Okay," I said. "I can take it."

It was Walt. He was back in the country and heard from his sources about my situation and how Mob/commie connection was now broken and the Waves all but shut down.

None of this seemed important to me anymore. I found that I was in a foul mood, wanting answers. "What about my parent's death?" I asked him.

He stalled out. "What do you mean?" he asked.

"You keep dumping these cases in my lap for a reason. Did my parents work for you and the FBI when they were at Lockheed? Is that why they died?"

He was quiet for about a thousand years. "This is not something we should discuss over the phone."

I fought off the residual effects of the medication. "If they went undercover for you like I did, I have to know. Is that why the mini-avionics plans didn't work for the communists back in the 1940s?"

"A major part of this is classified and—"

"Is that why they died? Is that why you're always dumping these cases on me?" I felt water welling up in my eyes. "You feel guilt, Walt. You're trying to clear your conscience. It's causing too much pain. It's putting too many people in jeopardy."

His usually warm voice held a chill. "Come see me after you've rested up, Stan. We can talk more then."

I wished I had a snappy comeback. The best I could do was to hang up on him.

☙❧

I lay there a long time, thinking about guilt. I found a box of tissues near the bed and cleared my sinuses. My stomach grumbled and my teeth chattered again for a moment. The drip bag was empty. I unplugged it and let the tube dangle from my arm. I hobbled over to the bathroom and relieved myself. I saw an old man in the mirror over the sink. I told him to go lay down.

As I was sliding back under the sheets, Suzi came in, cooing, "There he is. There's my guy."

I thought she meant her cat, so I said, "Phooey."

She laughed and sat in a metal chair next to the bed. "No, I'm talking about you, you big dope."

I blinked at her, hoping my eyes didn't look too red, and feeling uneasy about what I'd done in the cave, again.

"The Old Duck has quacked up," I told her.

"That's a terrible joke," she said.

"No more jokes."

She didn't seem to notice the shift in my tone. "I ran into an FBI man who knows you," she said, running a finger under the gold chain she wore around her neck. "He helped me find Lin Millar. She was staying with friends during finals week. Your buddy, Max and I compared notes on your case, too, and he decided to call in some official backup for you." That's when she caught the look on my face. "What is it, Standy?"

I tried to get out of bed again, but the room didn't want that. "Everything's a joke, because the grim reaper will have the last laugh," I said. "Until then, it's our turn."

Her forehead tightened and she stared at me. "I take it back," she said. "Sometimes, you're not funny at all."

"I'm afraid this is one of those times."

"Because of your injuries? I don't care—"

"No. Because I've been lying to you. I just don't think that it's right for us to be together anymore. I'm not the man you think I am. I've killed two people. And I've hidden the truth of it from you."

She hesitated, naturally. It was a lot to take in all at once. But it was the only way I could do it. "This doesn't feel right," she said. "Call it woman's intuition, Standy, but you haven't thought this through."

"Look," I said. "I'm a PI. It's all I know and you yourself said that I'm good at it. But it comes with a cost—a responsibility, almost a curse." .

"Is that you, or the stress and medication talking, Standy?"

"Stop calling me that," I roared. "We're not kids anymore. I live in a miserable world now and I don't want you in it."

A tear begin to form in her eye.

I aimed directly for it. "You don't know me as well as you think. I'm not one of those process-serving detectives. My life somehow keeps becoming more dangerous than simple skip traces and common keyhole photography. I've crossed a line into I-don't-know-what's-next and I keep putting my friends at risk. I don't want that for you."

"You don't get to decide," she said coldly.

"I've been lucky too many times, Suzi. When my number comes up, I don't want you anywhere around. So, leave, now. Please."

She looked as if she were listening to a voice I couldn't hear. "I—I can't think," she said.

Rage began building in her face. The storm was coming. It suddenly felt like she would fight this more than I'd expected, but, instead, without another word, she stood up and left the room.

I almost called her back, but I had aimed directly at a distant target and, despite what Millar had said, had hit it dead center.

# CHAPTER 26



*Saturday, July fourth:*

The last strains of "America the Beautiful" came over the airwaves on the TV in the coffee shop of the Brown Derby. A news bulletin broke in: American Workers Alliance was being investigated by the government for corruption. Robert Kennedy was rumored to suspect "nefarious communist dealings" within the west-coast union.

After this terse announcement, viewers were returned to our regularly scheduled broadcast: *American Bandstand*. Dick Clark held a microphone below his chin. "This song goes out to our unknown friend at the Santa Anita track." The kids in the studio audience applauded and Connie Francis began singing, "Who's sorry now."

"Where the hell have you been?"

I set my coffee mug down on the counter next to a piece of grapefruit cake, a specialty of the house, and gave an open-mouthed smile to restaurant owner, Robert Cobb. "It's been almost two weeks," he steamed, neck bulging over the edge of his starched collar. I thought he was going to shout, "Great Caesar's Ghost."

Swiveling on my stool, I told him, "I was due some vacation, so I took it. Simple as that."

People were starting to take notice of our conversation.

"Well," he grumbled, reaching to align a set of salt and pepper shakers next to a napkin holder, "I guess it's okay. Nothing important happened during the two weeks. Anyway, welcome back, Wade." He patted my shoulder, as if to dust off dandruff. "They want you outside."

"Yeah? Who does?"

He gave a Groucho waggle of his eyebrows, pretending to knock the ash off a nonexistent cigar with his pinky finger. "Everybody. Ha. Ha."

I'd been transported that morning back to LA and the parking lot of the Blue Phrog, where I plucked the hidden key from the wheel well of my Kaiser and drove to my boat for a change of clothes. Then I went on to my meager office at the back of the restaurant to try and put my life back together after having lost my wallet and nearly my life a hundred miles up the coast.

Cindy came in wearing a purple business suit and whispered something into Cobb's ear. The rotund restaurant manager turned a little ashen and left without another word. She leaned on the Formica and chrome counter and smiled down at me. "There really is someone out front, asking for you."

I swallowed a couple of Darvons, got up and walked out to the maître d's station. There were wide banners hanging from the ceiling, declaring the Derby's thirtieth anniversary. Beneath one, stood Francis Bergen, who wanted to thank me again for having helped her and Edgar a few months back when Candy had lost a diamond tennis bracelet and been blackmailed by her coach. The father and daughter waved at us from a booth in the back. Edgar was on the phone between courses. It looked like the Silver Fox, Duke Snider, was seated in the next booth with that odd-looking actor, Charlie Bronson.

I waved back and thanked Mrs. Bergen for thinking of me, just as Norman came through the front entrance, pushing Lex in a wheelchair and singing out the theme from Mighty Mouse, "Here we come to save the day…"

Suzi trailed behind in a cool lime skirt and cream-colored blouse. She had her hair pinned back like Audrey Hepburn. Just like a boomerang, the woman kept coming back. She lightly nudged Lex's shoulder. "Doesn't she heal good?"

I studied my friend's lean features, admiring her new pearl stud earrings. She stifled a cough and got out a few words: "Doc says it's an acquired trait."

I looked again at Suzi and began feeling like an ass, which might have been her whole point for being there.

"Hey, I've got one for you," Norm said. "On her back is the battle of Waterloo. Beside it the wreck of the Hesperus, too…"

Being Independence Day, I knew immediately what the next line was: "And proudly above, waves the red, white, and blue." Everybody, including one of the restaurant patrons, joined in the song. "You can learn a lot from Lydia." That's when I began to suspect a plot.

Cobb rushed up applauding, but wanting to know if we were going to be seated, or stand here forever.

As we all moved to booth eighteen, Suzi said that Lex was out of danger and the finder's fee from the state for locating the sunken gold would more than pay her medical bills.

Cindy approached our group and said there was an urgent call for me back in my office. I turned in that direction, as Suzi asked, "Do you want me to order you a drink?"

I looked into Lex's eyes and walked away, tossing

over my shoulder, "Canada Dry." Then, to sound tough, I added, "Neat."

I almost slipped getting into the roller chair behind my tiny desk in my tiny office, but managed to grasp the phone and admit, "This is Stan."

The receiver spoke back to me. "And this is Mickey. You owe me."

"For what?"

"Who do you think contacted the coast guard? Who do you think ratted out that damn union to the FBI? Who do you think shut down Reed's gambling concession? Me, that's who."

I rubbed at the itching bandage on my arm. "How'd you get all that done so quickly?"

"How? How do you think, shamus? I bought me an inside man."

No one had ever called me shamus before. "Who?"

"Some fathead named Petrovich. Cost me plenty. And now you owe me."

Pinky.

"Okay." I sighed. "What do I have to do to get even?"

"I want you to find some limey bastard for me."

Feeling a bit like an owl, I again said, "Who?"

"Guy named Fleming. Irving Fleming."

"Irving?"

"Something like that. You're the detective, figure it out."

❦

After getting a few more details from Cohen I went back to where my friends were gathered. Weezie had joined the party. She had on a polka dot skirt and blouse combination with a small scarf tied at the collar. She also wore an awkward expression. So did Suzi. I was sure they had talked.

"We've learned the truth," Weezie said, "and actually understand your feelings."

"Everyone has a little death in their lives and we're honored to be part of yours." Norman said. He blushed. "Life, not death."

Suzi dipped down as if to curtsey to me. "Stan Wade, marry me, you big dope."

I looked at her clear, loving eyes and expectant mouth. Like me, she was fighter. And neither of us really wanted to quit.

"Say yes, Squirrel," Lex said.

"Kiss her, dammit," Weezie added,

"Wowee," Norm said. "Get your kicks on Route 66."

Both Suzi and I shot him a weird glance. Then she rose on tiptoes and spread into my arms as easily as Peter Pan peanut butter.

I let her have one on the mouth, hard.

We came up for air among cheers from across the entire restaurant.

"What the hell. Yes," I said. "If you're sure you'll have me."

"You've been had, Standy," she said.

We kissed again and the fireworks began. Snap, crackle, pop.

The Facts Behind the Fiction

George Reeves: Lived a full life in {REDACTED BLACK TEXT}, working as a {REDACTED BLACK TEXT}. He looked up into the sky for the last time early in the twenty-first century.

Bobby Darin: Gained fame as an actor/writer/singer triple-threat and is adored by fans to this day. He went "beyond the sea" in 1973 during a heart operation and is now playing to a whole new audience.

Capitol Records Tower: Some think it an eyesore, others a landmark, but the building still stands. It is now part of the Universal Music Group and the less said the better.

Walt Disney: Continued his work with the FBI, graduating, some say, into a CIA operative called "The Grey Seal."

Marineland: Died a slow death, killed mainly by the growth of Sea World. The aquarium tanks and arenas are gone now and the entire complex has been replaced by a luxury resort—yet, the ocean cliffs are still there and some nights you can hear the forlorn calls of the friends and family of Orky and Corky.

Ken Millar (Ross Macdonald): Succeeded in writing a dozen more novels, most featuring Lew Archer, his socially-conscious PI played in two films by Paul Newman. Alzheimer's struck Millar in 1971 and he finally faced the Chill in 1983.

*Superman*, issue 128, April, 1959: This ten-cent comic book featured a two-part story of the Man of Steel versus the Futuremen. It is currently worth $120 in fine condition.

George Burns: Entertained the public in all forms of

media until 1996, when he passed away of cardiac arrest at the age of 100. Many thought that he was Hollywood's *Oh, God!*

Lloyd Bridges: Despite being typecast for years from his underwater TV role, Bridges acted successfully until his death in 1998. His greatest legacy is his two actor sons, Beau and Jeff, who are active today, ensuring that Lloyd is the original "Dude."

Mickey Cohen: Went on with his mob and media activities in LA until he was put away for good in 1976 by stomach cancer.

*Untouchables* and RKO/Desilu Studios: The studio of Howard Hughes, Orson Welles, and Lucy got passed around and broken up into a half-dozen corporations. The curtain finally came down completely in 1967 and the back lot in Culver City was razed in the mid-1970s.

John Reed: John Silas "Jack" Reed was an American journalist, poet, and socialist activist, best remembered for his first-hand account of the Bolshevik Revolution, died in Moscow, Russia, during the October Revolution in 1920.

The Kingston Trio: These "worried men" continue to "sing a worried song." At this point, it appears that they will go on forever, like a zombie jamboree.

Kenpo: This "martial art" was first promoted by Ed Parker in 1959 and is still practiced today, even though its open-hand chop to the back of the neck was beat to death repeatedly in television action shows.

Two-Way Radios: Eventually evolved into today's smartphones. Grandpa Norman Weirick loves them.

Hollywood Playhouse: Later became the Hollywood Palace and saw headliner acts from Groucho Marx, Bing Crosby, and Jimmy Durante, among many others. Today it hosts the popular Avalon nightclub.

Peter Lawford: His beach house on Palisades Beach

Road would become famous a year after these events as the trysting place between JFK and Marilyn Monroe.

Darvon: Once a commonly prescribed pain killer, the drug was banned by the FDA in 2010, due to concerns of fatal overdoses associated with depression.

*Plan 9 from Outer Space*: Ed Wood's notoriously bad film starring Vampira, Tor Johnson, and a dead Bela.

Charles Manson: Thief, pimp, and one of the creeepist individuals in America. He was later convicted for the murder of eight-and-a-half-month pregnant actress, Sharon Tate, among others.

The *Santa Marta*: This ship went down in 1582 with millions of gold aboard and is still sunk somewhere between Santa Catalina and the coast of Southern California. Good luck.

July 4, 1959: President Eisenhower spoke in Washington DC about the never-ending battle between Freedom and Despotism. Standing before the Stars and Strips, he made a passing reference to truth and justice while proudly advocating the American way.

If you enjoyed

**SUPERFALL**

By John Hegenberger

continue reading for a preview
of the next book in the series

**STORMFALL**

Coming early 2017
from
John Hegenberger
and
Black Opal Books

# PROLOGUE

*October, 1959*:

Thunder rumbled outside the rented apartment as Chet thought he sure could use a wet sloppy kiss.

He giggled the way he always did when he was high. He knew that the dope had made him slow and clumsy, but he didn't care. The price had been right and he was feeling the singing in his veins and head.

Jean floated in. She bent and scooped up her copy of the script from the coffee table where his feet were propped in front of the snow-filled TV set.

He made a pass at grabbing her arm, but missed. "Hey, where you going, baby? It's after three in the goddamn morning?"

"I told you. I'm leaving, Chet. You slobs are never going to amount to anything. Hank and Doug are happy to sleep together and you—you drink and take too many pills."

"Nahhh…" was all he could say. "I—I love you, sugerbabe, you know that." The old excitement was starting to rise. It happened whenever he saw her. "Let's do it here. On the couch."

Jean tossed her blonde hair and screwed up her face. "I told you, Chet. I'm leaving." And she took her sweet butt into the bedroom, emerging seconds later with a suitcase and arm-load of coat-hangered clothes.

His mouth felt dry as old newspaper. He struggled to his feet. "You—you can't do that."

"I'm doing it. Wayne has a room for me closer to the set. He's expanding my part, giving me more lines. You guys are weighing me down." She dropped her luggage and dresses beside the apartment's front door and went back into the bedroom for another load.

Chet felt the rage bubbling up. His hands flexed as his gaze wobbled across the room to the sharp prop they had given him for his role in the picture. The blade was only five inches long, shaped like a Bowie knife. It would go all the way into the cheating bitch's heart.

Someone said, "Kill her," or maybe it was just another roll of thunder. Chet saw he was alone with only the sound of the TV's hissing static.

His hand was drawn to the knife. He studied an eye in its reflective surface. *No,* he thought, *no I didn't, but— How did it get into my hand? And why am I carrying it toward—toward the bedroom?*

She acted startled to see him so close. *Acted.*

His palm itched. He rotated the handle and drove the blade all the way into her chest.

Her mouth and eyes widened, like tulips. She flailed for a second and seemed to turn into a fawn in his arms. *Soft brown eyes. Sweet small tongue.*

Then she folded and a low moan slid out of her. She said that she loved him, and his hand grew wet and warm and red. The doctor's finest drugs sang to them.

"I love you too, sugarbabe. Gimme a kiss."

Outside, the rain beat down in sheets on the roof. *Or is that someone pounding on the door?*

# PART 1

# DUST STORM

# CHAPTER 1

I had no way of knowing then, but the next week of my life would be filled with dust storms, snow storms, and brain storms. How? Easy. It began in the arid, windswept valleys of Texas and ended on top of Mount Baldy, and in between, I was drugged to the gills by an intellectual who hated the way our country treated "his people."

On a Tuesday in mid-October 1959, I was on page seventy-one of the digest version of *Woman in the Dark*, where "Conroy fell away from the fist rigidly, with un-bent knees," when my phone rang. I hadn't read a lot of Hammett, but this tale didn't impress me as much as the one earlier that afternoon; a Continental Op story called, *Slippery Fingers*.

I flexed my own fingers, put the paperback on the edge of my desk, and answered the phone, feeling hard-boiled due to my choice of reading material. "Stan Wade, Private Investigations. We never blink."

The female voice on the end of the line commanded sweetly, "Hold for Mr. Ford." Then in a more submissive tone, I heard, "He's on the phone, sir."

"Is this Wade?"

I acknowledged my last name, and the gruff guy went on. "I need you here now. Drop what you're damn-well doin' and get to the airport out in Anaheim. There'll be a flight waiting for you on the executive runway tomorrow morning at seven o'clock."

The paperback tilted, about to flop on the floor. "Excuse me—A flight? To where?"

The book dropped into the wastebasket on top of the remains of a slice of raspberry pie—a la mode.

"San Antonio. I'll have a man meet you there with a car and a check for eight hundred dollars. That ought to cover your first week."

I was fighting the first signs of a cold and sore throat, so I popped another Smith Brother's cough drop in my mouth and talked around it. "Is this really John Ford, the director?"

The receiver rattled in my ear. "Hell, yes, I'm Ford. You returned my call and now I'm calling you back."

I tasted cherry on the back of my tongue and glanced through the open door as a waiter dashed by carrying a tray of heavenly-smelling sirloins. "I remember now. Sorry, I'm just finishing up with slippery case involving a woman…in the dark."

"What's wrong with you, boy? Say, do you want this job or not? Disney said you were a top investigator, but you sound out of focus to me."

I stifled a sneeze from the cold or the subtle scent of our LA smog. "Okay, take it easy." The mention of Walt finally sold me. I'd worked for the elder cartoonist on several discreet cases and if Ford knew even a smidgen about them, it meant this phone call was the real thing. "What am I expected to do for your eight hundred?"

"Christ on a stick, kid. You're supposed to show up and solve a murder." The line slammed shut with the sound of a cheap cap-gun.

I flexed a finger at the receiver and immediately felt stupid for doing it.

The soggy novel lay in the trash, and I wondered if Conroy ever got up.

ღღღ

The clock in the hall above the restaurant's time cards said it was half-past four. I'd need at least an hour to drive across town via Santa Monica Boulevard in rush-hour traffic to my boat in del Rey and pack a bag. My swivel chair creaked and almost tipped over as I got up. Damn, those steaks smelled good.

I opened a desk drawer and shrugged into my .38 shoulder holster. I slipped a worn sport jacket over the holster and gun and remembered that I had a change of clothes hanging in Suzi's closet. Going there, instead of the *Cervantes II*, would cut twenty minutes from the drive in the morning, since the 101 ran all the way from North Hollywood down to Orange County. Still, considering the morning traffic, it might be quicker if I just drove straight to San Antonio.

When I locked up my tiny office and ducked out the rear of the Brown Derby, I stopped to grab a steak sandwich and consider Ford's word "murder." The wide open spaces of Texas would be a welcome change from all the complex highway logistics of LA.

ღღღ

Suzi handed me a light-blue Oxford with a button-down collar. "He wants you to go to Texas?"

I didn't remember seeing this shirt before. She was always buying me clothes, as if somehow it would make a better man of me. Fat chance. "Eight-hundred a week," I reminded her. "That's better than our usual fifty per day."

We were both in the PI business. Only she was planning on raising her rates—for good reason. Suzi Sunset had a full-service agency with offices in the Taft building. I had a battered desk at the back of a restaurant where I gently enforced deadbeats who didn't pay their bar bills.

The love of my life and soon to be wife stepped back, tilting her honey-colored head to one side, inspecting me. "I've said it before, Standy, you should raise your rates. I told Jerry Lewis last night after his *Jazz Singer* show at NBC that I charged a hundred a day plus expenses for investigative work. He didn't bat an eye." She handed me a couple of pairs of socks and a small stack of handkerchiefs. I made certain that there were no frilly edges.

"That's probably because you batted those baby blues at him. Which, I can't do." I stuffed underwear into my suitcase and clicked the latches shut. "And wouldn't if I could."

Her face seemed to glow slightly. "And that's why I love and will miss you. Why have you been gone so much lately?" She let those same wild blue-yonders skewer me.

That was all it took. Within minutes, we were enjoying a frisky evening's skewering.

Later, we hugged long and sincerely—and drifted off together. I never did answer her question.

❦❦❦

There was a soft buttery glow in the east now. The car's radio beat out the latest rock-and-roll tunes on KFWB-98, and the sun would soon beat down on the shimmering concrete roadway. I hated heavy traffic, but this morning's didn't seem too bad.

I drove south on the Hollywood freeway around a Greyhound Bus and then got stuck behind a ratty pick-up full of Mexican day laborers. Despite the forty-mile-an-hour speed of several passing delivery trucks, the Latinos stood shoulder to shoulder in the back of their banged-up Dodge, chatting, laughing, and lighting cigarettes off each other's butts. I gave them a two-finger salute as I swung past, but they didn't seem to notice. They occupied a place in my world, but at the same time were in their own private version of it. *Vaya con Dios, amigos.*

I concentrated on steering through the interchange with Route 66 past the city proper. After navigating a knot of semi-stalled vehicles, I relaxed and began to reflect on what I knew of the crusty John Ford.

He was an ex-military man with a thirty-year career of directing motion pictures, thus accustomed to having his orders carried out without question. Working for Ford would be tricky, especially if I expected to handle the case my way, which is to say unhindered by his authority. I liked to follow each lead or hunch wherever it took me without "direction."

Once things started happening, there wasn't a lot of time to report every detail back to the client. I'd been cursed or blessed with a series of investigations lately that kept getting deeper and a bit out of hand. But I'd come through them all with some success, if not a lot of cold cash. October, 1959 would be…let's see…the fifth full year of operating the agency on my own.

A full year, too, with more things going wrong than a season of *I Love Lucy*. Since spring, I'd dealt with dead astronauts, sunken treasure, and Soviet spies. I'd flown a hover platform over Germany, run around Vegas with a supposedly dead TV star, and killed a woman intentionally. Now, I was "gone to Texas" to look into a murder that involved John Wayne and his new movie, *The Alamo*.

↜↝

I parked in the wide, flat lot outside the flat, concrete Orange County Airport and began walking in the warm sunlight toward the tiny terminal. Not all places in the LA basin were exciting and colorful for the tourists. For a second, I saw double—twin images aligned side-by-side like a movie special effect. Only it wasn't anything special. It was something the docs had warned me about, after I'd been slugged in the head one time too many.

I'd need to take it easy, they said. Maybe consider a new line of work, since my life as a detective had caused me to get knocked out more times than a heavy-weight fighter. Pretty soon, I'd have to start wearing a hard hat.

Occasionally, for no good reason, the world would go out of focus or slide to the right, and I'd hear a sharp ringing for a few seconds. I knew I should try and take it easy; relax for a few weeks on a quiet vacation, instead of taking on any new sleuthing clients. But I couldn't resist a good case when it came my way. Besides, I needed the dough for my upcoming wedding. So, like a dutiful mailman, I pressed on, no matter the climate, and kept my self-appointed rounds, this time with prepaid airfare.

The plane was little more than a puddle-jumper. It didn't have to be big, just fast enough to make the trip past Phoenix and El Paso to San Antonio. Most of the other passengers were employed in some capacity with the movie.

I was delighted to find that my old acquaintance, Joe Canutt, was aboard.

I knew Joe and his father from my brief spell as an apprentice stuntman in the early '50s. He was already enjoying a pre-flight scotch when I plunked down in the seat beside him.

Canutt smiled when he saw me and indicated his plastic cup of amber liquid. "Keeps me sane."

I never touched the stuff anymore and ordered a Pepsi. "Hey, Joe. You running a dangerous gag for Wayne's pic?"

"Not as dangerous as your job, Stan. I heard you almost fell off the Capitol Records Tower a month ago."

Joe knew I was a licensed snoop and kind of envied me for it. Anything near danger and death interested him. "Just another day of routine maintenance work." The stewardess brought my soda pop and I let the bubbles tickle my nose.

He half-turned in his seat. "Hey, how about that George Reeves dying, huh? I worked with him on a Disney western couple of years back. Even then, he'd packed on a lot of weight for a superman. Too bad he ate his gun, huh?"

"Too damn bad," I agreed as I buckled in.

After a bouncing roll out to the runway, our plane lunged up and accelerated away into the eastern sky. I knew that Reeves was still down there below us somewhere alive and kicking, but I couldn't tell Canutt or anyone else the true story.

Joe asked how I was involved with the Alamo movie and I told him I wouldn't know for sure until I met with John Ford.

Canutt gave me a nodding "yeah, yeah" and took a pack of Old Gold's from his shirt pocket and shook one out at me. "Smoke?"

"No thanks. I don't anymore."

He shrugged, put them away, and caught an attendant's eye, signaling for a refill of his drink. "Tread easy around Pappy, huh? And don't try any funny stuff with Wayne, either." He chuckled and shook his well-tanned head. "I once caught holy hell from Duke for not being man enough during a fight scene. He damn near knocked my block off with those big fists of his." He rubbed his jaw as if he'd just been slugged.

Joe was a good foot taller than me with wide shoulders and somewhat bowed legs inside his worn cowboy boots. He knew plenty about taking a punch and rolling down a hill from a galloping horse, but this was the first time I'd seen him with a worry line etched between his eyes.

I drained my cup of Pepsi and sucked on a piece of ice. "Okay, pard. I'll be sure and ack tough aron' bof Ford an Wayne." I learned a long time ago that I'd get further with most Hollywood types by suppressing my boyish charm. Acting hard-boiled was a cliché, but movie people expected it from a private eye. Cops, however, hated it, but knowing the correct stance to take with people often was half of my profession. Something like method acting.

They said you couldn't smell vodka on someone's breath, but I had found that not to be the case with scotch, and soon Joe was malevolently fragrant. He continued to drink and eventually dozed through most of the trip.

I noticed a complimentary copy of *Time Magazine*, but avoided it with disgust when I saw that the cover story was about "The Corpse in the Living Room." It featured Peter Gunn, Stuart Bailey, Philip Marlowe, and Richard Diamond in an article about the private lives of all the slick new TV private eyes. I almost gagged. That kind of publicity gave the public the wrong impression. Most of professional PI work involved mundane skip-tracing and process serving, although my last year *had* been uniquely adventurous.

Maybe someday someone would write about my "adventures."

If all else failed, I could always write it out long-hand myself in my old age. Hmmmm.

# About the Author

John Hegenberger writes adventure, mystery, science, and horror fiction. Born and raised in the heart of the heartland, Columbus, Ohio, he is the author of *Tripleye* series and the *Stan Wade LA PI* series from Black Opal Books. Father of three, a tennis enthusiast, collector of silent films and OTR, hiker, Francophile, BA Comparative Literature, ex-navy, ex-comic book dealer, ex-marketing exec at Exxon, AT&T, and IBM, he has been happily married for forty-six years.

Over the years, he's published two non-fiction books about collecting pop-culture movie memorabilia and comic books and sold a dozen novels and short story collections. Follow his adventures at johnhegenberger.com and have fun.